The Weight
of Stones

The Weight
of Stones

C.B. Forrest

RendezVous Crime

Cover design: Vasiliki Lenis / Emma Dolan

LE CONSEIL DES ARTS | THE CANADA COUNCIL
DU CANADA | FOR THE ARTS
DEPUIS 1957 | SINCE 1957

We acknowledge the support of the Canada Council for the Arts for our publishing program.

We acknowledge the financial support of the Government of Canada through the Book Publishing Industry Development Program for our publishing activities.

RendezVous Crime
an imprint of Napoleon & Company
Toronto, Ontario, Canada
www.napoleonandcompany.com

Printed in Canada

13 12 11 10 09   5 4 3 2 1

Library and Archives Canada Cataloguing in Publication

Forrest, C. B.
    The weight of stones / C.B. Forrest.

ISBN 978-1-894917-78-0

    I. Title.

PS8611.O77W43 2009   C813'.6   C2009-900675-8

For Tracy
'tears & laughter'

It is when your spirit goes wandering upon the wind,
that you, alone and unguarded, commit a wrong unto others
and therefore unto yourself.
And for that wrong committed must you knock
and wait a while unheeded at the gate of the blessed.
        -Kahlil Gibran

One

The meetings were held Tuesday nights in a small conference room tucked away down a maze of hallways at St. Michael's Hospital. McKelvey went as often as he could, which wasn't often these days. If he missed a session, he would lie to his wife about the meeting, waiting until they were in bed with the lights turned out, the quiet of the night interrupted only here and there by the barking of a neighbour's dog. He would carefully reconstruct the session as though he were on the witness stand, telling her about what this person had said, how it had helped him see something in a new light. These were harmless lies, bedtime stories told to soothe a wife. The truth was he hated the meetings, everything about them. The stuffy, stale heat of the room, the pale and lost faces of the other men around him; their *vulnerability*. These were tortures that dragged on for over an hour. But he went as often as he could. He went for her.

For the entire first year, they went together weekly to a psychologist specializing in grief and trauma of their specific variety. The sessions were intensive, intrusive and altogether more stressful than simply going for a long drive, which was what he much preferred. He felt a man could sort out almost anything on a long piece of open road. A highway let a man be a man on his own terms; there were no repudiations. But he went with Caroline, went for her. She did most of the talking, she did most of the crying, and he sat there like a pillar of flesh, Kleenex box on his lap. He got through it a minute at a time, gritting his teeth and nodding when he felt it was appropriate. He understood that opening the tap on this thing—that to turn the knob or flick the switch—would not signal the beginning of the *end* of grief as the professionals assured them, with their promises and their fifty-minute hours, their air of subtle superiority. It was, he knew, in fact just the opposite. The opening of the valve meant only the beginning of acute and chronic suffering, infinite in its scope. In his line of work he had learned and accepted the simplest truths of the human animal. There were places from which a person could not return. A wound becomes a scar, and the scar fades with time, but it will never be undone.

"The worst thing," Caroline confessed during one of the sessions, "is how he died. Alone like that. Away from us. I can't help feeling that we cast him out. Families aren't supposed to do that…"

For a husband to hear those words come from the mouth of his wife, to bear the silent weight of those goddamned words—*to hear it spoken and to be unable to do anything.* That was true powerlessness, an unnecessary cruelty to a man already on his knees. For in the light of day, and in his heart of hearts, McKelvey knew that things had not been good between him and Caroline for a long, long time. Even before *this,* there had been the distance between them. They had stumbled through the battlefield of marriage and come out the other side, a little battered and bruised, but still together, still standing. Negotiations were held, compromises brokered. As with all couples who weather the storm, they had found a spot of common ground and made a sort of quiet peace.

The routine had been shattered by a single late night

phone call. Their lives had shifted, buckled. The known world had collapsed around them, reinventing itself in muted colours, muted sounds. Days became a blur of handshakes and sympathetic looks, downcast eyes, hushed whispers as he walked through the halls at the office.

It was understood there was a *process* involved here, levels and phases to be negotiated. There were the stages of grief, as clearly outlined in the pamphlets and brochures. McKelvey wanted to break something or fix something, or simply run through to the other side. In the silence of his grief, he bore the weight of his guilt, the consequences of his decisions. For it was McKelvey who had pushed back hardest against the teen's drug use, the disrespect, the lack of appreciation for a home carved from the meagre bones McKelvey had gathered along the way. Nothing had come easy in his own life, so there was a desire to impart the lessons of a life learned the hard way.

After a time, Caroline had steered herself towards a group of mothers who gathered in alternating homes to discuss their grief from a distinctly female point of view. So it was that Charlie McKelvey found himself adrift for a time, driving away from the suffocating city, up through the lush farmland of Holland Marsh, the only sound in the car the soothing rush of tires on pavement or the beat of his own ragged heart. Long drives, tanks of gas, packages of cigarettes and wads of gum in a vain attempt to mask the reek of tobacco. It was ironic, he thought, how he had quit smoking a half dozen years earlier for the very reason that he wanted to ensure he would be around for his son's wedding day. Now there would be no wedding day. No grandchildren. The future, which only yesterday had hovered in the distance like the comforting and anticipated closing scene in a film, was now blurry and grainy, the storyline meandering without purpose. This was arthouse cinema. Their lives, both his and Caroline's, reduced to a series of comings and goings, a joint bank account, their future anchored entirely in memory.

Eventually, after much goading, McKelvey had agreed to participate in the men's grief group up at the hospital. He saved gas money but found no solace in the depressing room that smelled of cheap aftershave and burned coffee stewing in the aluminum percolator they also used for AA meetings. The men were all ages, from the youngest, a thirty-year-old named Tim, to the eldest, an eighty-three year old with the antiquated name Bartholomew. They represented all walks of life, too, from a shoe salesman to a cop. They were balding or they had hair, they were overweight, and they were tall and short, and they were just a bunch of idiots sitting in a room trying to do something that—in McKelvey's estimation—was akin to fucking around with a Ouija board in a darkened closet. He was not hardwired for this, and nothing good could come from it.

Most of the men in the group drifted in and out of attendance, likely just as uncomfortable in the dredging of grief as McKelvey found himself. A rare few shared regularly, wept openly, and curled balls of tissue in their moist, clenched fists while the moderator knelt before them, rubbing a hand across their back. McKelvey hated it most when a crying man's nose began to run, as though this physiological reaction somehow represented total and final *defeat*, a threshold breached. He felt sorry for them, and yet conversely he admired their ability to weep openly in a room full of strangers. It was beyond his grasp.

Two

On this Tuesday evening, the wind was lifting bits of garbage, the detritus of the city, and whirling it around the visitor's lot. Early December, the sky dark as coal and glowing at its edges from the burning lights of the city, the air thick with the dampness of coming snow. Upstairs in the meeting room, seated at the corner of a long conference table, Charlie McKelvey was chewing the skin on the side of his thumb. This was a habit his father had also possessed, one of the few things he remembered fondly about the man, an indelible impression. That and tearing his hangnails with his teeth. Caroline was always at him when his own thumbs were cracked and bleeding. Then McKelvey remembered it was something he'd seen Gavin doing on a number of occasions, this automaton's movement of thumb to mouth, and he wondered then if it was possible for a quirky family trait to be so deeply embedded in the coils of genes and DNA. A sort of torch of the generations. *And what other surprises had he passed along in that weathered packet?*

The meeting room was always too hot, and this day there was a pong of body odour, a lingering sour ripeness. McKelvey was not paying attention to the words unfolding around him. He was thinking about something his wife had asked him to do, and now he couldn't quite remember the details. They had shared a rare moment during breakfast that morning, McKelvey guzzling a coffee while standing over the kitchen sink, Caroline up early and eating a bowl of granola at the table. She had raised her head to him, yes. Words spoken. But now he was at a loss.

"Charlie?"

McKelvey startled, and said, "Sorry?"

He lifted his head and smiled benignly at Paul, the group moderator. McKelvey had been doing this since he was a child, the same quick little boy's smile that carried him through school when his grades weren't good enough. It was simply a part of his physical character now, like chewing the skin of his thumbs.

"I said, 'Did you want to say anything to Tim?' From your experience?"

McKelvey blinked at Paul, then looked over at Tim. Tim was a young man, much younger than McKelvey. A widower at thirty, a crime by any stretch of the imagination. The details were unclear to McKelvey. He believed there had been an accident.

McKelvey shrugged and said, "Maybe next week I'll think of something."

The moderator regarded him for a long moment, then he said, "That's what you said last week. And perhaps even the week before."

McKelvey smiled and let the little poke roll off him. Then he shrugged and looked over at the young widower. He was a handsome kid, handsome in the fashion of a high school teacher, which is what he was. Sandy hair was swept back over a high forehead, and his clear eyes were framed by modern eyeglasses, small rectangles. McKelvey saw himself at thirty, intense blue eyes burning beneath a lid of thick black curls cropped short, already a married working stiff weighed down with the long shifts and routines of a life. Even back then he and Caroline had owned the choreography of roommates, roommates who happened to be intimate on a regular schedule. Even then it was only to answer a physical need, and it was in reality something they felt they could do for the other without losing ground one way or the other. He couldn't imagine the house without her.

McKelvey lowered his head and said, "I wish there was something I could say, you know. It's just that...I mean, with my job and everything, I see what happens to people every day. It happened to me. It happened to us. I can't change anything. And I don't know how I'm going to live to be eighty if every day is like this."

Paul nodded and smiled. He said, "That was *something*, Charlie. See, you did have something to say." Then he moved on to the man on McKelvey's right.

The men's voices melted to a murmur then, the vague sound of a TV bleeding through the wall of a cheap motel room, and McKelvey got lost in himself. He drifted out and beyond the confines of his physical body, eyes closed, blood hammering in his ears, until finally it was the only sound he could detect, soothing as the methodical *whoosh* of wipers sliding across a windshield. *Shook shook, shook shook.* There was nothing for a long time, and it was good, just the blackness of the back of his skull, of the deepest part of himself, and when he squeezed his eyes there was a burst of fireworks, coloured pins, geometrical designs. Then he was pulled to a specific place and time, an earmarked memory. As easy as closing your eyes and moving through time.

*   *   *

He is a boy standing in the sunshine on the sidewalk, squinting as he strains to look all the way up at his father, Grey McKelvey. There is another man standing on the sidewalk, someone who knows McKelvey's father, another miner, and while this man's features and voice are blurred, McKelvey understands there is a level of admiration here for his father.

"Al Brooks at the Legion was sayin' you might run for the union," the man says.

Grey McKelvey laughs with just the right amount of humility. Flashes his smile and dips his head, the modest and practiced gesture of a man well used to an easy sell.

"Oh no," Grey chuckles, "I don't think I'm cut out for that racket. No sir, not me."

"Well, anyway, Grey, where are you two boys headed?"

McKelvey's face is warm in the sunshine, his eyes blinded by the soaring yellow light, the sky above them as liquid blue as the combat knife his father keeps in his top dresser drawer, nestled in with his wool socks and strange square packages with rigid rings at the centre. He feels his father's big hand squeeze his own small hand. He feels his father take a step closer to him, a wall of human security, sixteen feet high, eight feet thick.

"Taking Charlie here to get his hair cut over at Bud's..."

Then they are transported, and McKelvey sees and smells the inside of the old barbershop on the main street, the multi-coloured bottles of after-shave and hair tonic, the neon blue disinfectant for the black combs, the lather creams, the strong manly scent of sandalwood and alcohol, tobacco smoke and sweat.

Old Bud sets a board across the chair, hefts him up, ties a red apron around his neck, pushes his head forward and begins to work with the scissors. The sound of stainless steel parts working in concert. All the while McKelvey keeps his eyes closed, pretending not to follow the conversation between his father and Bud and the other men assembled in the barber shop, this sanctuary of all things male. They speak in loose code about local women, about their physical attributes, then on to hunting, drinking, eventually coming back around to a war story, for they all, with the exception of Bud, due to his age, had fought in the war in one way or another. Whether soldier, sailor or airman, the war is their generational bond.

Then the haircut is done, and he opens his eyes to the world once again. Bud takes a hard-bristled brush and whisks away the hair trimmings from the back of his neck, and the brush hurts, but he doesn't say anything, not ever. Bud with his big boxer's face that reminds McKelvey of an old bulldog with sad bloodshot eyes. Then Bud gives him a lollipop from an old coffee tin he keeps under the cash...and he can right now taste the sugary orange...

* * *

McKelvey opened his eyes. Like waking up. The meeting was closing in its traditional fashion, some of the men hugging, others patting one another on the back, congratulating each other for progress made in this battle against *grief*—or perhaps simply for making it through one more Tuesday night. McKelvey was one of them, and yet he was *apart*. He found it impossible to imagine himself slumped forward in his chair, head in hands, crying in front of strangers. He couldn't do it; it wasn't *in* him. He slipped out the door and was down the hall before the moderator finally caught up to him.

"Charlie," he called, "Charlie, wait up. I'm glad I caught you," Paul said, pausing for a breath. He smiled. "I wanted to talk to you about something."

"Listen, about tonight—"

"No, no. I wanted to ask a favour. It's Tim, he's..."

McKelvey glanced at his watch, but not really. He said, "It's just I'm running late and..."

Paul moved a hand to McKelvey's shoulder and looked into his eyes, unblinking.

"My daughter was hit by a car on her way to school six years ago, Charlie."

"I know, Paul," McKelvey said, "I know, I know."

"We're in the same club, you and me. All the guys in that room. We're all on the same side of the street watching everybody else go on about their lives over on the other side." Paul was a tall, slender, soft-spoken man. His eyes were hazel, moist. His eyelids fluttered when he spoke. He struck McKelvey as the sort of rare man who manoeuvred easily and completely without shame in the realms of emotion, *sensitivity*. It was for this reason a certain type of man—a man like McKelvey, say— often assumed at first glance that a man like Paul must be weak.

"Nobody else knows what it's like. How can they?" Paul said.

McKelvey said, "I know..."

"I need you to help Tim. He's not doing so well. Will you have a coffee with him, maybe go for a beer? I think you could help him. Maybe help yourself while you're at it," Paul said.

"I guess," McKelvey said. "It's busy right now at work, but maybe in a week or so."

Paul reached into his pocket and handed McKelvey a folded square of paper.

"Give him a call, Charlie."

McKelvey held the note between his thumb and forefinger, as though he had been handed a summons to appear. So the whole thing was pre-meditated, planned before the meeting had even begun. Paul was no fool, McKelvey knew. He knew the man had a way of getting more out of the group members than they set out to divulge, putting on this act of the eye-fluttering half-wit. The man possessed the sort of quiet intelligence that could not be underestimated by a police detective. McKelvey was always on guard in the presence of psychologists and social workers and group therapy moderators. Their craft was emotional sorcery.

"All right," McKelvey said, shoving the paper in his pocket, "if it'll get you off my back."

He turned and walked away, wishing he'd rounded that last corner about thirty seconds sooner. That was the truth of it, and he felt a pang of guilt for even considering the request a burden. It was a privilege to be asked. *You're such an asshole, Charlie.*

Three

McKelvey came through the door of his home, the simple abode he and Caroline had purchased on a quaint little drive off Queen Street East long before the east end neighborhood known somewhat piously as "The Beach" was out of the price range of a working class family. The tiny old white-washed cottages nestled across from the beaches of Woodbine, Kew Gardens, Scarborough, Victoria Park, had over the decades been bought and sold a dozen times, renovated for the yuppies of the 1980s, renovated yet again for the high tastes of the urban young in the 1990s. At the very closing of the twentieth century, the old cottages wore skylights, their innards gutted to accommodate open concept lofts, kitchen islands beaming with marble and slate, walls smooshed in the latest designer colours, and owners could be overheard on the local Starbucks terrace dropping names like Gluckstein. The McKelvey home was finished with a newer kitchen and hardwood flooring in the hallway and living room, but that was where the upgrades ceased. All else was preserved in its original simplicity. McKelvey did not see the sense in replacing a functioning faucet simply because it didn't *look* a certain way. Caroline, in her continual frustration, said it was one thing to change just for the sake of change, but another thing altogether to forget that time moves forward. She said one look at his collection of blazers and ties was evidence enough that McKelvey did not buy into the myth of first appearances.

He put his coat on its hook and stepped lightly down the hall to find her seated at the kitchen table. He watched her there for a moment, unnoticed, a voyeur. She was an attractive woman, plain and confident in her beauty, at ease in sloppy clothes, old fraying pyjamas. She was writing in her "healing journal", a cup of herbal tea at hand. He longed for her patience, for her ability to pause and sit like this, to be quiet and still, to listen to the beat of her own heart against the din of the city. It was half past nine in the evening. The room smelled of toast made some hours earlier, the lingering scent of burned bread. She looked up. Their eyes locked, and for the first time in a long time, they were in the same room together at the same time.

"Home," he said.

She glanced at the clock. The Tuesday night meetings ended at eight. He caught her eye and followed her gaze to the timepiece on the wall. He blinked. Like a kid caught, getting ready to explain.

"I went for a drive after the meeting," he said with a shrug. And he was chewing gum, which confirmed everything. He coughed, too, and cleared his throat on cue.

"You need to quit, Charlie," she said. But there was an indifference to it. Or perhaps it was simply exasperation. A lifetime with McKelvey and his bad habits, broken promises.

"I'm working on it," he said. "Christ."

She tilted her head a little but didn't say anything.

"Listen, I was going to tell you after I got the confirmation," he said, "but I have a meeting with Aoki tomorrow morning. To find out what the Crown plans to do with...you know, with all the information I've been putting together."

She stopped and looked at him, this strange expression on her face; it was a look he had not seen in a long time. A place where hope meets possibility.

"They're going to make an arrest? In Gavin's murder?" she said.

"I don't know. I mean, I don't see how they can't." His thumb went to his mouth, and he chewed it for a second, a nibble between the canines. "Or at least it opens them up to spending some goddamned man hours on this thing. I swear, Balani's done almost no work on this in the past six months. Let it go cold."

She looked at him. "If it was this man you say—"

"Duguay," he said. "Pierre Duguay."

"If it is this man, this Duguay, what will happen to him?"

McKelvey said, "Face trial, likely for second degree murder. If convicted, he'd get life. Maximum twenty-five, minimum ten. In reality, he'd probably serve eight to ten years behind bars, the last two in a halfway house or a minimum security health club."

"So he could be free in as little as ten years."

"It's the system," he said, as though it explained everything. "We've got a system run by liberal judges. You know all this, Caroline. The frustration we face every goddamned day on the job. Make an arrest and see it chucked out the window because you said something that hurt the perp's feelings."

"That's not enough time," she said. "Not for my boy's life."

"Listen," he said, "it's too early to be talking about specifics here. Let me get through this meeting with the Crown and see where we're headed. Okay?"

"It's funny, isn't it?"

"What's that," he said.

"How at first it's all you think about. Punishment and prison. Even the death penalty. And then after a while it's gone, it just doesn't matter any more. You come to the point where you lose your mind or you learn how to get past it. I stopped thinking about an arrest a while ago. It won't bring Gavin back. It won't *change* anything. It's a cliché I heard from some of the other survivors, but I didn't realize it was true until just now. I didn't realize that I would feel this way. Unchanged."

Survivors. He hated it when she used that word to describe their predicament. There were all sorts of words the counsellors were fond of tossing out as though it would win them points in a game of Psycho Scrabble. McKelvey cleared his throat again and said, "There will be justice; I promise you that."

"You don't know that," she said. "Don't make promises you can't keep."

"I already said it. So there."

She looked at him like a sister to a brother, a friend to a friend. She *knew* him. She knew Charlie McKelvey better than anyone else. Knew the weight behind those words he had spoken, knew there wasn't a day that went by that he didn't envision revenge. For things were black and white for Charlie. She looked at him, and he saw in her eyes how the past couple of years had changed her. They had both changed. McKelvey knew he had gained weight, all of his shirts stretched and his sports coats too tight, and his face looked heavy and tired, and what little empathy or humour he had left after almost thirty years on the job was long gone. With Caroline the change was inner, as though through the darkest days of the struggle she had discovered within herself a new reservoir of strength and hope. And *peace.* He understood in that moment that they were standing on opposite sides of a river, the water was rising, and it was getting harder to decipher the other shoreline.

McKelvey wanted to change the subject, in fact wished he hadn't brought it up at all. He said, as he moved to the cupboard and pulled down a mug, "I spoke with Paul after the meeting.

I guess he wants me to help this kid out a little, talk to him. Guy lost his wife after two years of marriage."

"Are you going to do it?" she said.

"I don't know what I'd say that would change anything."

He went and took the pot from the stove and poured some tea into his cup. He held the pot for a moment, recalling the day Caroline had brought it home from a pottery night class at the high school. It was hand-painted, and the colours ran, and when glanced at quickly, it appeared to be the handiwork of a kindergarten student. It was during remembered moments such as these that McKelvey found enough feeling for his wife, enough shared days, to see him through.

"It's healthy," she said. "That's what people do when they're hurting, they come together, they share. People have been doing it since forever. Sitting in caves talking about their—oh my god, their *feelings...*"

He replaced the pot on its pad on the counter. "Listen." He stopped for a moment, looking for words. "Paul seems to think everyone has the ability or the desire to sit down and discuss this kind of stuff with complete strangers. What the fuck am I going to say to this kid?"

She looked at him, and he felt smaller. But it was the truth.

"God almighty, I've delivered that kind of news in person enough times, Caroline. You know what I'm saying? Standing on someone's front step at midnight, hat in hand. I don't need to come home and do it in my spare time, thank you very much."

Caroline went to speak but stopped herself. She looked at him for a long minute then lowered her head to her journal. He turned and stood against the counter, nursing the hot tea. It was peppermint. He kept smacking his lips in an attempt to like it. He wasn't a fan of tea to begin with. It seemed to McKelvey that you could divide the world into two groups: tea drinkers and coffee drinkers. There were lifestyle and philosophical differences, an attitudinal *chasm*. He drank black coffee, six to eight cups a day, starting with the first cup grabbed on the way to the office for seven a.m. His guts were cramped and boiling by evening, requiring a bedtime shot of PeptoBismol, a sleeping pill, perhaps two. Caroline used to read aloud to him studies published in the newspaper about how coffee caused cancer of the bladder or blindness or erectile dysfunction, insanity or death. It was always something. But now it seemed to McKelvey that the joke was on anyone who thought they could cheat death simply by eating a certain way, cutting this or that out of a life, by following the so-called rules laid out in schools and in churches. No, death comes when death damn well pleases, and you often don't even have time to put your underpants on.

"This tastes like somebody's chewed gum," he said and spat a mouthful into the sink. He poured the rest of it down the drain and moved to the fridge to wash the taste away with Diet Coke. He drank straight from the plastic bottle, four big swallows that burned and fizzed down his throat.

"I hate when you do that," Caroline said without looking up. "Ever heard of germs?"

"You should see some of the stuff I touch in a day," he said, wiping his mouth with the cuff of his dress shirt.

And he saw himself through a vivid and stark lens, all the places he had been in a lifetime on the job, the rooms and hallways, all the things his hands had touched, the bloodied doorknobs and the bloodied cribs...

"I can just imagine."

"Oh," he said, "I don't know that you can."

She finished the line she was writing, then she closed the book and held it to her chest, saying, "I'm going to go draw a bath. Do you want it after I'm done?"

McKelvey shook his head.

Four

In the sombre hours between midnight and dawn, within the sleep that falls like the weight of the dead, McKelvey lost himself completely. It was the best destination, his one luxury at the end of a day that seemed to last a lifetime, hour by hour, minute by minute. Sometimes he saw the rest of his life in this way, as a series of days stacked like folded card chairs against some long table. It was his job to walk along that table, unfolding a single chair at a time, preparing a place for guests unknown, and the table had no end; it faded to infinity. It was just something to do. The way he saw his job lately, the endless hours logged to lay charges that would be turned into plea bargains or else dropped altogether. The way he saw his life at home. Hour by hour, minute by minute. Nothing came easy.

Then McKelvey startled awake from the same dream he'd been having every few weeks since his son's murder. There was no schedule to the dream, but it always returned, and it never changed. It was a dream of innuendo, shadows and murmured voices. There was no direction to it, no line to follow, as though it had been conjured in the mind of a drunk. There was only the residue of something not quite right, the pressure of impending doom, unnameable yet undeniable. Like the sick feeling he'd got in his belly as a child when he knew he'd done *something* to *someone*, but couldn't quite recall the particulars of the trespass.

He woke in a cold sweat, the sheets twisted around his legs, his breath raspy and chest clenched like a fist.

The neighbour's dogs barked and howled at the night, their empty-belly sounds made all the more stark by the late night silence of the street. Maybe somebody's cat was passing along the fence line, raising its arse in a taunt the way cats taunt a dog that is safely penned or chained. Then the barking ceased, and silence fell once again. McKelvey blinked to orient himself, wiped his face, turned to be sure his wife was still sleeping, and slipped out of the bed and down the hall to the room that had been his son's bedroom for seventeen years—up to and until the teen's poor attitude, anti-social behavior and escalating drug use had popped the McKelvey family bubble of security and success. This was, they were assured, happening all the time inside seemingly happy suburban homes, a family's dream of earned contentment ripped open when a child or children passed with great difficulty beyond the stage of cute smiles and teeth too big for their mouths. Most kids made it through the minefield of adolescence a little wiser but without much serious trouble. They talked back a little, tried their hand at shoplifting or drew detention for skipping classes, got sick from smoking a joint at lunch in somebody's garage. But there was a minority, McKelvey knew from his day job and his own life, that entered a surreal zone of angst that could not be fully comprehended by anyone, professional or amateur. All parents felt responsible, but as a cop—especially as a cop—McKelvey felt a terrible burden of failure. It was the ultimate irony in life, akin to the local minister's daughter strolling around town with a swollen belly.

If a cop can't keep his own son off drugs, then who can?

The room had remained for two years as Gavin had left it

when he took off at seventeen. No clear memory remained of that day for McKelvey, only a series of impressions: a muddle of angry voices, a plate shattered against a wall, threats uttered in hatred and confusion. He had lost himself that day, and his son and his wife, too. Within the tightly coiled mess of his incomprehensible frustration, there came forth the variety of anger that was buried within the memories of his own young life. He had put his hand through the drywall in the hallway, again in the master bedroom. And their boy was gone from their home.

For two years, Caroline had dusted the room without disturbing the contents. For two years, she had believed the boy would return home, eventually, when things got bad enough out there (and here was a source of constant friction between mother and father, for the mother believed the father's stubborn and hard-nosed approach, his "school-of-hard-knocks" and all of that idiotic police logic was the reason their child stayed away, despite the hardness of life lived on the fringe).

Two years later, and just a few months after Gavin's death, Caroline tore through the room like a twister with a green garbage bag. There was raw purpose to her movements. She was a robot programmed to remove every last trace of the child... *Erase*. She tore down the posters of punk rockers and gothic freaks, threw away the magazines and books, and left the remnants of her son's life at the curb for the regular Wednesday trash pickup. McKelvey had come home to find his wife curled in a ball on the boy's stripped mattress, thumb tacks peppered across the naked walls with bits of poster stuck beneath them. She was exhausted, and she wouldn't speak a word to him for four days. It terrified him to the point of inaction. He understood they were on a precipice of some sort. He felt everything shift within the deepest parts of himself, and it was frightening at first then somehow liberating. He felt as though he had little left to lose. What else was there?

Now the house was still and lonely, and McKelvey stretched out on the bed in Gavin's old room—which was referred to simply as "the guestroom", as though they ever welcomed visitors into their museum of grief. He closed his eyes, and he remembered the time when Gavin was four and had asked for a bunk bed.

"Bunk bed? What do you need a bunk bed for?" McKelvey had asked.

He saw Gavin's little face, four or five freckles on each cheek, the same thick coal-black waves that would one day become a majestic head of hair.

"My friend Gorley Robinson needs a place to sleep, you know," Gavin said.

"Gorley Robinson, and who's that?"

"My friend. He lives in the closet right now. But it's too crowded with my shoes."

"Ah, I see. Gorley Robinson who lives in the closet. Well, we'll see..."

McKelvey could reach out and touch the little boy's face, smell the chocolate milk on his breath—*he was there, just there, and for a moment his mind played the cruelest trick.* He sat up in the bed. The room was silent save for the quiet tick of a clock on a night table. Soft light from the street lamps outside bled through the Venetian blinds, painting slanted shadows across the wall. McKelvey lifted a wavering hand and reached out, blinking to clear his sight, but then Gavin was gone, faded or retreated. And he was left alone with the tormented thoughts of a guilty man, all of the rhetorical questions gathered across a lifetime hanging there in an empty room. Why had he not even considered getting bunk beds?

If I could go back, he thought, *I would build the thing myself. The best bunk bed in the neighbourhood, all the kids would want to sleep over at Gavin McKelvey's...*

He could see the lengths of pine, how the ladder would fit against the side with a set of brackets, and a runner so that you could slide it back and forth. He settled back onto the bed and closed his eyes tight. He felt the sting of a tear roll from the corner of his eye and slide down his cheek to the pillow. He tucked his hands between his knees to rock himself, and in this way he negotiated sleep.

Five

The alarm sounds, and McKelvey slaps the top of the little black box, giving himself the gift of another eight minutes of lostness. When the second buzzer sounds, he finally opens his eyes and stares at the stucco on the ceiling with its familiar shadows. He collects his bearings; is it Tuesday or Wednesday? Time shifts, and days melt into weeks. Mondays are born and suddenly bloom into Friday afternoons. There is comfort to be found in the mundane routines.

He pulls himself from the cocoon of covers, steps numbly into the shower, slides a razor down his face, pats his cheeks with whatever cologne Caroline bought him for Christmas last year. He stands in front of the fogged mirror dabbing a piece of tissue on a nick. Stands back to adjust the sports coat that is too tight in the armpits. He feels hot, stuffy. He practices nodding, smiling a few times, until he feels like a meteorologist on a local cable channel, searching for a middle ground between contrived and genuine. And so he meets the day...

*   *   *

McKelvey stood there in front of the mirror the same as he did every morning, adjusting and re-adjusting his tie. And still it was too short, three inches above his belt line. He undid the tangle and worked at it again. His thick fingers—ode to a few generations of McKelvey manual laborers, miners mostly—were not designed for this sort of fine work. He had never slipped a tie around his neck and made it the correct length in one attempt; it was always an event, a flail of silk. How many years had he been doing this, for godsake? Caroline used to laugh at him and, when he was old enough, Gavin, too. The kid said his fingers were like fat sausages...

"Sausages," McKelvey said aloud, and was startled by the sound of his own voice.

Finally satisfied with the result, he brushed a few flakes of dandruff from the shoulders of his navy sports coat and regarded himself for a moment. He thought he looked old and heavy, and he *was* heavy, over two-fifteen now. There were pouches beneath his blue eyes, dark circles, bloodshot eyes. His face was evolving, morphing into his father's face. The same width, the same creases at the jowls, the same wrinkles across the forehead from a lifetime of scowling. He leaned in to check his teeth, and they looked the way old people's teeth begin to look: narrowing, dying. He hadn't slept well, his mind working through the coming events of the day. It was to be a day of reckoning. At last, a beacon at the end of the long dark road. All of the work, all of the tears, all of the silent angst bottled under pressure. Two years of bulldog determination, countless hours of unpaid overtime logged pouring over files, drawing the connections. He had pushed it as far as he could push it, working angles from the sidelines, and the doggedness had brought him to the point of being written up for accessing files without *authorization.* The files concerned the murder investigation of his *son,* so Aoki had let the infraction begin and end at her desk. It was one cop doing another cop a favour. Any father would be interested in his son's murder investigation, more so if the father happened to *be* the police. But even so,

McKelvey believed there was some word out there about his level of interest in the whole thing, the way he came at things. He was aware that some people spoke of him in a certain light.

He passed through the kitchen and downed the last of his cold black coffee. He set the mug in the sink and grabbed his long coat from its hook in the hall. He was warming up his old red Mazda pickup when he was startled by a knock on the window. He turned and looked into the face of his neighbour, Carl Seeburger, who was standing there with his wispy silver hair glowing like a baby's down in the back light of the rising dawn. The old German had been their neighbour for just eighteen months now, having replaced a longtime and affable family by the name of Dewar. For eighteen months, he and McKelvey and some of the others on the street had battled sporadically, and sometimes loudly, over the trio of dogs that Seeburger kept, without much apparent attention, in his backyard. McKelvey rolled the window down without smiling.

"Did I forget my lunch bag again?" McKelvey said.

Seeburger's lips began to work and, as always, a tiny white froth appeared at the corners of his mouth. He crossed his long arms across his chest and said, although it sounded more like a direct accusation, "Did you call the city about my dogs?"

"Jesus Christ. It's seven o'clock, Carl, you should be in bed," McKelvey said, and immediately began to roll the window back up, move his foot to the clutch.

Seeburger, dressed in faded grey work pants that were a little too short, and a worn red and blue flannel shirt and suspenders, stepped closer to the truck. He was a tall man, and he had to bend down to level his face with the window. McKelvey caught a whiff of strong cheese and wool. Even though he had apparently been living in the country for forty years now, Seeburger's accent was still thick and harsh. Is sounded to McKelvey like a machine cutting and splicing. McKelvey believed it spoke to the man's stubborn refusal to go with the flow.

"Just because you work for the city, you think that gives you the right to use your connections to hassle tax-paying citizens? This is a free country, Mr. McKelvey, and I will not be treated like a criminal. If I choose to own dogs, that is my right. Protected by the Constitution. And if you have any more problems with my dogs, I would wish that you would be man enough to address me directly rather than use your connections to have me harassed by the city by-law office."

It was the right morning, or it was the alignment of the stars. Or it was just the way McKelvey felt lately. As though he were functioning in a sort of suspended animation. Everything was as in a dream, and he couldn't think anything through with clarity. Anything could happen. McKelvey moved his right hand to ensure the stick shift was in park, then popped his seatbelt and was out of the vehicle standing toe to toe with his neighbour. Seeburger stepped back, his eyes blinking with anticipation.

"Listen, let's get something straight here," McKelvey said and pointed an index finger. "I hate your fucking dogs, Carl. I really do. I wish death upon their ugly howling heads every night when I close my eyes and try to fall asleep in a neighbourhood that until eighteen months ago was a goddamned piece of heaven. Secondly, I don't have any connections with the bylaw office, and even if I did, I wouldn't require the use of said connections, because I would take care of things myself. I'm not beyond getting my hands dirty. In fact, I enjoy it from time to time."

"Oh, yes? Is that a threat, Mr. McKelvey?"

"Oh no, it's not a threat," McKelvey said, "it's a guarantee." Then he opened the door and held it there for a moment before sliding behind the wheel. Something within himself, a coiled spring or a bottled surge, *wanted* his neighbour to do something wild and crazy, take a swing perhaps. McKelvey saw himself connecting with that big Teutonic chin, a blow for glory, a blow for every goddamned neighbour within earshot of those barking sons of bitches. His gaggle of thick sausages was already curled into a tight fist, jaw clenched. He looked up at the morning beginning to spread across the skyline in a deep, dark orange of early winter, then looked back to the old man standing before him, and said, "You know, Carl, it's a very thin line. A very thin line."

"What is?" Seeburger said.

"The precise location," McKelvey said, "where your right to own dogs intersects with my right to a peaceful sleep."

McKelvey closed the door and put his seatbelt on. Seeburger stood there wagging a finger and said in a hoarse voice, "I'll find out who called the city. That is my right as a tax-paying citizen!"

"Have a nice day," McKelvey said, smiling broadly and waving as he rolled away.

*   *   *

He felt like a tourist at the office these days, somebody passing through. The police headquarters had at one time been located in a little shithole over on Jarvis Street, but now it was next to a Starbucks on College. There remained very little of the "old" building McKelvey knew from his first days on the force. Back then, the interview rooms were choked blue with smoke, and more than a few lockers in the change room held a pint of rum or brandy tucked beneath a pair of dirty gym shorts for an end-of-shift "happy hour". And women were just beginning to make their bold entry into the strange universe that was "The Police". Hard to believe. A lifetime ago and just the other day.

Now the interview rooms were painted in soothing pastels based on psychological consultations, and McKelvey's boss was a thirty-eight-year-old woman named *Inspector* Tina Aoki. A university graduate with degrees in criminology and law, Aoki was right now working on her own time towards some sort of Masters. While many of his silver-haired peers were genuinely frustrated, perhaps even angered, by the seeming tendency to put greater stock in framed degrees over hours spent in the blood and filth of the streets, McKelvey took it all in stride. He accepted the fact that everything in life, if given time, changes to the point where you eventually don't recognize it. We look upon our lives in a sort of warped hindsight, he knew, everything taken in our own unique context, set against our own criteria. He knew any tradesman was declared obsolete if he didn't keep up with the latest tools. The knowledge didn't prevent a man from longing, from time to time, for the old days, the old ways.

Detective-Constable Charlie McKelvey made his second coffee of the morning at the refreshment stand in the Hold-Up Squad. This place had been his home for five years now, having transferred from a half dozen years on the Fraud Squad and, before that, a lifetime on the beat across four divisions that spanned the full spectrum of a city that never stopped growing. It was only the nature of the crime that changed with each transfer. The people he dealt with were invariably the same; whether he was pulling a guy over for running a red light, or forcing a known drug dealer to empty the pockets of his cargo pants across the hood of a cruiser up at Jane and Finch, everybody thought he was born last Sunday. They believed with a fervent religious conviction that their lies and excuses were brilliantly unique. It got to the point, and pretty soon into the job, where McKelvey went into every situation—whether a break-in at a hardware store or a stabbing at an after-hours booze can—ready to offer absolutely zero benefit of the doubt. It got to the point sometimes, he knew, where he took this view back home with him. And to Gavin. A teenager with a goddamned cop for a dad. *You never believed him. And so, through this lack of trust or faith, the boy necessarily wandered and pushed the limits of a life, real or imagined...in this way did you fail your son...*

"Morning, Detective."

McKelvey looked up from the cup he was stirring and stirring, endlessly stirring, and he smiled at the youthful face of the administrative assistant who had been hired just a short while ago. Amy—he couldn't remember her last name. She was standing in the hallway, a stack of files clenched under an arm. She was a striking young woman dressed in a form-fitting skirt and blazer combination. The guys were always giving her a hard time, kids in a playground. They disguised their lust for her behind jokes and pranks, and McKelvey believed she didn't mind the attention.

"Good morning, Amy," he said. "You look nice today."

And she did. She was beautiful and young. She was perfect. And McKelvey felt a twinge of sadness for something he had lost within himself somewhere along the way.

"Thank you, sir," she said, and McKelvey thought she blushed.

Sir. That's what she called him. It stung, but he was pleased with the show of respect.

"I'm just on my way to see the boss," he said. "Is she in a good mood this morning?"

Amy smiled, rolled her eyes, and continued on down the hallway without a word. McKelvey took his coffee to Aoki's office. Her door was always open. She was talking on the phone when he popped his head inside. She motioned him in, and he took a seat across from her, sipping his coffee. The office was small and unglamorous—*beige*—but he knew she wouldn't inhabit it for long. She would be heading up Detective Services before her hair began its turn toward grey, that was his bet.

"Morning, Charlie," Aoki said, setting the phone down.

"You look pissed," he said.

She shook her head, leaning back in her chair. "These prosecutors, they think we can just pull evidence out of our *assholes.* They say 'is that all you've got?' and I feel like saying 'no, we thought we'd keep some of the good stuff until we get to court'."

Aoki made him smile. She was wiry, all sinewy muscle, her dark hair cropped short. And she swore like a longshoreman. It was as though every movement, every mannerism was aimed at destroying the myth of her diminutive stature. She had confided in him over a drink a couple of years earlier about how her father had been interned at a camp on the west coast during the Second World War. She spoke of how he hadn't been angry with his new country for assuming he was a possible collaborator, saying instead that "everyone has a role to play when their country is at war". McKelvey believed she both admired and detested this vein of deep stoicism within her father. Knowing Aoki, she wouldn't have taken it on the chin for king and country.

McKelvey was anxious, and he caught himself chewing at his ragged thumb. In a matter of weeks, the Crown would kick off the trial of a bank robber, drug dealer, extortionist, suspected killer and known biker named Pierre Duguay. The trial was attracting media attention due to Duguay's alleged connections to the Blades, an upstart Quebec biker gang with roots in the southern United States and South America. The Blades had battled the Hell's Angels in Quebec for a few years at the closing of the nineties, fighting to control the lucrative drugs, prostitution and fraud rings. The body count was high. Car bombings, pipe bombs, shootings. The Angels were too big, too well-entrenched, too well-organized and managed, so the war eventually ran out of steam, and a large faction of Blades patched over to their rivals rather than face certain annihilation. But there remained a faithful few who drifted from Quebec in search of new frontiers out west and up north in the mining towns, places like Sudbury and Thunder Bay, Winnipeg, but like all pioneers, they stopped somewhere to catch their breath, and it ended up becoming home for a while.

The Blades bought a house in the west end of Toronto, installed security cameras and raised a new flag. They also bought an old strip joint near the airport, a place in which to conduct business, to launder their soiled cash. New kids on the block come to carve out a little corner amidst the Asian street gangs, the Jamaicans, and yes, always the Hell's.

And it was Duguay, McKelvey knew, who was responsible for his boy's death. Duguay, whose method of operation was to get his hangarounds and foot soldiers to befriend and recruit street kids to peddle his crack, run his errands, get his army of the lost moving across the landscape of parks and transit stops, malls and arcades. It was what he had done in Montreal, how he had ended up in Joliette for a number of years. He had recruited McKelvey's boy, who exchanged the roof over his head for a fetid bed of rags beneath the Gardiner Expressway, the dangerous missions and shelters. Exchanged school textbooks for a goddamned squeegee rag and a bucket. Doc Martens and black eyeliner, a dozen pieces of steel attached to his head, tattoos, a whole warped and negative outlook on the world.

Then, just as McKelvey had prognosticated and warned, his boy had died alone, his body left in a vacant lot beneath the expressway. A piece of garbage tossed from a passing vehicle. That's all.

"How is Caroline?" Aoki said, leaning forward.

He blinked, brought himself back. He said, "Fine. She has good days and bad days."

"And you?"

He took a sip of coffee, shrugged and smiled.

"You're always fine, right Charlie?" she said. "Good old Charlie, straight as an arrow, cool as a fucking cucumber."

"Go easy," he said, "my neighbour already chewed my ass this morning."

She said, "You stopped seeing the department psychologist, I understand. That's okay, though, because between you and me, I don't think she's very good at her job. She's got nice hair, but she's a bit of a twat. That would be my reasoning. So what about you, why did you stop going? You got everything sewn up?"

He sighed, fumbling to put into words how he felt. How *did* he feel about sitting in a closet-sized office, opening up to a woman practically young enough to be his *daughter? Felt. Feel. Express. Breathe in, breathe out. Let's hold hands and explore the stages of grief, Charlie.*

"You can only talk about things for so long," he said.

"Sounds to me like you didn't do much talking."

"You get to the point where it starts doing the opposite of what it's supposed to do. At first, sure, it makes you feel a little better, spilling all this poison. But then they want you to keep digging deeper and deeper...and there's nothing else *down there.* There's nothing there. You've scooped it all out, everything, and now you're just...empty."

Like cleaning a Halloween pumpkin, he wanted to explain. But in picturing that, he was reminded of the years he and Gavin had carved pumpkins a day or two before Halloween, trying to find new ways to smear the greasy pumpkin guts on each other. He saw the various farmers' fields and Sunday markets they had visited in search of the annual pumpkin. *The smell of those slippery insides, rich, fecund scent of fall.* And then he didn't want to think about that any more. He blinked and saw that Aoki was still talking. Her mouth was moving as he brought himself back into the conversation, like flipping to a channel midway through a show.

"...other things that you can look into, like out-patient counselling and..."

His mind suddenly flashed with an image of old Seeburger standing there like the king of goddamned Kensington, and he gritted his teeth and imagined tying those dogs from hell to the back of his truck and taking them for a run all the way to the Humber River.

"You should take advantage of the employee assistance folks," Aoki said.

"I'll see about all that," McKelvey said, nodding.

"I hope you do."

He shifted his weight, rubbed the back of his neck, and said, "So."

She reached for a paperclip and began to uncoil it. Not a good sign. He knew her too well and recognized the mannerisms. "I spoke with the Assistant-Crown attorney, Laura Wright. She understands your personal interest with regards to this particular suspect. They feel the best shot at a conviction against

Duguay is with the charges he's currently sitting on."

"I see," McKelvey said.

"People here don't want to see what happened in Quebec a few years ago, when that little boy was killed in the car bombing. There's pressure on the mayor, the chief, on all of us," Aoki said. "The joint task force logged an incredible amount of time getting one of them to roll over. They got Marcel Leroux by the balls, caught red-handed with a couple ounces of coke shoved down his cowboy boot leaving the Dove strip club. He's been persuaded to testify against Duguay on the extortion, money laundering and organized crime charges. With Duguay out of the picture, the local chapter of the Blades will suffer a major loss in their command structure. The task force can use the momentum to effectively shut them down before they even get a foothold. And with Duguay's record, he'll pull a dozen years at least. It's a simple cost-benefit scenario."

"They're not willing to take a closer look at the file I pulled together?"

"Charlie. You're a respected investigator on my Hold-up Squad. I think you're a very fine cop. But you're not a homicide investigator. You have to trust that your colleagues are as good at their job as you are at yours."

"I'm just saying, boss, what I've been saying all along. I don't think Balani and Gilmartin made the right connections here from day one. I know what I know because I went down there and talked to these kids. For hours. I know Gavin was selling dope for the Blades. Out of Moss Park there, and the Eaton Centre, the Yonge Line. That new apartment he was in up off Jane Street, it was a drug house for the bikers. Crack, E, weed. Duguay was known for getting guys like Leroux to get the street kids in on the hustle," he said. "All we need is one of them to come forward and say that, yes, they saw

Duguay with Gavin on the night he was killed. It'll take some coaxing. They've got their street code. Just get him positioned there at the scene, and we can make the rest of it work."

McKelvey wanted to mention also the evidence of a woman in Gavin's apartment, a bag in the bathroom with a brush and makeup, items that disappeared from the time they were tagged and the time he checked the evidence lockup. Trying to match the inventory sheet with the physical property, coming up empty. A small thing, perhaps, but still. It was something he'd mentioned to Balani more than once. The senior detective brushing it off—*stick to your holdups, McKelvey, stick to your old lady muggings…*

"I wanted to talk to you about something else," Aoki said. "An offer. After your current files are closed up, I'm going to ask you to consider taking the department's early retirement package. I spoke with the head of HR last week, and he said with your years of service and accumulated lieu days, you could leave with almost a full year's pay before your pension would kick in. That means full benefits, everything."

An old rotted dory finally cut from its dock, he understood for the first time that without this place to come to, without something to keep his mind in check, he was a man adrift. Lost and perhaps dangerous. *What would he do with his days?* His mind flashed with an image of Charlie McKelvey dressed in a blue vest and polyester slacks, smiling as he passed shopping carts towards customers…a big round button on his chest that declared: "Have a Nice Day!"

"I thought for a minute you were going to give me a promotion," he said, smiling.

"Listen, don't take it personally. You're *eligible,* Charlie. The same offer's being made to four others in Detective Services, a bunch over in administration and special services. The department's trying to balance a budget while hiring more patrol officers. Anyway, it's not a negative, Charlie. I'd love to see you leave this business with a good package and all your wiring still intact," and here she tapped the side of her head for effect. "You did more than your share, and you deserve to get on with your life. I think the timing's right, to be honest."

"What if I don't want to retire? I've got a few more good years."

"Right now they're *asking*. If you push this, they'll be *telling* you."

"Who's 'they'?"

"There's more to this than..." She took a moment to find the right words. "Don't sit there and tell me you didn't see this coming. Your head and your heart aren't on this job any more. I've been very patient, Charlie. I've let a lot of things slide. You come and go from this place like it's a fucking train station. You stopped seeing the department psychologist. You harassed Balani while he was the lead investigator..."

"Is that what Balani said, I *harassed* him? Jesus Christ, Tina. I just want to keep up on developments. He hasn't followed up on any of the angles I've tossed out. And now that he kissed ass and got himself recruited onto that biker task force, what happens to the file? I guess closing this one isn't a priority."

"You don't mean that. We look after our own, and Gavin was one of ours. I can only imagine how frustrating this is for you, but you've got to leave it alone. You have this hypothesis, Charlie, but nobody else can connect the dots. Balani doesn't agree with you, and quite frankly, neither do I. Motive, maybe, but the evidence just isn't there. The Crown has finite resources. We can get by sometimes on our gut instinct. Crown doesn't have the same luxury once they get to court."

"Duguay did this," he said, "or else it was on his word. Either way, it was him. The guys who were buying dope all say the same thing. That Duguay was running that apartment Gavin was in. Something went down, and he was seen in the vicinity."

She went to respond but had to answer her ringing phone. She paused before picking up and said, "Talk to Caroline about the offer, Charlie."

Six

The first flakes of the season began to fall gently as McKelvey wound his way through the streets of the lower downtown, edging the lakeshore. Always the lake was out there, great dull silver horizon. It was a soft and slow snowfall, the kind he remembered from childhood, the snow just falling and falling so you couldn't tell whether the sky was up or down. Winters up north were so different from here in the city. He couldn't remember a green Christmas back home, but down here it wasn't unusual at all.

He didn't want to think about life back there, back at home, and so he pushed it from his mind and focused on the city streets moving with people and traffic, and soon enough his mind came back, as it always did, to the place where it got stuck, the groove worn deep. Every circuit, every synapse, every cell within the complex machinery of his grey matter seemed always to be working in the background on his son's file. It didn't matter what he tried to do in order to reign in his concentration; the wiring was splayed now, and the message wasn't getting through.

On mornings like this, he could not sit at his desk without his knee pumping in agitation, his fingers drumming a meandering and aimless beat, a million thoughts running through his head. Figuring things, remembering things. He would stand up and sit down, walk to the coffee machine a dozen times, visit the men's room and stare at his face in the row of long mirrors, anxious as a small boy waiting for *something.* Like a swimmer at the bottom of a pool, he could see the shimmering green-yellow lights of the surface dancing just beyond his reach, a whole universe taking place above that cloudy, formless horizon. Each morning he pointed his arms skyward, pushed off with both feet, and jettisoned himself toward the surface, his lungs aching for oxygen, fingers anticipating the first freshness of open air...

The falling flakes were hypnotic. He drove through the business heart of the city, blocks of chrome and glass, stone and concrete, University and Bay, then on down past the iconic train station with its weathered pillars and arches, the first view of the city offered to freshly landed European immigrants. This, too, had been McKelvey's first view of life in a metropolis, a smooth-faced kid stepping from the northern train with a duffel over his shoulder and a pocketful of hope. Now the immigrant taxi drivers lined up outside the station as well-dressed men and women flowed in and out of the brass-plated doors on their way to and from commuter trains hauling them in from 'burbs that were spreading like dark wine across a tablecloth, east and west, north and south.

Across from Union Station, the old Royal York Hotel appeared frozen in time, monolithic matriarch of hospitality from a forgotten era of crisp white table cloths, heavy silverware, and doormen dressed in rich burgundy coats and hats. McKelvey moved eastward, down side streets he hadn't been on in years, not since his days in a radio car. Back then he had known every street in his division, every corner where someone might hide. Those long ago days when he never seemed to question his physical ability to wrestle another man's hands into a set a cuffs, to put him to the ground like

40

a dog, knee in his back. Was this a brand of unquestioning confidence unique to police officers, or was it simply youthful ignorance or arrogance? He couldn't say. And while he still believed he could handle himself, there were no illusions of infinite strength. He felt the energy of his life force waning.

The radio in the car thrummed and snapped with activity, but after a while McKelvey tuned it out. He noticed the subtle and not-so-subtle changes to the geography, the transformation of old apartment blocks into trendy loft condos. When you lived and worked in the city, as McKelvey had since the age of eighteen, you eventually stopped noticing any changes until they were entirely completed. Massive structures simply appeared as though set there overnight by a child building a train set village. Urban change was overwhelming in its velocity; there was simply too much of it to absorb. There was something going on around you all the time, a minute by minute transformation of the city, renovations, new glass, paint, scaffolds rising and falling like rusted skeletons, jackhammers and trucks backing up, apartment buildings blooming like strange orchids among the grasslands of the war-time bungalows and row houses. McKelvey remembered the old days of the warehouses along the train tracks, the low thick buildings that resembled concentration camps, the smashed distillery house windows staring like black empty eyes, the vacant lots where poor kids played stick ball long before there were million-dollar condos. Today wealthy young executives ate salmon steaks overlooking the train yards and back alleys where the original urban immigrants lived in shacks insulated with newspapers. Evolution.

He wound his way northward, meandering through the old neighborhoods where he had worked, specific coordinates bringing forth the memory of vivid calls: a stabbing at this corner, a bloody armed robbery at that convenience store, all the while his mind running through the meeting with Aoki. Caroline would ask about the news from the Crown, and he would tell her that not only would there be no charges brought in Gavin's murder, but the sun had set on Charlie McKelvey's mediocre police career. Hell of a day. So many things to think about. A man could get lost in the details without even knowing it.

And then he was stopped. Stopped and staring at a traffic light.

Red.

Flakes falling almost horizontal now, mesmerizing.

McKelvey stared at the traffic light. Green now. It had changed from yellow to red to green without his even noticing. He was staring at the light, yet he was also watching himself as a young man, a kid riding in a patrol car with no experience. *And then the kid was Gavin, and he was on that first bike they bought him, and then Gavin was just lying there lifeless on the table, a single bullet hole to the upper left forehead...the gunshot wound the colour of black cherry...*

Someone honked.

McKelvey blinked, checked the rear view. A guy in a delivery van behind him. Honked again. *Fucking idiot.* McKelvey slid the unmarked cruiser into park, undid his seatbelt, and was out of the vehicle and approaching the delivery van, the wet flakes swirling, and he could hear himself, hear his voice, hoarse and distant. It sounded like it belonged to someone else. The driver of the van just shook his head and pulled around the car, leaving McKelvey standing there in the road with the snow stinging his eyes.

Like a magnet drawn to its inevitable destination, he pulled the car up alongside the wrought iron fence surrounding the cemetery. The snow had stopped now, and the sky was muted, grey as putty, still and cold. What a day, he thought. *The world is talking to you, Charlie,* is what Caroline would say. She'd said it all the time when they were kids in their twenties, failing miserably in that first basement apartment they rented. A real dive. All they had back then was a futon on the floor, books and a turntable supported by milk crates and bricks. He saw an image of Caroline and himself at that age, sitting up in bed after making love, a bottle of cheap wine wedged in the tangle of covers between them, the air thick with the scent of their bodies. He saw the image, but he couldn't connect himself with the man in the picture. There was nothing.

In the summertime, he would sit in the car on days like this and watch people come and go from the cemetery, human traffic manoeuvering through the landscape of grief. He rolled the window down, and he could taste the city in the back of his throat, wet dirt and ash. He sat in the car, where not so long ago he would get out of the vehicle to walk across the emerald lawns manicured to perfection, walk through those rows of stones, through generations of families laid to rest, and believe with utter conviction that the soil beneath his feet was the dust of living beings, who, at one point, had laughed and cried, won and lost, and taken for granted the dependability of the blood running through their bodies. He would understand that because he was made of the same bone and blood as those who had gone before, there could be no hope for escape; the soil patiently awaited his embrace.

He had once possessed the ability, indeed perhaps the courage, to step from the vehicle, to make the long walk to the place where his boy rested in perpetuity. To kneel and touch the soft grass there, find the mettle to speak a few words. All the long moments Caroline never knew about, all the secret promises and pledges he made with himself, the lost hours parked at the cemetery. He sat there now, and he

43

searched for the thrust to propel him up and out through the door of the car, through those rows of stones. He glanced in the rear view and saw a stranger's set of eyes, a stranger caught in mid-life, in mid-stride, entangled in the lines and nets of his own setting. He understood this was the point of embarkation; he squinted and made out a door—slightly ajar—just up ahead. It bled a little light.

He opened the car door and walked through rows of stones, his dress shoes and pant legs wet from the fresh snow. The place was empty, lonely as only a cemetery could be. The headstones rose up from the earth like stoic grey perennials. The trees that ringed the perimeter were dusted like the trees on the front of a Christmas greeting card. His body found the stone it sought through the remembered geography of the heart and soul. He stood there before it. A simple stone, simple but right. He turned and crouched and touched it.

His boy.

He touched the face of the stone, the letters of one life etched for all time. *We build monuments,* he thought, *to prove we have come through this place. Or perhaps for the false comfort of those who remain.* He touched the grooves of the letters and dates, the bare statistics of a life stamped in granite. The natural rhythm of the lives of those who are left behind is necessarily set off-kilter; yes, he had lost his balance there for a long time, but now he felt himself coming through to the other side of something, a new window opening within himself. He couldn't say what it was exactly, or even where things were headed. But it was something different to feel, something besides the feeling of utter helplessness. It wasn't optimism, no. It was something more like hope born of desperation. And it was okay. It was okay. Anything but *this,* the status quo of hauling grief around like a bag of stones.

"It's okay," he said, and stood. He took a deep haul of the chilled air, and it felt like being born again. He brushed some snow from his knees. "It's okay, my boy. I'll do this one on my own."

Seven

He walked back to the car, and his breath was visible in small clouds. It was getting dark out already, the afternoon fading imperceptibly. He went back to the office, parked the vehicle, checked his messages and had made up a few lies when Hattie stopped by his cubicle with a stack of files under her arm.

Detective Mary-Ann Hattie had transferred in from Halifax a couple of years earlier, and she and McKelvey had worked together on a series of armed robberies. They'd been printed up in the *Star* together for netting the so-called "Royal Bank Bandit". She was a genuine fisherman's daughter. She was lanky, owned unruly red hair, and her skin was as white as milk. McKelvey always thought she looked like somebody's kindergarten teacher.

"Want to grab a beer and burger up at Fran's after work?" she said. "First snowfall always makes me a little lonesome for home. Looks so pretty falling out there on the ocean."

"Could always go look at the lake," he said, fiddling with some yellow stick-it notes.

"Just doesn't have the same magic," she said, smiling.

He checked his watch and said, "I'll have to take a rain check."

They talked for a minute about some of the cases that were on the go, the usual suspects holding up Chinese convenience stores, lottery booths, a recent and violent trend towards armed robberies at the after hours booze cans. Then Hattie smiled at him, a sort of sad smile he thought, and she moved on to her cluttered desk. McKelvey called his wife at home, but Caroline did not answer. Then he remembered that she was out with four other women, fellow sufferers in grief. Drinking red wine—then, later, desserts and cappuccino—at a cozy Italian restaurant in Yorkville. She had told him all of this in the morning as he was getting ready for work, but he either didn't hear her or had forgotten. It hardly mattered.

McKelvey left a message, speaking quietly into his phone. "Hey," he said, "I'll be home late. You don't have to save supper."

He thought of telling her about his day but decided it would only cause her unnecessary worry. He waited awhile at his desk, fiddling with pens and papers, before turning off his desk light and slipping out. The sky was black, devoid of stars. The city was quilted in fresh white, which made everything look clean and new, as though the whole place had been built just a year ago. The dusting would be gone by mid-morning under the glare of the early December sun. But for now, at just after six, the new snow made the city almost look like a place where bad things never happened. It covered up the filth, McKelvey thought, the way a hooker covers up the bruises on her cheek with foundation.

He drove for a while before pulling into the parking lot of a convenience store a few blocks from his home, then he was standing in the phone booth in front of his car with his collar pulled up, the receiver cradled against an ear, reading the ads for chips and pop and candy bars posted over in the store window. Everything was on sale, two for one. Everything was a necessity. The use of payphones was not necessary, however, as the force supplied a cellular phone with which McKelvey had made a compromise: he would use it for work, but that was it. He could push himself towards the emerging technologies only so fast, so far. He still owned milk crates full of record albums, as yet unconvinced that the mysterious compact disc was here to stay. There was something about pushing a quarter into a phone, something about closing those folding doors off to the rest of the world. The streetlight overhead turned the flesh of his hand yellow as he dialed the number Paul had given him at the hospital group. A crumpled piece of paper dug from his pocket, words recalled. He couldn't say why he was calling, exactly, or what he hoped to accomplish.

A man answered on the third ring. "Hello?"

"This Tim Fielding?"

"Speaking."

McKelvey dug in his outer coat pocket for the package of cigarettes he'd bought after the meeting with Aoki. Player's Light Regular. His old friend the old sailor. He lifted the foil flap, fished out a smoke with his teeth. His stomach fluttered with the anticipation of the first nicotine rush, that sick twinge of guilt. All the things that kept him coming back.

"It's Charlie McKelvey from Tuesday nights. Tuesday nights at the hospital group," he said, fumbling for the two-cent matches that advertised rare coins. "I got your number from Paul there, the moderator."

He had thought about hanging up one ring before the man answered, and now McKelvey was wishing he had. He struck the match and lit the smoke, and with the first flood of nicotine and hovering tendril of blue smoke knew that he was in trouble now. No way to explain away the stench of smoke that would cling to him in this enclosed space. He supposed this carelessness meant he was beyond the point of caring now. In the end, that's what carelessness always boiled down to, an indifference to the consequences. It was how most criminals eventually got themselves caught.

"Oh, Charlie, right, right. The policeman," Tim said. "Paul gave you my number?"

"Well yeah, you know, he said you might help me with something I'm going through."

Tim laughed, and McKelvey took a long drag on the cigarette, holding the smoke until it began to burn his lungs like mustard gas. His eyes watered a little, and he released the smoke through his nostrils in two long funnels. Fuck it. He wasn't going to quit these.

"Me help you, right. He wants you to mentor *me,* I suppose. Sounds like something Paul would try to orchestrate behind the scenes. Anyway..." Tim said, and waited for the conversation to resume.

"Mmmm, that's right," McKelvey said. "So how about it. One night this week, maybe?"

"How about tonight?"

"Tonight?"

"Why not? Just stupid cop shows on TV," he said. "No offence."

"None taken. I can't stand to watch them myself," McKelvey said. "Everybody thinks we're running around with our guns drawn half the time."

"You mean you guys don't get to do that?"

"Sometimes. Most of the time I'm sitting at a computer for nine hours trying to learn some new software program so I can fill out my reports and upload them to an invisible mainframe, or whatever they call it..."

Tim laughed again. McKelvey glanced at his watch.

"Do you know Murph's on Bathurst?" McKelvey said.

"Sure," Tim said. "Who doesn't?"

"The one and only. I don't think Murph will ever retire," McKelvey said. "He must be going on ninety. I could meet you there in, say, twenty minutes."

"I'm on my way," Tim said and hung up.

McKelvey stood in the phone booth watching his breath fog up the scratched and gouged Plexiglass, smelling the stale air, the reek of tobacco. He wondered briefly about fate and what had moved him to call the young man. He wondered about fate quite often these days, how chance meetings seemed always in the end to be so much more than they first appeared. How there was no such thing as pure coincidence. How everything—even the murder of a child, say—was supposed to have a purpose behind it, something to be taught or gleaned. Or perhaps it was punishment. A lesson to be learned. What goes around comes around. Call it whatever you will; the notion gave McKelvey a chill. He opened the phone booth door and walked into the night.

⁎ ⁎ ⁎

Murph's was a bare bones tavern wedged between a dry cleaner's shop and a convenience store owned by a Korean family. It was an old and worn establishment that had stubbornly weathered the various decades and all the changing trends the city could throw at it. McKelvey thought of the place as an old sports jersey or a favourite hat that you loved and never wanted to put through the laundry, because everything that was special about it would be washed away. It had to stay the same, with the scuffs on the wood floor and the ages-old stains on the walls and the toilets that only worked half the time, a filthy plunger propped in the corner. Graffiti scrawled on the washroom cubicles stretched back to the 1940s, and that alone was worth the price of admission. For a good time call Gertie…

They didn't have much in common, it was true. Tim Fielding was a school teacher and an unapologetic socialist, and was not at all embarrassed to tell McKelvey over their first draft beer that he would have killed himself following his wife's death if it hadn't been for the Tuesday night meetings up at the hospital. No, they didn't have much in common except for the shared experience of loss, but McKelvey liked the younger man. He got a good reading from the kid, and he had been ruled by his gut instincts for so long now, it was about all he trusted.

"I pictured myself going through with it," Tim said, "you know, parking my car in the garage with a hose running from the exhaust. I went to the hardware store one day and checked out furnace hoses. After I left class. After I left my fucking students. I held it in my *hand,* turning it over. It was that real to me, that close. I can't even believe I'm saying this now. But you being a cop, I guess you've probably heard everything."

"What pulled you back?" McKelvey said.

Tim shrugged. "Responsibility won out in the end," he said. "I tried to imagine the impact on my class. I knew it was something that would stay with them forever, and it wasn't fair. It's hard enough to be a kid nowadays."

"You're right about that," McKelvey said. "I wouldn't be a kid today if you paid me. We used to spend all day out in the woods, shooting squirrels with a BB gun or breaking glass bottles with a slingshot. TV wasn't even an option most of the time. You used your imagination. You found something to do, or your father'd put you to work. And everybody wore the same jeans and the same cheap runners. Now you got nine-year-old girls dressing up like pop stars…" And they drank in silence in one another's company. McKelvey didn't have many friends outside of work, because he got a feeling for people right away, looked into their eyes in ways that his wife could never appreciate, always picking apart their reactions or actions, judging, measuring. "Can't you stop being a cop for one night?" Caroline would say. "Sometimes you treat our friends like suspects. Sometimes you treat Gavin like he's a suspect." He shivered now at the thought, and it stung. Remorse and regret.

"You're okay now, though?" McKelvey said after a mouthful of beer.

"Oh sure, I'm a poster boy for mental health," Tim said, and they laughed.

Tim drew the frothy head from his mug of draft beer. He was a tall man, with a thin, latent musculature, glasses with a modern dark frame, and sandy brown hair that was receding faster than its owner could likely accept. When the young man smiled, McKelvey thought he looked a little like the Hollywood actor Ed Harris. Seemed like the majority of men nowadays were going bald. Must have been something in the water or the milk, steroids or hormones or some other form of voodoo. Not that his own hair was showing any signs of disappearing. Even Hattie had once remarked that he had a beautiful head of hair for an older gentleman. *For an older gentleman,* that was the qualifier...

They watched the clientele ebb and flow. McKelvey remembered the times, when he was much younger, that Caroline had to call around to a series of neighbourhood bars just like this one in an attempt to locate him. McKelvey and his colleagues turning the after-work drink into a five- or six-hour run. Back when he was younger and unsure of what he was missing at home, all of them caught up in the male ego of it all, trading stories from the street, and the cigarettes and the laughs and the feeling that they were in a special club, the secret order of the brotherhood. Only a handful of the original crew were still ardent daily drinkers, unapologetic through three failed marriages and estranged children, and they wore the lifestyle on their faces. They were red-nosed and bloated, made old before their time. *All young men break a few bones to learn their lessons,* McKelvey thought. *Takes us so much longer than our wives and lovers to learn to be still.* How to pace the drinking, how to handle the testosterone and the anger and how to reconcile the day job with the home life. He understood that negotiations were required. The alternative was a life of lonely rooms and empty beds. Now it hardly seemed to matter.

McKelvey's moment of peaceful reflection was torn when he looked up and saw that Tim was crying. Like a small child, his eyes watered, and a few plump tears streaked down his cheeks. There was no sound. A man crying, it was one of the worst things, one of the most difficult parts of McKelvey's job, the crying and the crying. Suspects crying when they got pinched, begging and sobbing for just one more chance at freedom, crying until snot ran glistening from their noses. But the worst was the family of victims. It didn't matter the cause, not initially at least. Vehicle accidents, murders, drownings, drug overdoses, it was all the same when you were standing on a front step with your hat in your hand. It made McKelvey's stomach clench so that he couldn't eat for an entire day after he delivered a Notification of Death—N.O.D. The cop's worst task.

"What's up, Tim? What's up there, buddy?" he said. It didn't matter what McKelvey said at these times, it always sounded foolish to his own ear, an actor reading lines.

"Oh god, I'm sorry," Tim said. "I just get like this sometimes. It's the beer, I guess."

He wiped his nose and dried his eyes with a thumb.

"Listen, don't apologize, man. It's okay," McKelvey said. "Just let it go."

"I miss her so much," Tim said, and now the tears resumed. "I keep getting to this place where it feels like maybe I could build a life again, you know? Maybe I could have a life again some day. Wake up without this weight on my chest, her name running through my head. I had everything, Charlie. I had the greatest love. We were going to have children..."

McKelvey gritted his teeth, frustrated by his own awkwardness. He felt he ought to do *something*. It was the same when Caroline cried or began to reminisce about Gavin as a child, and McKelvey saw himself standing there like a big dummy with his hands at his sides. He felt like a statue—or worse, a man dead from the neck down. It wasn't enough that he possessed the genuine *desire* to do something, the innate reaction to reach out, to comfort. It wasn't enough, and he knew it. His wife deserved more. She always did.

"I have moments where I forget," McKelvey said, pushing the shadows from his mind. "I'll be doing something, mostly at work, and my head gets buried in the little details. And then all of a sudden it's like I'm coming up, breaking the surface, taking this huge mouthful of air. And that's it, that's when I realize that yeah, I had a son and he's gone now...but I had a son. He was real..."

"Do you think it'll ever get any easier?" Tim said, his red eyes searching.

McKelvey took the last mouthful of his beer. He held the beer in his mouth, buying a moment. It was dark draft, good and strong against his tongue. He felt he should tell this kid the way he saw it. Leave the lying to the grief counsellors and the facilitators like Paul up at the hospital group. Seven stages of grief? No, no. Grief was an onion. With each skin you peeled away, the thing just got softer, more delicate, and each layer burned your eyes a little more.

"No," McKelvey said, "I don't believe so."

Tim's face betrayed his surprise at McKelvey's bluntness. As a young widower, Tim had grown somewhat used to everyone telling him things would get better, that it was okay to start dating again, that yes, despite mounting evidence to the contrary, life does go on.

"I didn't mean to kick you in the balls there," McKelvey said and chuckled to lighten the moment. "You asked me a question, and I'm too tired to bullshit."

"No, no," Tim said, "I appreciate your honesty. I'm not being facetious. I wanted to ask you that question in the meeting a few weeks ago, but you didn't look like you wanted anybody to talk to you, to be honest."

McKelvey said, "My wife says I look like that a lot."

"Tell me something," Tim said. "Why do women, good women, tolerate jackasses like you and me?"

Tim was on his second large draft beer, about two and a half pints' worth, and McKelvey could see the man was not a heavy drinker. His eyes were already glazing over with that watery, faraway look. There was a time when McKelvey himself could have sat there and drunk six large draft beers then driven home—yes, driven, in spite of or perhaps because of the fact he was a cop—then crawled right into bed beside his already sleeping wife. Not every day, to be certain, but with enough consistency that it became an issue to be addressed, placated.

"Speak for yourself, young man," McKelvey said. "I'm an asshole, not a jackass."

Tim choked on his mouthful of beer, a big smile across his face. "Not to be confused with a garden variety dickhead."

"There are grades to these things, levels to be achieved,"

McKelvey said. "I don't really remember what it was like being a husband in my early thirties, but I can guess that I wasn't very good at it. You think you learn about women as you go along, but you don't learn anything. They're light years ahead of us."

"I never cheated on my wife, but I came close," Tim said, and it came out so fast that it reminded McKelvey of a typical amateur's confession. A breathless burst of information. "This supply teacher, she invited me to her place for a drink."

"Listen, you don't have to..."

"No, I want to tell you. I want to tell somebody, because it drives me crazy sometimes. I have to get it off my chest. There was this supply teacher, and we really hit it off, you know, joking around and being stupid. Getting caught up in the whole school flirt thing. She invited me to her place for a drink. She knew I was married, but I guess she didn't care." Tim paused, looked down into his drink, rolled the frothy remains in the bottom of the glass. "Anyway, we didn't do anything. I had a drink, and we fooled around a little, then I got my senses back. I felt sick about it. And then six months later, Jennifer was killed by a fucking drunk driver. She was hit walking across the street that she crossed every day when she was leaving work. The same street."

"Don't do that to yourself. You should be proud of the fact you got the hell out of there. Most men would have jumped at the opportunity without even thinking, then lived with the consequences," McKelvey said, and his mind flashed with childhood memories—listening with an ear to the floor while his mother and father argued below in the kitchen, accusations of infidelity, the awful words his mother spat. "Your tavern whores," she said. And then the arguments seemed to simply dissipate, and McKelvey was left to decipher the silences, the glances that fell between his mother and father. The male gossip at Bud's barbershop, the coded language that belonged to men of that era. Life in a small northern town. Every aspect of your life is everybody else's business. To believe otherwise is to be an elitist—like anyone who came from a city in southern Ontario or anyone perfectly willing to pay four dollars for a cappuccino.

"Listen, we're idiots. Face it," McKelvey said. "I used to think women had no place on the police force. I'll admit to that line of thinking at one time. But not now. I see that women come at things from a whole different angle. I can't tell you what that fucking angle is, mind you, but we need it. We need it."

Tim wanted to order another round, but McKelvey declined. He made an excuse about work, but the truth was his guts were on fire. The worst heartburn imaginable, like goddamned napalm cutting a line from his stomach to the back of his throat. It was a new sensation, a flash of heat and stabbing pain. Like something *tearing*. He was dizzy when he stood from the table, and he set a hand down to steady himself. It was the weight of the day, a bad day, and the fact he'd had too much coffee on an empty stomach. He did it to himself all the time.

"You look like you're getting the flu," Tim said, sitting forward to pull his wallet from his back pocket. "It's going around the school like wild fire. I got the free shot at the clinic."

"I'm fine," McKelvey said, though the room was beginning to undulate, the hazy lights fading, flickering. "Listen, this is on me."

He tossed a few bills on the table then wiped his forehead with the back of his hand.

"Next time I'll buy," Tim said. "If you're up for it, that is."

"Just give me a call," McKelvey said, and the two men shook hands.

Outside, the night was clear and cool with an early winter freshness that reminded McKelvey of the childhood nights spent at the outdoor rink just down from his house, old Eaton's catalogues shoved inside his wool socks as shin guards. He'd wanted to be Jean Beliveau, probably because it incensed his father that he would idolize a Montreal Canadiens player and not a Maple Leaf. As he walked up the sidewalk, he saw himself tearing down the ice on those crisp cold nights, playing the puck with his stick, somebody's older brother lining him up against the boards so that he saw explosions of stars and had the breath sucked from his lungs, but it was all worth that single moment of imagined glory.

*   *   *

It was past midnight when McKelvey slipped inside the master bedroom, walking on the balls of his feet across the hardwood. He knew the secret spots that would offer up a sound under his weight. The room was dark, save for a soft glow coming up from the street lamps outside, muted and altered in hue by the window blinds. He got out of his sweaty shirt and jacket, remembering to pull from the breast pocket the tie he had removed at Murph's. In the bathroom he bent over the sink and splashed water on his face, good and cold, then he paused there to grip the cold porcelain, fighting a wave of nausea. He cupped a mouthful of the cold tap water, to ease the burning in his chest before he brushed his teeth. He had been smoking like it was his new job, so he splashed a dab of cologne on his jaw. A false hope, perhaps, but hope all the same.

Caroline was sleeping on her side. He traced with his eye

the outline of her figure beneath the sheets, the hips that had widened with age, her ample bosom, and he was filled with a sudden desire to make love. It had been a long time. He tried to remember the last time he woke her in the middle of the night, their sleepy bodies moving, the bed creaking in the darkness. But not now, now she would think there was something wrong with him. He lifted the comforter and gently slid between the sheets, doing his best not to jostle the bed. He stretched out on his back and looked up at the dark shadows on the ceiling. His mind swirled with activity, connecting lines and fitting puzzle pieces like blocks of wood. His wife stirred.

"You're home," she said without turning.

"I met with that guy from the hospital group," he said.

"The young man," she whispered, "who lost his wife."

"Tim. He's a good kid," he said. "He's a teacher."

McKelvey listened to the sound of his own breathing. It was laboured, raspy, altogether noisier than he imagined it should sound. Was it the cigarettes? Was it the coming of a chest cold? A chest cold that would transform into pneumonia? Fill his lungs with fluid until breathing became not an automatic task, something you took completely for granted, but something to be thought about, worked at. Old people died from pneumonia all the time. They died in their sleep, a measure of peace. But he wasn't old. Not really. He was on the cusp...

"I said, you've been smoking," Caroline repeated.

"I had a few with my beer," he said.

He waited for it, but it did not come. He understood with a sense of finality they were beyond this now, and perhaps she had resigned herself to this backsliding to old habits. Was it worth arguing about? Was it the least of their concerns? McKelvey turned onto his side and put a hand on his paunch.

Whether it was the beer or the cigarettes or the coffee, something was eating at his insides. Like worms: nocturnal miners, tunnelling without rest. Dig it deeper, dig until you come out the other side...

"They made me an offer today," he said, his voice drowsy.

But Caroline had already fallen back to sleep. The room was dark and warm, and McKelvey felt himself teetering on the brink of the beautiful escape. *I could die in my sleep. A heart attack, a stroke, an aneurysm. This rattle in my chest, this burning in my stomach.*

Eight

The dressing room behind the stage was a whirlwind of garments and flailing limbs. Lanky girls wearing lingerie tops searched frantically for the missing bottoms as the bass line from the first song of their three-song set began to pound in their chests. Their scrawny legs were made all the more precarious in four-inch silver heels as they teetered about like strange, twittering giraffes. The cigarette smoke mixed with the blue language, the foul and candid mouths of the itinerant workers rising above the music like voices at a house party, or perhaps a sorority in full swing. The smells of strong perfumes and makeup, body glitters and glues, even the smell of body odour, everything blended together to produce this surreal orchestra of the lonely and the damned.

The girl with the coal black hair was seated on a stool in a corner. She rolled the black stockings open so she could slip her painted toes inside, then she uncoiled the roll as far as it would go, to mid thigh. She stood to smooth the short black skirt, then sat again. Suddenly she was a schoolgirl. *How ironic,* she thought, *for a Grade Nine dropout.* She had a cigarette going in an overflowing ashtray, and another dancer appeared out of nowhere from stage right, a petite black girl wrapped in a ratty house coat, who grabbed the cigarette and took it with her on her way through the room.

"Goddamn, Janine, buy your own," the girl said without much conviction.

She was olive-skinned, and she had her long black hair tied back while she finished with her makeup. She was just eighteen, but in this dim lighting, she passed easily for twenty-one, twenty-two. When she removed the makeup in the earliest hours of the morning, she looked like a teenager once again, perhaps as young as sixteen. Everything except for the eyes. For these green eyes had seen much. Sometimes, when she closed her eyes, she saw things that had happened but that didn't seem real any more. Time was all mixed up. Memories played tricks. The drugs didn't help matters. There were a couple of years in there, the years of the street, which were tangled together in a knot of memories, dreams. Stepping from the Greyhound downtown, nowhere to go, nobody to turn to. Fifteen years old. A thousand miles, a thousand regrets since then.

When she closed her eyes, silently willing the strange men labouring above her to reach the end of their lust, the blackness of her clenched eyelids gave up the secrets of her heart. The pictures came into focus then, the faces and places of home and family. It was too much sometimes, and this is what the drug counsellors did not understand, what her aunt did not understand. There were things from which a person could not return. Not whole, anyway. Once you'd seen or done something, you couldn't *undo* it. Once something had been done *to* you. No amount of bathing could ever wash away the physical memory. Sometimes when she got high, she pretended that certain things had never happened at all, that she would be discovered one night while dancing. An agent passing through the city on his way to Hollywood. Or perhaps a wealthy businessman who would marry her and give her a fancy home near a lake, a trip in an airplane. It happened, and it could happen to her. Why not? She was pretty enough.

"Are you ready yet?" a man called from down the hallway.

"Relax, Gerry," the girl said, using her compact mirror to adjust her eyeliner.

It was almost one in the morning, and the girl was just beginning her work for the night. The dancing was done now, the easiest part of the gig; it was so easy to pry cash from the men that sometimes she wondered why she hadn't tried this sooner. Much easier than washing windows or bumming pocket change down in the subway and beneath the overpass. When stacked against the alternatives, it was easy to bend and roll, to arch your back like a cat the way the men in the front row always liked, to put your ankles by your ears and drill holes with your eyes until the shy ones burned red and turned away, to put your hands on the brass pole and sway to the beat of the music, your tits dripping tequila. You got drunk or you got high, then you hit the stage, and it was dark, then it was over. Once you got past that first time, it was nothing. It was a joke, really. Something most girls, especially girls on the street, ended up doing for free anyway. So why not. Close your eyes and make believe. They're nobody to you; in these dark rooms everyone is a stranger and your best friend. The payoff came when a client particularly liked one of your assets and ended up dropping twenty dollars for a four-minute lap dance. Once you got them in a corner, it was easy to turn the twenty into eighty, a hundred. Give your share to the club, to the bouncer, and you were still making out. And in this regard at least, Duguay had been true to his word: it was the easiest money she had ever earned. She got paid to tell lies. And she was good at it.

The dancing was the easy part. What came after was often

much less pleasant, the sort of work that required the shutdown of entire lobes. And now that her patron Duguay was in the detention centre awaiting trial, the girl with the black hair found herself unprotected in a sea of sharks. Duguay had chosen her from all the girls, and in this way she was "his"; she didn't go with anyone unless it was on Duguay's word. It was usually only once or twice a week, and it was usually an associate of his, someone he wanted to impress. A free ride on Duguay's private yacht. Something like that. But lately her world had changed, and some of the other girls took great satisfaction in watching her get painted up the same as them. Painted, plastered and parted. But they didn't know. They didn't know *her*. What she had inside.

"We gotta go," the man called again, this time from the doorway.

The girl snapped the compact shut and put it in her small purse. She stood and brushed past the man, walking down the hallway towards the back door of the Dove Gentleman's Club, the effects of the vodka and O.J. and Oxycodone painkiller carrying her on the wings of something that could make life bearable.

The driver was a nice guy named Gerry. He was stocky, and there were thick grey scars along the ridges of his eyebrows that someone said were a commutative result of boxing, and his ears looked a little funny, too, lumps of twisted flesh, but he was soft-spoken, and she had never heard him so much as raise his voice. It's all he did, drive the girls to the dates which were arranged by the management. It was no secret that the club out by the airport hotels and convention centres was owned and operated by the Blades. The girl with the black hair liked Gerry because, unlike the doormen and bartenders at the club, he never tried to get one from her for free. She figured he was like all the guys who hung around the place, hoping one day the management would ask an errand of him, and in this way he would be initiated. Men were all the same in their desire for sex and power.

"You look nice," he said as he drove them up the Airport Road. Traffic was light at this hour. "You know the drill, eh. Call me when you get in and see that everything's okay. Call me again when you're ready for a pickup."

"Yeah, Gerry," she said, but she was looking out the windshield at a huge 747 gliding in for a landing. It seemed like magic that something so huge and heavy could be so graceful. She had never been on an airplane. She wondered what it would be like to sit in an airport all dressed up, or to tell people when they asked, "Oh, I'm leaving for Paris." To be *in between* destinations, to be nowhere really, and completely anonymous. She often wondered about the fancy hotels, too, and what it would be like to stay there as a guest. To call down for poached eggs and have them call you Miss So-and-So. She had slept in the nice beds with the big pillows, yes, but she hadn't seen very much. She had never been up the CN Tower, either. She wanted to go to a hockey game.

They moved away from the high-rise hotels, the Marriotts and the Deltas, past the industrial strips and storage units and all-night gas stations glowing like space stations, until finally the driver pulled into a two-level complex called Grand Motel. A big sign on the road promised cable TV and free local calls. It was a dive. She could already envision the polyester floral print comforter, the hideous artwork hanging crooked above the bed with the abused mattress, glasses with water stains turned upside down on the bathroom counter, the cheap rectangle of soap loosely wrapped in paper. The driver eased the car around the lot, reading the numbers on the doors. She watched him the whole time, waiting for him to let her in on the joke. This wasn't the kind of place she was used to. He stopped in front of Room 14.

"What is this?" she said.

"This is the place. Luc set it up."

"Perfect."

She wondered what Duguay would think of them sending her here to this place. Would he care? It didn't matter anyway, because Duguay wasn't here now, as Luc and the others had made clear. It was funny with these men, with their blue tattoos and thick arms, their big talk and swagger. All the talk of loyalty, brotherhood, death before dishonour. How quickly they forgot. Duguay wasn't inside a day before Luc and the others were already jostling for control.

"Are you okay?" Gerry said.

She didn't say anything. She had a bad feeling, which was unusual. Perhaps she wasn't drunk or high enough. That could be it. Three months—ninety-six days to be exact—off the rock, and nobody had a clue as to the true depth of that single achievement. Fucken Jezus. Like winning every award in the world all at once. At least *she* was proud of it, proud of herself. Everyone underestimated her. They didn't know that she was going with the flow until she could save enough money to get out. It wasn't her life, wasn't her future. Just a means to an end. She was resilient and had more guts than anyone could ever know. *Fuck them all. They'll find out one day when I'm long gone...*

She longed for a joint now and hoped whoever was inside Room 14 was a partaker. It would mellow her out, soften the rough edges of the night. Or another drink at least. *Something.* She fumbled in her purse for her cigarettes and lit one. She blew a line of smoke from the corner of her painted mouth directly at Gerry, who sat at the wheel with a pained look on his face.

"Sorry, eh," he said.

"It's okay," she said to him. *How, typical girl, soothe the asshole who drove you here to get laid by a stranger.* "It'll be fine," she said. "That's me. F.I.N.E. Fucked up, insecure, neurotic and emotional."

"What's that?" he said.

"Oh, just a stupid saying they had in the detox," she said.

"Be careful," he said.

She got out, put her mask on and went right up to the door. She knocked three times as Gerry moved around the corner. She knocked again and heard some noises from inside the room, something being knocked over, someone swearing at themselves, and she closed her eyes for a second and hoped with all her heart that the customer was drunk, too drunk.

*   *   *

Afterwards, the girl with the black hair stares at herself in the fogged mirror of the motel bathroom. Her face distorted by the steamy glass, she appears as a ghost to herself. And she *is* a ghost. It's how she feels inside most of the time. Just the trace of a girl, a charcoal sketch. She is an outline. *I've been waiting,* she thinks, *for someone to come and colour me in…*

Nine

The ringing of the phone on the night table tore McKelvey from the ether of a restless sleep. It was dark yet, and his fumbling hand set the clock radio blaring, a disembodied voice on the AM talk news station ranting about the Maple Leafs' final games to be played that year at the historic Gardens. He flicked the light on and hit the radio with the flat of his palm enough times to make it stop. It was only then that he realized Caroline was already up and out of bed. A return, perhaps, to those darkest days when McKelvey had woken to an empty bed and found her sitting in the living room staring out the bay window at nothing at all as the sun spread like honey across the darkened street. Now she came in from the kitchen, dressed in her robe, her hair tied back. She watched him and waited.

He grasped the receiver and made a noise. It was Aoki. That simple fact promised bad news. He made a motion with his hand to indicate it was about his work, and Caroline receded. He felt as though he were watching everything unfold in a Sunday night movie, looking down at his bloated body sitting on the side of the bed, hair tousled, face wrinkled by sleep.

"I wanted to tell you before you heard it on the news," she said. "The star witness Marcel Leroux was found hanging in his segregation cell late last night."

He cleared his throat. "I see."

"I'm sorry, Charlie."

How many times had he heard this same phrase? He couldn't stand to hear it any more.

"So," he said, "what happens with the Duguay trial? Everything was on Leroux."

"I'm not sure what their plans are at this point," she said.

He made a noise with his throat again, holding it in, and said, "Well…"

"But no, it doesn't look good. Without Leroux, there isn't much of a case. His lawyers will have a motion for dismissal drawn up before court's open today."

"I appreciate you calling like this, Tina," he said, nodding. Nodding, for he saw things laid out clearly now. How he had been a fool to place his trust in the system, when he knew what he knew. For the system *was* broken. He was part of the system, he was the system, and yet he knew in the deepest parts of his heart that it was a ruined machine. He had lost faith. It was not an easy conclusion to reach. But it was what it was.

"You're off today, so take some time, Charlie. Do something with Caroline to get your mind off all of this stuff," Aoki said. "I'll let you know as soon as I hear from the Crown. Okay?"

"That's right," he said, but his mind was already gone, already thinking ahead.

He hung up, fell back on the bed and closed his eyes in an effort to regain his focus. *Breathe, Charlie. Inhale, exhale.* The line of fire was stoked in his belly once again, rising like liquid flame. *Jesus Christ almighty.* He sat up and looked around the room, searching for something, anything. It was a necessity. Bottled up, a gas threatening to erupt. His hand grasped the clock radio, and he hurled it against the far wall, hurled it hard. It exploded in a spray of plastic shrapnel and electronic bits, coloured wires hanging, and the sharp sound sent

Caroline running back into the room. Her eyes moved between the dead appliance and the dent in the drywall, and finally settled on McKelvey, sitting there on the edge of the bed. He just looked back at her. The room was silent. She turned away, and he dropped back to the mattress, exhaling the poisoned breath of his life.

*　*　*

The witness Marcel Leroux had been found hanging in his cell, true, but he had not died. Not right away. His throat was a purple bruise, his brain destroyed by lack of oxygen. Officials began the difficult task of locating next of kin. His nearly lifeless body was removed from the jail in Owen Sound where he had been housed in secrecy awaiting the trial. McKelvey listened to the news as he drove his little truck to a coffee shop around the corner from the police headquarters. The all-news station reported there would be a significant and far-reaching investigation. How the witness had come to do the job—uninterrupted—was beyond fathoming. A so-called expert on organized bike gangs was explaining to the news reporter that Leroux was a "pioneer", the first member of the Blades to turn against his brethren. While the organization had deeper roots in the southern United States, they were new kids on the block up north. Eventually, the expert said, every organized crime faction must face this cold hard reality; personal survival trumps loyalty. The Hell's Angels had had their sellouts, and the Mafia, too. It was only a matter of time.

"I would imagine," the expert said, "it finally dawned on Mr. Leroux that, once he testified and was sent to prison as part of his plea bargain, he would require protective custody twenty-four hours a day. He would always look over his shoulder..."

Now it was Duguay who would be looking over his shoulder, McKelvey thought as he parked and walked up the sidewalk. The coffee shop was always busy with cops and office workers from the nearby towers. He breathed in the rich scent of freshly ground beans, soil and wood, the flash of chrome and hissing steam. Young men and women of university age joked and moved like dancers behind the counter, repeating orders in their sing-song voices. McKelvey spotted Hattie at the back, seated at a round table. She gave a wave when she saw him, and he made a drinking motion as he went to the counter. She held a mug aloft and shook her head. He ordered a large black coffee, bold as the law would allow, then went to the milk stand and poured a little sugar in, stirred and stirred. He took a sip as he negotiated his way to the table. Someone recognized him, an old duty sergeant, and McKelvey nodded in return.

"Thanks for meeting me," he said and took a seat.

"Any excuse for a coffee," she said.

He took a mouthful and waited for the furnace working in his belly to respond. It was quiet. He said, "Funny, I've never seen you drink anything but coffee. I thought all of you people from the east coast were tea drinkers. Like a religion or something."

She told him she was an unrepentant four-cup-a-day coffee drinker and how her mother completely ruined her for tea, practically pouring the stuff down her throat three or four times a day. They drank tea with breakfast and supper, they drank it to cure the common cold, hangovers, athlete's foot and unemployment. They simply guzzled the stuff, and "no excuse for a cup was ever too shady," she said.

McKelvey was tired, and he knew he looked worse than he

felt. Hattie had said as much. "Look like a drunk with a hangover and a bad cold," was how she had put it. Now the coffee shop began to bulge with the lunch crowd, and they ordered pre-wrapped deli sandwiches and more coffees. McKelvey picked at his roast beef sandwich but couldn't muster an appetite.

"Are you okay? You're a little pale," Hattie said, working on a mouthful of egg salad.

"Just some heartburn," he said.

"Did you get the flu shot this year?" she asked.

"Come on, Hattie, what are you, my mother?"

"I wish you'd call me Mary-Ann sometimes," she said and licked at a dab of egg at the corner of her mouth.

"And yet you call me 'McKelvey'. Always have," he said.

She shrugged and smiled. With her red hair and freckled cheekbones, she struck McKelvey as the sort of woman who forever remained a little girl at heart. Despite her best attempts to alter perceptions, despite even the fact that she carried a gun and was a damned fine shot on the range, she hadn't let the job completely snuff that softer side buried in there. He wondered if she struggled at times with the evil things men do within this world of violent crime. And it *was* men, almost entirely. McKelvey could see her clearly as a precocious eight-year-old with pigtails asking a million questions and driving her parents around the bend. She had been a tomboy, he bet. He saw her wearing a dress with a tear in it from a nail down at the dock, watching her father fix the netting on the boat, or simply waiting for him to come back from the sea.

"It's more acceptable to call a guy by his last name," she explained. "It doesn't take anything away from his machismo. In fact, I would argue that it adds to his image as a gruff, unemotional male. Like in team sports, everybody calls out the player's last name. For a woman, on the other hand, calling her by her last name erodes a little of her...I don't know, her *femininity*."

They looked at each other until their little smirks grew to smiles.

He said, "Is that your rousing manifesto for woman's lib on the edge of the twenty-first century?"

She shrugged. "I don't know. It sounded better in my head."

He pushed his plate aside and asked her about Balani. McKelvey had an impression of the man that was somewhat tainted by something he'd heard on the street.

"You guys have a little bad blood?" she said.

"Who said that?"

"Just something I heard. How he didn't appreciate your involvement. Who knows. Cops are gossip whores, right. Everybody talks about everybody behind their back. Like high school, except we get to carry guns."

"Balani's problem is he focuses on the big show. He wants the glory of the big-name case so he gets his name in the *Star* and the *Sun*, and he forgets about the little details that make a case. All I ever wanted was for them to take a look at some of the information I was pulling together. I spent hours out there on the street, talking to people, to some of these kids. You think I don't know what happened here? He treated me like I'm some fucking beat cop."

She shifted a little, looking into his eyes, and said, in a voice absent of malice or accusation, "We're all guilty at times of letting our hunches lead us around by the nose. Even when the evidence isn't there or it points somewhere else. We're only human."

But it had been upside down from the very start, something off about the whole thing. McKelvey had watched as Gilmartin and Balani bumbled their way through what they ignorantly assumed was an open-and-shut drug murder that would likely never be solved. McKelvey stopped getting information. He pushed things farther than he should have, he saw that now. He got aggressive because something in Balani's ego brought out the worst in him. Words were exchanged on more than one occasion. McKelvey finally reached the limit of his frustration. He put Balani against the wall of a corridor one day, used the strength of anger coursing through his body like an electric pulse to hold the bigger man in his place. Everything started and ended that day.

"This is my son," McKelvey had said. "Don't cut me out!"

Hattie wiped her mouth with a napkin then neatly folded it in two and set it beside her plate. "Sometimes," she said gently, "we're too close to something. To see it clearly."

McKelvey opted not to share the rumours he'd heard on the street concerning Balani. About his years on the Drug Squad. How he liked his dope. How his work on the joint task force would now allow for the perfect mixture of power and lack of accountability. But kids on the street said stuff like that about cops on the Drug Squad all the time. It was a grey area, word against word. He drained the mug and said, "Let me ask you something. Between you and me. Okay?"

She nodded and waited.

"Are you still friends with that woman over in Court Services?" he said.

"Gail," she said. "We're still friends, yes. Why?"

But she knew. She knew why. She knew him, and she knew his mind. He chewed his thumb a little, playing through the words in his mind. He needed to be careful here. It was a fine line. But she didn't wait for him.

"Hey," she said, leaning in, "I know what you're thinking."

"Is that so?"

"They're going to release Duguay. You and I both know it. But let the joint task force do its job, Charlie. They'll probably have a tail on him the minute he steps outside the courthouse. These guys have spent a year and a half working on this project, you think they'll stand by and watch a scumbag like Duguay sail off into the sunset? He won't be able to take a piss without someone writing down the time and location."

"I'm tired of waiting," he said. "Waiting for Balani. Waiting for the Crown. I can't wait any more. Christ, I'm not getting any younger."

"What are you looking for?" she said, resigned to the fact that she would have to offer whatever help she could.

"You can bet they'll have a tight wrap on the proceedings for this," he said. "I'd appreciate knowing when and where. That's all. I just want to make sure this asshole doesn't slip away. I want to be there to look at his face."

"That's it, eh?"

That, and to begin the process of following this man. He would become Duguay's shadow. Watching, waiting.

"That's it," he said. "Cross my heart and pinky promise."

He held out his crooked pinky, and she smiled and brought hers in until the digits were intertwined, locked in a schoolyard pledge of the ages.

"Well, I'm off to an interview," Hattie said. "How about you?"

"Guess I'll go over and do a little paperwork. Since I'm down here," he said.

She shook her head as she got up from the table. He put his hand out and she smiled again and moved past it, giving him a light kiss on the cheek.

"Be good," she said.

He felt his face rush with blood, and he looked quickly around the coffee shop.

"Don't worry," she said. "I kept my tongue in my mouth."

At the police station, McKelvey started to fix a coffee at the stand, but it had been brewing since seven that morning. It smelled like a blend of old tires and burnt plastic. He tried it, shivered, and tossed the cup in the garbage. In the washroom, he was bent over the sink to splash some water on his face when the door opened and someone came in. It was Rogers, a young and recent addition to the Hold-up Squad. Probably the one who would take McKelvey's job. The department was big on succession planning.

"What are you doing in?" Rogers said, moving to the urinal. "Thought you were off for a couple of days."

McKelvey raised his head, water dripping from his pasty face. He felt awful and looked even worse. His body was in the throes of a fever, or else something was shutting down. Rotting from the inside out.

"Yeah, well, I was born here," McKelvey said. He grabbed some paper towels, wiped his face, dried his hands and tossed the balls of paper in the waste basket.

Rogers was unzipped, his head tilted back, and he said, "You're dedicated, that's why. Old school. All of you guys, you treat it like the army or something. The Marine Corps. My generation, we're not interested in working eighty hours a week. Loyalty only goes so far, right. We want a gym and a cafeteria that serves salad. Flex time." He laughed as he zipped up his pants and turned to the counter to wash his hands. McKelvey ran his fingers through his hair and regarded the younger man. He was thirty years old if a day, and the rest of his life was spread before him like a buffet. *The things I thought I knew back then,* McKelvey thought. And with each day he lived, with each year that passed, it became all the clearer that nobody had a goddamned clue.

"You don't look so good, if you don't mind me saying," Rogers said. "You got that flu?"

"What the fuck is it with everybody? I'm fine," McKelvey said.

"Right. Well, you have an awesome day, Detective," Rogers said on his way out, giving McKelvey a pat on the shoulder.

"An awesome day," McKelvey answered, nodding. "I'll do that."

He sat at his desk looking through the thick file that contained all the information he had gathered on Gavin's case. Names and dates, locations and co-ordinates, time-frames stacked against witness statements, photocopies of crime scene photos. Always going back and looking for something he might have missed, his greatest fear, to miss an obvious link in this thing.

He scanned the autopsy report again, for the hundred and sixth time:

City: Toronto

Name of Deceased: Gavin Charles McKelvey

What followed were nearly two pages of cold specs regarding Gavin's height and weight, hair colour, distinguishing features, every square inch of his flesh catalogued for posterity. He recalled the mixture of surprise and regret as he stood there looking down at the body, discovering for the first time the tattoos the boy had kept hidden beneath his shirt.

Manner of death: Homicide

Cause of death: Gunshot wound, head

Body identified by: Father

Autopsy authorized by: Coroner, Chief Medical Examiner

Photographs by: Dr. Harold Manners

Investigating Officers: D/S Raj Balani (lead); Constable Kevin Gilmartin (responding)

Summary of gunshot wound: The entry site is situated on the left upper forehead where it measures 0.6 inches to the right of the anterior midline. The wound is circular, having a diameter of 0.21 inches. Gunpowder residue is located in the wound and the immediately underlying tissue. The course of the projectile runs through the skin and soft tissue, producing hemorrhage to the left frontal lobe. Several curvilinear lead fragments retrieved from the wound. Projectile proceeded through the frontal pole of the brain in a downward direction to perforate the cerebral peduncles and pontine region. The projectile then impacts with the occipital bone. A large calibre, mushroom-shaped projectile is retrieved and forwarded to Forensics for Ballistics Identification.

Shot in the head. Face to face with his killer. The trajectory suggests the killer is taller than the victim—*or else the victim was forced to kneel.* His punishment for a drug debt or an argument, or nothing. His boy died for nothing, and that knowledge was what tortured McKelvey's soul with each breath that he drew; that his boy died for absolutely goddamned nothing, and here he was, still alive in spite of himself, in spite of all the places he had been, the risks he had taken. And it was true, absolutely true, that McKelvey would have exchanged his life for that of his son—without hesitation. It was what he wanted more than anything, to be able to deliver that gift for his wife and his son. The midnight pacts made with god and devil both.

It was in these moments when he sat with his file of papers, his ragged clutch of faint hope, that he understood with a sense of shame what had happened to him. To them all. His family. In many ways what he had *allowed* to happen to them, the three of them. Whether through his direct negligence or inadequate fathering, or through the anger he had displayed when his son's course veered from the track, this was his failure to bear alone. Caroline had been a good mother. She had tried to be a good wife. But it is impossible to be a wife to a stone. And now, just like the family members of crime victims who overnight begin sporting photo buttons of their loved one and calling for the police to take action, this was all McKelvey was left with: the residue of memory, regret. His file folder, his papers, the single-minded drive towards justice and revenge. This was what came to a man who was filled with self-loathing for words left unsaid, a touch left undone. A bitterness and anger, a deep disappointment with himself, that boiled in his veins like a toxin.

Sometimes he saw the face of his boy as a young child, the ever-present cowlick and the boundless energy and curiosity, and he would close his own eyes and try to reach back there and hold the boy or kiss his forehead, physically reach back there through time and once again hold the body close to his chest, the body of his boy forever sleeping on that bed of steel...

It was after seven when McKelvey looked up from the file. He'd gotten lost again. He gathered the papers back in order, put the file in his briefcase. He said goodnight to those still labouring at their desks, making calls, doing paperwork. He felt momentarily unburdened, as though the fog was finally lifting, and he could see an end to the suffering, a finite point on the horizon that promised peace. For he knew what he must do. For his boy. For himself. For Caroline. For the ghost of a family. A more lucid thought had never been conceived.

*　　*　　*

The night is cold and clear. It occurs to McKelvey that he has not started his Christmas shopping. But Christmas for the past two years has seemed less like a holiday and more like a black hole. The days are long, the nights even longer. He sometimes drinks too much and Caroline gives him a look...

Now his stomach flares as he slides behind the wheel of his truck.

He tastes blood. A scent of what—gauze? Razor blades in his stomach, a mouthful of rust. Head spins with an intoxicated dizziness. He brings a few fingers to his lips, then pulls them away; they shine with blood, greasy like fingerpaints. He is weak, and he can't turn the engine on.

McKelvey fumbles with his seatbelt, stumbles from behind the wheel.

The open door buzzes in the night, the drone of an alarm.

He gropes at the seat in an attempt to locate the files, teetering there like a drunk leaving a bar after last call. He makes out a blurry form moving at an angle across the lot, but he is already sliding down the side of the truck.

And he goes down, down, down, the pavement good and cold on his face.

Ten

Twenty past four in the morning, straddling the shadow that falls between the end of darkness and the beginning of light. The girl with the black hair made sure the other girls who shared the small apartment overlooking a Park 'n Ride lot were asleep before she got down on her hands and knees and used a key to raise a slat of hardwood in the entry closet. She kept picking and picking and finally got purchase with the key and lifted the slat of hardwood to reveal a white deposit envelope. Quickly counted the stash of cash inside—four eighty, five hundred, five twenty—then added eighty to the wad. *Six hundred*. With the piece of hardwood out, the envelope right there, the apartment silent, she felt as though she were the last person alive. The whole world had been destroyed by a nuclear bomb. Yeah, and that'd be okay with her. Start it all over again, and maybe this time they could get it right. It was people that wrecked everything. Animals didn't hurt each other like people did. They didn't own that sort of nastiness. She wanted a house filled with stray animals, the wounded animals abandoned to shelters. She eyed the envelope, getting thicker all the time. Eyed it and did the fast, automatic calculations of the addict. Six hundred bucks, and she could get rock for ten a piece. She'd rent a room and be high around the clock for three days…

She quickly put the envelope back and replaced the piece of hardwood. Temptations were just bad ideas disguised as good ones. She had a plan, and nobody and nothing was going to pull her from its course. *They'll all find out a little too late,* she thought, *when I'm already long gone.* The Greyhound to Vancouver with a savings account and a new name, a whole new past. She would get set up in an apartment, then she could be a mother, a wife. Imagine. She'd get a library card and a station wagon, and she'd shop for tasteful women's clothing and nobody would ever know who she had been. It made her smile sometimes to picture herself in a house with a husband, a couple of kids, a dog, roast beef on Sunday nights, growing grey with grandchildren running around asking for her to tell them wild stories of the crazy old days.

Sometimes her mind got stuck, and she saw the boy's face, the dark hair and the blue eyes, and she felt him near her, a physical presence falling like a shadow across the rest of her life, and she saw all the things they had done, were going to do. But then she hurt so bad, she had to forget him or make him into something else, something she could hate...

She sat there with her back against the wall in the hallway and lit a cigarette. A band of light bled from a crack in the bathroom door down the hallway. She thought about the new past she could create. She could be anybody again. The way she'd been at five, six years old. The future a clean slate, anything you could make of it. The pain couldn't be undone, no. But she'd get so far away from it that it seemed like a movie she had watched a long, long time ago.

Do you think I'm pretty, mama? Do you think I'd make a good vet?

She drew on the cigarette, and she sat in the silence.

The last person alive in the world. This was the best time of the day.

Charlie McKelvey pulled himself, against his own will and his better judgement, through the murky slumber of unconsciousness. His mouth was dry. His body thrummed. They had him shot up with painkillers, the good stuff. He was *weightless,* and when he came around the first time, he briefly wondered if this is what death was like, a final freedom from the burden of your own body, of all the things you'd carried with you through a life. *It would be good if it were like that…*

He blinked at the ceiling tiles, the steel safety guard at the side of the bed, the yellow institutional curtains drawn like a tent. His mind flashed with snapshots, recalled images: the lights in the parking lot glowing like halos above his head as he felt himself sinking, giving in to the promise of lostness, and then the strobe of ambulance lights, disembodied voices, his body being lifted, carried…the scattered sounds of the emergency room, a taste of blood in his mouth like old pennies.

Is there anybody we can call?

His eyes were raw, buzzing. He slipped away for a while then came back, like waking from a hundred-year sleep. The first face that came into focus was Hattie's. She was smiling, or trying to, and her red hair was pulled back in a bun. A few wayward strands had escaped the confines of the hairpin and were swept across her shoulder, licks of flame. She was dressed in jeans and a green hooded sweat shirt that said "Dalhousie Tigers Hockey".

"You're cute after you've had a heart attack," Hattie said.

"Thanks," he said weakly, "but it wasn't a heart attack."

"I know. The doctor told me," she said. "Heart attack just sounds—I don't know."

"More dramatic?"

"Gastrointestinal hemorrhage just doesn't have the same ring," she smiled.

"That's just your east coast sense of humour," he said.

"Looks like you got yourself a nasty peptic ulcer there, Detective," she said.

The young doctor who'd visited when McKelvey had first come around had mentioned something about the combination of the ulcer and stress—or perhaps he had used the word "exhaustion". His body's immune system weakened, ravaged.

"How do you feel?" Hattie asked.

"Probably not as bad as I look."

The room smelled of disinfectant, bandages and industrial floor wax. It was a sickly perfume, and McKelvey remembered it the same way a dog remembers the scent of the vet's office. This smell was associated with vulnerability, weakness... endings. McKelvey had watched his mother wither away from cancer in a room not unlike this one. Machines and IVs, Hallmark greeting cards and cheap grocery store flowers lining the window sill; his father in the tavern, unable to face the day, an old man hiding from his life. McKelvey sat in that room because it was what he had to do, but every part of him wanted to get up and run down the hall, keep on running until he came to the end of something, the end of himself.

"Is Caroline here?" he asked. "Did anybody call her?"

She nodded then picked up a small plastic container from the table beside his bed, and began to fiddle with it. She replaced the container and looked at McKelvey. His hair was slicked back from sweat, and she saw what he must have looked like as a little boy, staying home sick from school, his mother touching his forehead, stroking his curly hair. A cute boy he must have been.

"The nurses in the emergency department kept trying to

84

reach Caroline, but they couldn't get through," she said. Then her expression betrayed her. "So I went over, you know. While they had you out. You were out for a long time. I hope you don't mind, I got your keys…"

McKelvey waited. Hattie fiddled with something else on the table.

"Charlie…" she said—and that was enough for him, enough and more. "There was a note."

"Let me see it," he said and extended a wavering hand. He watched it tremble the way his father's hand had trembled the last time he'd seen the man alive. He felt weak now, and his stomach began to glow with a strange new sensation. He wondered briefly if this was a sign of things to come. Is this what it meant to grow old, your body folding in like a card chair after the last hand has been played? There was so much left to do. Singleness of purpose.

"I don't want to upset you. In your condition," she said. "I could read it to you."

"Give me the fuckin' note," he said and wagged his fingers.

Hattie reached into her back pocket and produced a small square of lavender paper. He recognized it as Caroline's writing paper, used for sending notes to friends and relatives. Sometimes she sprayed a scent on it, just a trace of fine mist. And sometimes she used a small stamp to cut out various shapes in the corners, an angel or a heart. He saw his wife sitting at the kitchen table to write this note. What it must have taken for her to come to this… Even before he opened the note, he knew it would kill her inside, hearing where he'd been when he read it. He wanted to spare her this pain; he had never meant to hurt her. Not in a million years…

Then he read the lines so carefully written in Caroline's beautiful handwriting. And it was strange. Everything seemed somehow so inevitable. The only possible conclusion to *The Story of Charlie and Caroline.* Of course Caroline had slipped away to visit her sister on the west coast for an indefinite period, "to sort things out". Of course, she had escaped from their dead home, their mausoleum. He didn't blame her. Christ, how could he? He loved her, and yet he was happy for her. She had seen a small window of opportunity, perhaps her last shot at a life, and so she dove through it. She had escaped, and how could he hold that against her? *Keep running, and don't look back,* he thought.

"I'm sorry, god," was all Hattie could say.

"Listen," he said, and he flushed with embarrassment. "I knew I should've stayed in bed today. My horoscope said something about all this."

It made her laugh just a little, but it was something. He tucked the note beneath the covers at his side. He was tired again, drifting. *Jesus, what a mess of things I've made.* McKelvey groaned as he adjusted his weight, a sliver of pain shooting through his torso. The painkillers were waning now. The real world was waiting for him. *Run, Caroline…run.*

"I'm going to sit here for a little bit," Hattie said. "If you don't mind."

He mumbled something, then he was gone.

Eleven

The prisoner was seated on the hard bunk of his protective custody cell, eyes closed. He slowed his breathing, drawing a bead on a point of light at the centre of the blackness. This was something he had been doing since his first long stretch inside, back when he was eighteen and staring down a sentence of two years less a day. "A deuce less" is what the cons called it. It wasn't much time, not when stacked against subsequent stints and now this, the threat of a virtual lifetime. But it had seemed like a lifetime to a kid back then. It was an older con named Gervais who had taught him all he'd ever need to know about making life work on the inside. It was all about pacing, not counting the days... *Time is meaningless for you in here...time is for the regular citizens, the moms rushing home from work to pick up kids at daycare, the dads coaching little league. Sooner you forget about the clock on the wall, about the calendar on your wall, the pussy sitting at home all alone, the better off you'll be…*

A voice broke his concentration. Visit up. Shackles and leg irons on the slow jangly shuffle to the visitor's cubicles. It was his lawyer. Slick suit, slick smile. What he got paid to do, to look like. Called Duguay "buddy" until Duguay had told him not to call him that. But that was yesterday, and this was today. A few words, a little bit of Latin, and everything changed. The hemispheres flipped, revealing a bright new day. A smile and a nod of the head as acknowledgment of the continued sweetness of karma. The rat Leroux, it made Duguay smile to picture the motherfucker hanging by a bedsheet, his ugly face turned purple.

Paperwork, appearances, signatures, and now Duguay stood on the street outside the courthouse, the air good on his face, and he looked around, half expecting it to come from out of nowhere as it always did, just something that hit you like the hand of God. Unseen, omnipotent. One of his own or a rival from the Quebec days, it hardly mattered. Get in line, take your pick. But there was nothing. Just the regular citizens in motion, trapped in their mini-vans and hum-drum, moving back and forth across the landscape of their lives.

His buddy Danny there with the car, waiting. Good old Danny. Duguay jumped in and looked around, fully expecting to spot a surveillance vehicle. There was nothing. Not yet, anyway. Danny put a CD on and pulled out, slipping inside the stream of traffic.

He said, "How was stir?"

"Rather do time back home," Duguay said. "Least the screws speak the language."

Danny said, "Come on, let me buy you a special dinner. What do you want, a big fucking steak? Spaghetti? And I guess you gotta get laid. But you don't need my help with that."

Duguay took the package of cigarettes from the console and lit one. He coughed at first, then sent a nearly perfect smoke ring floating towards the windshield. He watched it hover and glide then finally disappear as it met the glass. Like magic, how you could never be sure the smoke hadn't just slipped right on through. One of many tricks gleaned in juvie hall. Fourteen years old and thrown to the wolves.

"I want to see my dog," Duguay said. "And find me a good poutine in this fucking city."

They settled on Greek, and Danny took them to the Danforth strip, a little taverna that was owned by a hundred-and-sixty-year-old man named Gus, who liked Danny because he had restored the old man's Cordoba to its original stature, great blue whale of the streets. They took a table at the back, tucked away in a dark corner, and ordered plates of moussaka, grilled octopus and roast lamb, and Duguay told his old friend how he was thinking about distancing himself from the Blades, going back out on his own.

"The Internet, that's where the next big money is coming from," Duguay said, washing his food down with a splash of ouzo. "I know a guy down in Virginia, he set up a room with a bunch of computer hard drives and put up websites. He pays strippers and whores to screw on camera, and guys all over the goddamned world pay to watch. I mean these assholes are willing to give their fucking credit card numbers just to see some tits and ass in the privacy of their own home. You can turn around, sell their cards on top of what you're bringing in from the site. It's the way of the future, man. Who needs all the heat with dope and guns if you can sit back and run a business from your fucking bedroom?"

"Sounds like easy money," Danny said.

"The best kind," Duguay said, and smiled. He raised his glass, and Danny raised his, and they clinked. "To new horizons, man."

Twelve

It was a strange period, a time of significant adjustments, during which McKelvey came to certain resolutions. These were the variety of conclusions a man arrived at when he stood still long enough to face the truth of his mortality. Beyond the scope of a mid-life crisis, this was constitutional, akin to a government reopening laws and charters, setting a course for a new era. It swept a man along on its own energy, the stark realization that he might leave this place before his work was done. It reminded him of a poem the teachers had his class memorize back in grade school, about a man walking in the snow, miles to go, miles to go. He couldn't remember much of it, just those lines. He felt he could relate to that sort of propulsion.

On the morning he was discharged, McKelvey stood in the washroom of his hospital room looking at the sudden transformation of his face. Much of the weight gone from it, a new cut of sharper angles, lines now visible around the eyes, and he understood he had been re-born, he had been delivered another chance to make peace with himself, settle the score with his son's killer. He needed to get in shape and stay in shape. He needed to close his eyes to all else, put blinders on to block the periphery. One foot in front of the other. Follow the fading line to its end point. It was, in the end, all there was to do.

In the time between his discharge and full recovery, his wife returned twice to their home. The purpose of the first visit was to check in on him following his release from hospital, but Caroline stayed longer than she had planned. They fell into a quiet and comfortable routine. She prepared food for him, moved about the house doing this or cleaning that. They rarely spoke, but it was okay. He slept, and she read in bed at his side. There was something indestructible about Charlie and Caroline. And he thought, *it doesn't matter that she won't stay, because we remain forever.* He understood with a sense of sufferance that he would not take another wife. These days spent together as old friends were to be among the final memories McKelvey would carry with him.

There was a month between visits. During this time he adhered to the strict nutritional guidelines as set out for him by a platoon of doctors. He stood at the kitchen counter to slice and dice fresh carrots, turnips, onions, the mysterious eggplant, items he had barely considered in his previous incarnation, items he passed by in the grocery store because he felt they were the tools of the trade for those earthy "hippies" who seemed always to be vehement recyclers and drove bicycles to work even in the snow. He became acquainted with a broad selection of herbs— oregano, rosemary, dill, garlic. He gave up coffee and cigarettes entirely; a recorded miracle. There was a desire here to see how far he could run with this new life, take it to the limit. When the doctor allowed it, he began a careful regimen of sit-ups, push-ups, small hand weights of fifteen pounds, twenty pounds. He embarrassed himself on the first attempt, lifting his body from the floor a mere six, seven times. But he could feel the strength returning, flowing back into his body. He lost four inches around his waist and had to buy new pants. There was a notion of early man morphing, evolving, crawling from the primordial ooze to stand upright and beat his fists against his chest.

The longest days of winter came to pass, and with it the arrival of a new century. There were no computer meltdowns as the doomsayers had predicted; the world simply sighed and shuffled forward. Now and then Hattie would stop by for a visit, and she would laugh when he poured himself a tea, taking great satisfaction in watching McKelvey perform the brewing ritual as though it were a religious ceremony. He seemed so centred, so calm. There had been a shift in polarities.

"Chamomile," she said. "My god, it's the seventh sign. What's next—locusts?"

She always made him laugh with her unpretentious ways, the ways of a Maritime girl.

"You have such a nice smile, Charlie," she said. "You should use it more."

He shrugged, held the cup to his lips and sipped.

"And you've lost weight. God, you must be down to what, one ninety?"

"One eighty-eight, actually," he said. "I was pushing two-fifteen."

She smiled. "I know you were. You look good."

They would talk about work, but only in a peripheral sort of way. McKelvey seemed to show a lack of interest in staying abreast of the police work that continued despite his absence. But Hattie knew McKelvey followed the Duguay proceedings in the newspaper, saw the articles he clipped and set aside.

"Leroux's family authorized it," she told him one day towards the end of February. "They're pulling the plug. It's official." She searched his face for a sign, anything, but it was blank. "I guess that ends that," she said. But she didn't really believe it.

When Leroux was declared dead, finally and completely dead, the charges were stayed against Duguay, and the man was released to the world. The *Sun* ran a photo of Duguay on page three. "Blade walks free," the headline declared. There was Duguay, coming out of the court dressed in a nice suit, one of the city's notorious defence attorneys at his side. McKelvey cut the photo out, folded it in half, and tucked it inside his wallet.

She said, "You've got it for this guy, don't you?"

"These idiots think they're classy like the old-style mobsters," McKelvey said. "They don't see themselves for what they really are, which is a bunch of low-lifes. They've got no honour, they've got no plan. It's all about what they can get right here and right now. Duguay thinks he's Al Capone, waltzing out of court in a thousand dollar suit..."

Hattie stirred sugar into her coffee and let McKelvey's harsh tone simmer. She felt the sting and the choke like a lingering vapour. Sometimes it happened, she knew. A cop came to a point where he couldn't get past something, he couldn't let go of a perp or a case or a victim. Happened to the best prosecutors, too. Something got *stuck* and just kept looping. She understood that, for right or for wrong, McKelvey had fingered Duguay and Leroux for Gavin's death. Now Leroux was dead, and Duguay was a free man. She did not want to listen to the whispers of those who spoke of other motives at work here, a foreshadowing of darker things to come. She wanted to believe in McKelvey and in the way that she saw him.

When Caroline returned for the second and final time, it was with a moving truck. There was an understanding of conclusion here, a quiet acceptance of the facts. They went to the lawyer together and worked out the details. It was a legal separation; divorce was not mentioned. McKelvey wanted to give her everything, but he knew Caroline wouldn't take more than her fair share. The retirement savings were figured out, and they came to an agreement on the home they had paid off together; for the time being McKelvey would rent the home, with the funds being deposited in a separate account to be calculated and halved upon the sale of the home at a later date. It was all very business-like, as though the two of them were almost irrelevant in the whole process of valuing savings accounts, RRSPs, mutual funds, capital assets. They were a corporation. Charlie and Caroline Incorporated. McKelvey couldn't bring himself to make eye contact with his wife as they signed reams of paperwork.

He could see the change in her. Caroline looked young again, the darkness gone from her eyes, a burden lifted. She was dressed in new clothes. Her hair was done. It was a geographical cure, McKelvey believed, this transfer to the west coast, but who was he to judge? It was a strange and sad irony, though, both of them standing there in the living room looking healthier and altogether more content than they had in years, that their mutual regeneration was made possible only through separation.

"I have an interview next week," she told him, "for a job in a women's shelter. I'll be doing public outreach again, and helping out with the administration."

"That sounds great," he said. "They'd be lucky to have you."

He wanted to reach out and touch her glowing face, touch it perhaps for the last time. They would promise to stay in contact, to call now and then, write letters, but he had no long range plans; he just wanted this done. Like ripping a bandage from the flesh, do it quickly and don't think twice.

He said instead, "Listen, I want you to know I don't hold any of this against you. I mean, you leaving." He paused, unsatisfied. "No, that's not what I meant to say."

But Caroline reached out and touched his face, and she said, "Shhhh, Charlie."

She was crying, and he gave her a hug, rubbing her back.

He smelled her perfume, her hair, and he tried to recall the last time they had made love. He wanted to preserve a date, a context, but his mind came up blank. They stepped apart.

"It's nobody's fault," she said, which he accepted as a small kindness. "I just…I couldn't breathe, Charlie. I was suffocating..."

"I didn't come through for you, and I am sorry for that," he said.

"You need to look after yourself, Charlie. You're so angry, so filled with hatred. Treat yourself with love and kindness. You need to get some help with all of this. It's too much to carry around. There's no shame in admitting that. But even as I say that, I know it doesn't come easy for you. I know that, Charlie."

She went to pack the last of her things. The two young movers busied themselves removing furniture and boxes. McKelvey made them take more than his wife wanted, until there remained little more than the kitchen table and chairs. The master bedroom was stripped except for the bed itself. McKelvey stood in the middle of the living room once the movers were locking up the gate on the truck, and he nodded his acceptance of this new world order, this cosmic ripple.

"So what now, Charlie?" Caroline said.

She startled him, coming up from behind. He turned and saw her standing there, a final box at her feet. It was marked "Books". He smiled and felt something catch in his throat. He almost cried, but he didn't. It was over before it began.

"I used up all of my sick time and vacation days. So I guess I'll retire," he said with a shrug.

"Oh, I'll believe that when I see it," she said. "Promise me you'll take your medication and stay on the diet. You know how you drift away from things after a while."

She went to touch his face again but stopped herself. Old habits.

"I'll take a trip out that way next summer, stop in and visit," he said. "If that's okay."

"That would be nice," she said. "That would be just fine."

They looked at each other. They both smiled sadly, understanding they were too old to pretend. He stood at the living room window and watched as her cab pulled away. She did not turn back as he thought she might, a last little wave. Then the moving truck revved, shifting into gear with a guttural moan, and disappeared down the street, taking a good portion of his life with it. McKelvey experienced no pangs of regret or longing for the items in the back of that truck; it was just *stuff*. What was gone was his wife. His wife and son. His family. Everything he had worked for all these years, all those midnight shifts in the cold patrol cars, all the arguments over bills, the vacations and the Christmas mornings, all of it gone with the flicker of the brake lights on the moving truck.

Like a snake shedding its skin, he moved through the house to the garage, and pulled an old chair up to the high shelves along the wall. He reached with his hand, adjusting the rags and the oil cans and the garden fertilizer, until his hand found a small grey lockbox and pulled it down from its hiding place. In the kitchen he set the box on the table and opened it with a tiny key on a string that he kept in the bottom of his underwear drawer. The box was filled with newspaper clippings in which he was quoted in court, a few old photos, and at the bottom, wrapped in an old tea towel, there was a small .25 pistol. Black, what they used to call a lady's gun. Something he'd kept hidden from Caroline for years and years. The black metal pistol had belonged to a friend. He had kept it while the license was sorted out for the guy, but somewhere along the line it had become his property. It rested in a leather holster that you slipped onto your belt, the little bundle wrapped in the old stained towel. He unwrapped the gun, weighed it with his palm, this tiny weapon, then set it aside. With his green tea steaming, he sat alone leafing through the old clippings about armed robberies, arrests, acquittals. The story of his life set out in fading newsprint.

Thirteen

The air tasted in the back of Pierre Duguay's throat like crack cocaine. Its chemical residue clung to his tongue like baking soda and burnt plastic, and he hadn't even partaken. It was just after six o'clock in the morning, and Duguay was staring at the bedroom ceiling in the apartment unit located above the Dove Gentleman's Club. The sun was breaking open, spreading across the eastern horizon the colour of burnt marmalade. But in here it was still midnight. In this place it was perpetual midnight. The windows were covered in tinting, and the blinds were drawn. There had been a party, a series of never-ending celebrations following his release. His townhouse had been leased out during his confinement, so he was here like a kid starting all over again. Something he'd been doing his whole life, starting over again once the cuffs came off and the gates opened up. His throat burned from too many cigarettes, and his lungs ached from the abuse. On mornings like this, he felt the full weight of his age, the consequences of a lifetime lived on the fringe, the unpaid bills from his youth now stacked and awaiting payment. This year he would turn thirty-eight, a milestone in terms of morbidity rates in his profession. His father had made it to thirty-four. In this way he was already something of a generational success story.

There had been another party, and now the mood was

sombre, the hollow come-down mood of a strip joint at daybreak. The vampires were asleep, spread around the apartment, passed out on the long leather couch in the living room or curled up on reclining chairs. This one at his side had come to rest there as much by chance as any design. There were young girls new to the club, and his memory was unclear concerning this one. Nothing brought home the fact of his aging more clearly than the requirement of a few lines, once he had too many beers into him, to get hard and stay hard. The white was something he had tried to stay away from; once tasted, it was a talon in his shoulder blade. It came and went from his life in short, sharp bursts. He did what he did, and things were what they were. He never smoked it or shot it, a compromise of sorts.

He looked at the girl's back now, her tanned flesh smooth and dotted with tiny freckles across the shoulder blades. A tattoo at the base of her neck, some sort of Asian symbol. He figured it was her birth sign or perhaps a meaningful phrase in some mystical language: "courage" or "faith", something like that. All the young girls were getting the same tattoos in all the same places. They all wanted to look the same, dress the same. She stirred slightly, rolled over so he could see her face. She was not unattractive, but the evening had taken its toll. Her long copper hair was tangled, and her face was puffy from sleep. Her breath was sour and strong. He slid from beneath the sheets and walked naked across the floor, stooping for his jeans and t-shirt on his way to the bathroom.

Duguay lifted the toilet lid, tilted his head back and pissed a long golden stream. He shivered and ran fingers across the blue-black lines inked to his chest and belly, evil incantations, swords and skulls. He dropped the lid with his foot and hit the flush. He coughed and drew a mouthful of phlegm, spat in the sink and washed it away. He splashed cold water on his face then ran his wet fingers through his brown hair that fell to just above collar length, a little shaggy but a generation removed from the waist-length hair he had sported in the early Eighties. Tied back or let loose, for better or for worse, it had been something of a wild trademark, back when he'd tucked his jeans into his goddamned cowboy boots and taken himself so seriously. Driving around Montreal and Sherbrooke and way up in Val D'Or in a yellow Camaro. *Jesus,* he thought. *The days we had, the days.*

In the bedroom he found his watch on the night table and slipped it over his wrist. The girl was awake now and sitting up with her back against the headboard, a few white crumbs in her palm. He watched as she put the tiny glass pipe to her lips, a one-hitter, the glass blackened and stained from the burning chemicals. She held a lighter to the end, and in this way she was delivered from the collapse of her spirit. It was what she needed, what she wanted, what she had become. The first hit was a jolt, a dog bark in her ear, and she woke up. The ease crawled across her internal organs, system to system, cell to cell, then out through her limbs, some kind of a cure. It was the only game in town.

"*Tabernac.* Hitting the pipe before her eyes are open. You better watch that shit, sister. You're no good to me, you're no good to nobody. Fucking junkies…"

Her head was back now, lolling side to side. Duguay shook his head and reached for his cigarettes. He freed one from the package and tapped it a few times against his Zippo lighter, popped it in his mouth and fired it up. He drew a long haul, then exhaled the smoke through his nostrils in two long funnels.

"Cops probably sitting outside right now, watching this place," Duguay said. "Looking for any excuse they can get just to come in here."

He walked towards the door, and the girl opened her eyes, groggy. "Where you going?" she said.

"You should know better than to ask questions like that," he said.

"Can't it wait till morning?"

"It *is* morning, *bijou,*" he said. "You girls better be showered and have this fucking place cleaned up by the time I get back."

He walked out through the living room, past the empty beer bottles and stuffed ashtrays, an open pizza box with four or five cold slices that turned his empty stomach, past a girl curled and crashed on the couch. In a small refrigerator in the kitchen he dug his hand into a large package of deli end cuts, old heels of mock chicken and pork roast and spiced salami, then he unlocked the door to the spare bedroom. The room was empty save for a large comforter coiled into a bed, a bowl of water and a food dish. Too many luxuries spoiled a dog. Diablo, a Red Nose American Pit Bull, was waiting on his haunches, his thick body packed with muscle, translucent grey eyes glimmering, liquid.

"Daddy'll be back," he said, and tossed the handful of meat into the bowl.

He wiped his hand down his jeans and closed and locked the door to the spare room. He was closing the main door behind him just as a toilet flushed in the washroom down the hall, and the girl with the coal black hair stepped into the hallway, the hangover headache coming on like timpani as she gathered her clothes.

The sunshine was like arrows in his eyes as Duguay walked across the parking lot. It was a perfect early spring morning. It was still cold enough to see his breath, but the sun was warm on his face even at this early hour. It made him think about being a kid, a specific memory of walking to the corner store—the *dépanneur*—to buy milk for his cereal. A Sunday morning. The sun shining and making him squint like the cowboys in those Saturday afternoon movies. The streets were always dead on a Sunday morning, everybody sleeping off their Saturday night. It was a memory that came with a good feeling, like he was a man of independent means, a buck fifty in his front pocket, money filched from the asshole sleeping on his mom's couch. The little boy Duguay squared his shoulders and walked straight down the middle of the sidewalk.

The past wasn't something Duguay had much use for. To him, life was right here, right now. It had always made sense that way to him, as far back as he could remember. *Now* was all that mattered—getting through the next hour, having enough money in your pocket, a bed to sleep in, a woman to lie with. The counsellors in the prisons were always offering up diagnoses as a means to explain his chosen life, this path which alternated between periods of wickedness and penitence. Some said he had a personality disorder, or borderline personality, although he read the brochures and figured he owned only about half of the necessary characteristics. Was it true that he had no conscience? No, it wasn't true. Not the way they made it sound. When he was righteous, when he was wronged, then he could and would take care of business without hesitation. He had hurt people in different ways, it was true. He would probably hurt many more before his time was through. One time he'd tried to explain it to a counsellor by saying it this way: "If it comes down to me or another guy, it's going to be the other guy who falls every time. I'm gonna be the one who makes it out. See, you sit in an office, and you don't understand. You can't understand. You don't come from the same place as me."

There were things they tried to get him to talk about, and he gave them just enough to get his papers signed and make parole.

Sometimes he made up stories, telling the counsellors things he thought they wanted to hear. It wasn't until the range was mostly silent and he was on the bunk in his cell that his mind drifted back to the fragments of childhood, the worst secrets of those crazy days. The faces of the men his mother brought home, the sickness from booze and drugs hanging over the whole place like a weather pattern, the endless disappointments of birthdays and holidays. And always the memories started and stopped with the man named Duvalier, who stayed with him and his mother for a few weeks when Duguay was nine or ten. Duguay hated him more than the other dregs his mother brought home. These men were for the most part harmless fools, drunks and petty ex-cons, a parade of losers, men who had let life slip through their fingers and now sat in rented rooms with quart bottles of beer, their fingers stained yellow from tobacco, teeth rotting out of their head. But he particularly hated Duvalier because the man gave off a vibration of *meanness*, as though with him anything was possible. Duguay hated his little round beer belly, hated his thin brown hair slicked back across his high round forehead, hated the way he looked at Duguay. There was something not right about the man, about the way his eyes held the boy.

It happened one day while Duguay was in the bathroom brushing his teeth. A Saturday morning, his mother passed out and cartoons buzzing on the little TV in the living room. Bugs Bunny and Elmer Fudd teaching him American English. Duvalier came in, closed and locked the door behind him. Duguay smelled the day-old booze on the man, seeping through his flesh in a greasy film. The man's breath was sour, as though he had been sick to his stomach.

"I knew your dad," Duvalier said. "I bet you didn't know that, did you?"

Duguay didn't say anything. He kept brushing. It was the first new toothbrush he'd gotten in what seemed like forever, a gift from a nurse who had visited his school. He was brushing in circles, the way she had showed his class with the help of an oversized brush and a large set of choppers. He didn't want cavities. He didn't want them to stick a drill in his mouth.

"Sure I did," Duvalier said. "Yessir, we did time together up at Archambault. Same range, me and your old man."

Duguay understood the reference to the penitentiary in the same way a child of privilege might recognize the names of country clubs or dance studios. Names of institutions like Donnacona or Dorchester were simply place names that belonged to the resumes of the fathers and uncles and older brothers, the men who lived along his street, populated his universe.

"I could tell you stories about your daddy. Would you like that?"

Duguay wanted to hear stories, yes. He didn't know his father, owned only a vague memory of a man taking him for an ice cream at a city park when he was what, three or four? A man with sideburns and a cigarette package in the front pocket of his white T-shirt. Large hands with big knuckles. The car was black, and the seats were hot in the sun, wide as a bench. That was all, fragments. He wanted to learn things about his father beyond the lies his mother told. But not from this man. He didn't want to hear any stories from this man.

"He was a cool cat. A big guy. You know, before he got himself killed and all that."

Duguay didn't say anything still. But he watched the man from the corner of his eye, his body tensed, expecting.

"You should be nice to me, kid," Duvalier said, resting a hand on the sink, running fingers through his limp hair. "I just might be your new daddy, you know, if things work out between your momma and me. Could be."

Duguay leaned over the sink and spat. He was aware that the man's eyes followed him as though he found every movement entirely captivating.

"You little shit. You was inside," Duvalier said and made a clucking sound, pulling his tongue against a tooth, "you was inside, kid, I'd have you turned out before you could say 'papa'."

The tiny bathroom got too close, too hot, and the stink from the ex-convict was like a poison gas that made Duguay's eyes water. He had to breathe through his mouth. *How could his mother let this pig into her bed?* The man had known his father, or so he said, and this was how he repaid that friendship? Duvalier took a step, almost invisibly, a slick and quick slide. Duguay thought for a second that the man was getting ready to move a hand to him, to touch his body. Saw the events unfolding as though in a movie, and he was ready for it before anything even happened. He tapped his toothbrush against the side of the sink, casual as a Sunday afternoon. The low watt bulb above the faded mirror flickered for an instant. He felt his heart pushing against his rib cage.

Then Duvalier did it, moved his hand, never taking his red eyes from Duguay. The hand was warm, moist, and it squeezed Duguay's shoulder. Once, then again. Duvalier made a sound like hauling air through clenched teeth, excited.

"C'mon buddy, nothing to be afraid of. All the tough guys do it," he said. "Let me pop that cherry for you...turn you into a real man..."

Duguay looked him in the eye, staring, his jaw clenched and set. Duvalier stepped in and made his move, both of his skinny arms coming around at once, the limp strands of his greasy hair falling forward now across his twisted face, and Duguay pushed back and made a noise, then there was a hand down the back of his pants, fingers wiggling in his rear end, and he brought his knee up...

The doorknob rattled, and Duguay's mother called out in her hoarse morning growl. "Pierre, what are you doing? I've gotta get in there. *Open the fucking door!*"

Duvalier turned to watch as Duguay slipped out of his grasp, flicked the lock and stepped through the door in one liquid motion, as though he had been in command of the situation all along, determining its beginning and end. Then Duguay was gone, and so too was Duvalier, but not before leaving Duguay's mother a black eye with which to remember him by. It wasn't until a couple of years later that Duguay understood with complete comprehension what would have unfolded that day, how his life would have been changed.

All of the men who passed through their lives were invariably the same, and they came carrying the same weight through a tortured life: forearms speckled with sloppy homemade tattoos, a missing tooth, a grey scar across the bridge of the nose, they usually smoked and they always drank, and it was the rare individual who did not turn mean as the evening crashed headlong toward morning. Raised voices, broken plates, his mother crying, then the slow creaking of her bedsprings as the two wounded souls thrashed away their torment.

He learned how to steal cigarettes from packages left on the coffee table, learned later how to steal money from pants left coiled on the bedroom floor, and later still he learned how to take a punch and how to give one right back. He had his nose broken at age twelve by an unemployed construction worker named Giroux. Duguay had sassed his mother over something one night, something insignificant, and Giroux levelled the kid with a backhand without so much as getting up from the kitchen table where he was sitting drinking his

Labatt 50. Duguay crashed backwards, saw an explosion of stars, tasted blood like rust in the back of his throat. It hurt, *it hurt like hell,* numbness spreading across his face like a spider's web, but he was up and ready to roll almost instantly. He had some size to him by that point, too, developing into his father's body, his father's temperament. There was a rage spinning inside, a whirlwind rushing him headlong towards the world. Giroux turned just in time to catch a looping haymaker to the mouth. Bloody-lipped, but more embarrassed than wounded, he spun and tried to get a footing, but he was sloppy drunk, and anyway Duguay had already grabbed a full beer bottle from the case on the kitchen counter, and he was swinging it like a Louisville Slugger across the man's jaw.

"Pierre! Stop kicking the man, he's down, he's down!"

He could hear his mother's high-pitched voice, see the man's face twisted in pain, his jaw broken, teeth stained with blood, his arms wrapped protectively around his head as Duguay stood there working his feet. He couldn't stop himself.

At the age of fourteen, Duguay was whisked away to a juvenile detention centre upon being caught for the third time attempting to steal a car. It wasn't until he was actually inside the detention centre that he discovered what he had been doing wrong all along, and in this way he learned some invaluable lessons in wiring, circuitry. The older boys taught him how "the system" worked, what a kid could expect to draw in terms of sentencing for the various crimes, taught him how to roll a cigarette with three fingers and a thumb, but most of all they taught him how to swagger and act like he didn't care about *anything.*

Upon his release from juvie hall, Duguay stole a brand new Lincoln Town Car from a lot off Ste. Catherine Street. Sat at the wheel like he was some kind of mobster, the window down and his arm cocked out like he drove a frigging Town Car every day. He swung by the fringes of Verdun and picked up two friends he had met in the detention centre. Together, at the age of sixteen, they robbed their first *dépanneur* with a rusty pocket knife. That was really something. It was the beginning of all that was to follow. The rush of adrenaline, the wail of sirens, the look of respect and fear in the eyes of the other boys as they were returned to the juvie hall. Duguay learned two things from the foray: that he possessed the rare brand of courage required to face down the odds of a life lived on the narrow margins; and that he was a natural leader. He was born for this.

Eventually, after a couple more years of watching all the Duvaliers and the Girouxs and the Dionnes and the Phenoufs come tumbling through his apartment as though they owned the fucking place, as though they owned his mother and him also by proxy, after just a few more years of that, Duguay himself would be gone for good, too. He escaped from the street, he rose above the petty thieves who fenced their own junk in local taverns, the pathetic burglars who ran from suburban homes clutching VCRs and cassette decks to trade at pawn shops for a fraction of their resale value. He rose above it all, finally broke away from the myth of a mother's unconditional love for her child, and he became a man who was known and feared. He never looked back, and his mother followed his life through the police tabloids.

*   *   *

On this morning, the parking lot was mostly empty. There were a few vehicles which had been left the night before by those too drunk to drive. He slid behind the wheel of his car and paused before turning the engine. He sat there for a moment. Then he got out of the car, put a knee on the pavement and looked beneath the vehicle for anything that didn't belong. Wires and things. He reached in and popped the hood, then hefted the lid and scanned the engine components, all the places where it could be done. Satisfied, he let the hood drop, started the car and pulled out of the lot. He lit a new cigarette and steered himself towards the highway and the east end of the city.

The highway was sparse with car traffic this early on a Sunday, but alive with transport trucks of monolithic proportion. Cigarettes dangled from the faces of the truck drivers who appeared like zombies at the wheel, staring straight ahead at the infinite black unfurling beneath their wheels as they hauled their mundane cargo between Detroit and Montreal. Duguay steered the blue Mercury Mystique towards Danny Madill's auto body garage out in the industrial strips of Scarborough. He'd bought the car used, picked it up from the mother of a friend of a friend, a clean car with no history. Despite its name, there was nothing mysterious about the vehicle at all. It was a no-nonsense sedan, something a suburban mother might drive, and for this reason alone it was ideal. Now that he had been released to the world, there was no sense in attracting heat for vanity's sake. The guys made fun of his ride, but they were idiots. Too many of his contemporaries flaunted their all-cash income by driving around town in souped up new Mustangs, sporty BMWs.

He drove, and he tried to imagine waltzing back into the life he had been building before the take-down, before a colleague had turned rat. As though it could be that easy. Too many variables had changed. Leroux dying had perhaps spared him a lifetime in prison, but it presented other problems. He was tainted now. His value to the organization was dropping in direct relation to his exposure to both the media and the police. He saw that he was perhaps a liability to them now. Danny's call, while it shook him from a deep sleep, was not a surprise. That Bouchard, the boss, the national boss, was coming to Toronto—in fact, was *in* Toronto, and seeking a place to meet—was not a shock in and of itself. Duguay had been expecting the call from the moment he was released. There were issues to discuss, plans to be made. He suspected Bouchard would want him to lie low for a while, or perhaps take a job down south, get out of the city. Everyone knew the task force would keep tabs on him, and it was for that reason he took lefts and rights, zigged and zagged. There was nobody around him now.

The call that morning had set Duguay's mind in motion. Danny had said, "Pete. They left a message on the machine. Lookin' for a place to meet."

"Call them back. Tell them I'll be at the shop in an hour."

"I'll go unlock it for you," Danny said.

"Do me another favour, Dan. Stick around the shop for me?"

"I'll be there," Danny said.

As he drove, all the deaths back in Quebec flooded his mind. A wasteland. The bodies piled up week after week. Guys you sat and laughed with and drank with, blown to vapor the instant they turned the ignition in their car, shot in the face turning a corner, killed in their beds, killed by the other guys or their own guys; in the end it had been too murky to decipher. All the heat that came down on all of them with the formation of the *Carcajou*—or Wolverine—squadron, these cops who played a new game without rules. The RCMP, the SQ, the Montreal Urban, they were all working in their own way to win the prize, to be the first to wipe an entire gang off the map. In Duguay's mind, he could not return to the paranoia and violence of those days. He could fight and he could die, but it had to be for something. So many of his friends had died for nothing. All the long years he'd worked as an independent, or associate, carving out his own territory in the neighbourhoods of Montreal, buying bad debts from the various chapters and collecting the payments one way or another. Like a moth to a flame, you could propel the advances and the opportunities for so long, and eventually you got pulled all the way in. And then you burned up.

He'd been friends with some of the guys in the Laval chapter of the Hells when the Sorel chapter cleaned them out. The "Lennoxville Massacre", one chapter wiping out another chapter that was drawing heat to the organization. It was then Duguay had seen that there was no real brotherhood, not in the Hells or the Rock Machine either, and while the talk was of making him a full prospect in the Sorel chapter, he made his decision to stand alone. It was a decision, he now realized, that had only delayed the inevitable. He was good at what he did, he was solid, and with the casualties piling up, a dependable soldier was in high demand. The Rockers, the muscle branch of the Hells, finally gave him an ultimatum: sign up or retire. Duguay was his own man, and he favoured neither of the options, choosing instead to take a full patch with the upstart Blades, who had swallowed up the last of the renegade Satan's Choice, and a few Outlaws chapters.

All the big guys, the old guys who acted like generals in a field war, safe from the front lines, were willing to kill their own soldiers on the whisper of a rumour, the thread of a connection. All it took in this world was for someone to *think* you had a made a deal, and it was more than enough to get you blown apart.

When he became certain many of his activities were under investigation, just prior to his arrest, Duguay had begun to communicate through Danny. He didn't trust anyone, not after Leroux. Survival was the only thing on his mind. He could walk into Danny's garage knowing that he hadn't been set up. But Duguay knew the landscape was changing, and with it, his place in the order of things. It was this line of thinking that kept bringing him back to his emergency fund—an envelope with ten grand sitting in a deposit box in a little bank up in the small town of Midland. He'd set himself up with the plan during those last days of paranoia, taking half a day to drive at odd angles across the south-western Ontario countryside, just to be sure he wasn't being followed. The envelope provided a limited sense of security, to be sure. A few grand didn't go far these days. But it was there if things went sideways. It would be enough to get somewhere, get started again.

The east end industrial complex was populated with self-serve storage units painted yellow, freight forwarding warehouses with tractor trailers pulled up to loading docks, all-night printing plants, sign shops. He parked just down from Danny's garage, scanning the lot as he pulled in. It was empty save for two vehicles. The souped up Charger was Danny's. The black Chevy Blazer would belong to the man he was to meet. Duguay spotted a guy sitting in the passenger seat, there to ensure the vehicle's continued integrity. The man he was to meet was called 'Ti'Noir, or Little Black, but his given name was Jean Bouchard.

There was a single garage bay with two windows, and beside it a heavy grey steel door. It was unlocked. Duguay slipped inside. There was movement to his right, at the door leading into the garage bay, and Duguay paused. A man he didn't recognize stepped in. He was six and a half feet, three hundred pounds. One of Bouchard's new bodyguards. Duguay nodded as the goliath felt him for weapons. In truth, Duguay knew it was not a gun the man was searching for but a wire. Duguay sensed Bouchard's increasing paranoia since Leroux had flipped, and now all of their photographs were stacked in files, posted on computers.

"You should wrestle," Duguay said to the man.

"Used to," the man said.

"No doubt."

"Clean," the man called down the hall.

Duguay walked past the garage bay. He smelled tobacco and a hint of marijuana, and followed the smell to the back office. He stood along the side of the wall, close, listening for a moment before turning his head in. Danny was slumped lazily in his chair, Bouchard across from him.

"Boys," Duguay said, stepping inside.

Danny nodded, and Bouchard stood. He and Duguay were close to the same size, both tall men, broad-shouldered. They looked into each other's eyes for a moment, and Duguay thought he saw a glimpse of the man's mood.

"Just catching up with Dan here. I was just saying I remember his older brother from the west end Irish crew in the old days. Crazy sons of bitches, the Madills, the Murphys. I always got job openings for a crazy Irishman, but Danny here says he likes his cars these days," Bouchard said. "Anyway, maybe we can work something out. This is a good spot, tucked away. Still, I don't like driving all the fucking way out here."

Duguay shrugged, and said, "I don't like being frisked like some rat. Anyway, this is the way I do it, Jean. Don't know who you can trust any more. I'm still not sure I wasn't set up this last time. Little too much of a fluke getting pulled over like that."

"Doesn't matter now, you got your get-out-of-jail-free card.

We settled with the lawyer. You're welcome for that. Those guys are worse than the Montreal mob, what they charge."

"I appreciate it," Duguay said, despising the notion that he might be in the debt of any man.

Bouchard held out a hand, and Duguay accepted. Both men offered a formidable handshake, as though presenting the other a preview of the strength to be found within.

"It's good to be sprung," Duguay said and fumbled in his pocket for his cigarettes.

"That's why I left you alone for a few days there, get cleaned up and get laid. Luc's been running the show while you were away. He wants your job, you know. Better be careful."

"Good thing I'm not insecure," Duguay said.

Bouchard said, "Let's talk. Just the two of us."

Duguay looked over to Danny, sitting there like the little brother left out of every good conversation. Danny shrugged, dug into the overflowing ashtray for the remnant of his spliff, and shuffled out of the room and into the garage bay, where a 1970 Corvette sat on blocks awaiting restorative body work. Duguay heard the low voices of Danny and the bodyguard as they began to talk about the car.

Bouchard sat back and folded his arms. Black eyes looked out from beneath a head of short grey hair, cropped military-style. He looked like somebody's grandfather. Somebody's grandfather you didn't want to fuck with.

"We have some problems," Bouchard said.

Duguay said, "Tell me about it."

"No, no, this is a new problem, my friend. Courtesy of the cop friend we've been paying for two years now."

"Balani," Duguay said. He shifted his weight and leaned with his back against the opposite wall. "I haven't talked to the pig in six months, maybe more."

"He's on the biker task force now," Bouchard said.

"That's good for us then," Duguay said.

"You brought him in, eh?"

"I brought him in, yeah, and then he saddled up with Leroux. Two cokeheads."

Bouchard found his own cigarettes and lit one. He smiled a little. "He's got balls, I'll give him that. Gave me a heads-up from down the line. Says there's a cop dogging a case. He's got it in his head that you killed his son. The cop's son..."

Duguay saw it before him now, the links set out. Leroux. Balani. Probably some of the others, the junior jacks waiting to be patched. Bouchard was staring down the business end of an internal cleansing here. Everything was sideways. Bouchard reached to his shirt pocket and pulled out a folded square of white note paper. He unfolded it and read, "McKelvey. Do you know this guy?"

"Never heard of him."

Bouchard stared. "Maybe it was Leroux?" he said.

Duguay said, "He was cutting some of his own deals, Jean. I told you that six months before he fucked me over. I should've kept a better handle on him."

"You're right, you should have," Bouchard said, then stood and reached out to slide the piece of notepaper into the pocket of Duguay's jacket. "Anyway, this is your mess now. This cop McKelvey thinks he has a problem with *you,* he's got a problem with *us.* And I'm not going to spend thirty years in the joint because of any more fucking rats like Leroux. Understand me?"

Duguay dropped his butt, squashing it with a twist of his boot. "I'm not some kid looking to get patched here, Jean. I lost time sitting in there waiting for someone to sew Leroux's mouth shut. I'll take the hit for letting Leroux and Balani jump in bed together, but that's where my responsibility ends.

Half these guys you sent me from the South Shore are crackheads, a bunch of amateurs who draw heat every time they open their goddamned mouths, bragging in the bars. I can't get set up with a bunch of losers. Not in this city. Everything's different here. The Hells own this place…"

He stared into Bouchard's black eyes, both men unblinking. Bouchard twisted at the waist and tamped out his unfinished cigarette in the overflowing ashtray on the desk. His fingers rooted through the mess of butts, something amusing him.

"Your friend likes the weed, eh?" he said over his shoulder.

Duguay didn't say anything. Bouchard turned back, resuming his serious pose. "The Hells don't know whether to think we're a fucking joke or a bunch of loose cannons. We need to clean up our own backyard before we can take them on. Leroux is dead now, and that's a start. But we got some things to look after before we can make any big moves around here. I talked to Cortez the other day. He's on standby."

Duguay shook his head. The last thing he needed was the hitman from the southern States bringing his Special Forces bullshit to their backyard. It would be a bloodbath. He said, "We don't need a big show here. Let me take care of things my way."

Bouchard stood and surveyed the room one final time, taking in the pin-ups and the tool calendars. "We'll do things your way for a little while. In the meantime, Luc will stay in charge. Just stay out of the business until all of this is taken care of. Run your agency and whatever you've got going at the Dove, but keep your face out of the fucking newspaper. The heat's everywhere."

Bouchard held out his hand. The two men clasped their arms and settled upon their mutual honour, respect. Bouchard took a step for the door. He paused and turned, something still on his mind. He said, "Tell Danny boy I'm serious about the offer. We can always use more family."

"I'll let him know," Duguay said.

Bouchard disappeared around the corner and down the hallway. Duguay heard him stop at the garage bay, say a few words, then slip outside into the morning. Duguay waited a minute or two then followed the same path. At the garage he found Danny rubbing a piece of sandpaper in slow, circular motions across the front quarter panel, an artist at his methodical work. Danny could take a month to do what other body artists did in a week, but nobody came close to matching his level of perfection. It always amazed Duguay how his friend could do this sort of work while continually dipping into his pocket to puff on a joint. If it were him, he wouldn't get past the first joint before he'd want to order in a pizza and sit back and just think.

"Hey sweet cheeks, you new in here?" Duguay said, repeating the infamous line uttered by a hulking seventeen-year-old—whom they would later discover was aptly named Meat—upon their arrival at the juvenile detention centre.

Danny turned, a tight smile on his face, and he straightened. "Yeah," he said, continuing on with the dialogue, "and I'm looking for a girlfriend about your size."

Duguay laughed, and the memory of that episode came back as clearly as a scene recalled from a favorite movie. How the slab of a teen named "Meat" had broken Duguay's nose with one hard jab and one of Danny's hands, but how in the end the two of them, working together, both of them covered in tears and blood, had managed to beat the gargantuan bully down to the ground, their feet working in unison. How after that day nobody bothered to get in their face, and every step of the way they earned their reputation as "solid".

"Remember the look on Meat's face when he hit you, and

you didn't go down, you just stood there with blood gushing from your nose? Like he couldn't believe it," Danny said, "big kid like that probably used to watching kids piss their pants and run away. Man, you looked like Paul Newman in *Cool Hand Luke.*"

"That's how we got Meat to work with us, on our side," Duguay said. "Respect."

Danny looked up to Duguay, always had, ever since that first day when Duguay had stood there and taken a punch that rightfully belonged to Danny. But now, looking at Duguay with the dim light painting dark shadows across his face, Danny wondered if something had shifted within the man. He saw the same stance, the same attitude, but something told him there was a diminishing will.

"Let's get some breakfast," Duguay said. "I'll buy you steak and eggs at that all night joint up the road. That big-titted waitress still work there?"

"Last time I checked," Danny said.

The all-night diner was a low-budget place nestled among the industrial complexes. Laminate tables, cheap plastic seats. It served breakfast all day or full meals for the working men, broiled pork chops and potatoes, flavourless spaghetti and dry shepherd's pie. They took a table along the window and ordered fried eggs and hash browns. The waitress told them it would be better to order the breakfast special and get some bacon thrown in. Duguay gave her a smile, and she smiled back.

"What a guy," Danny said. He shook his head. "Still charming the ladies wherever he goes. I wish I had a quarter of the luck you have with women, man."

"What are you talking about, Dan? Look at you, you're a good-looking guy, you got your own shop. You do good work, you make a decent buck. No reason a guy like you shouldn't

118

have a nice woman. You see the way some of the dancers flirt with you."

The two friends looked at each other. There was only truth between them, and for this reason Duguay said, "Maybe you smoke too much, Danny. Nobody can say you don't do good work, but…"

Danny looked down at the black coffee in front of him, looked into the mug so that he could see his face, distorted so that he looked somehow much younger than he was, his child's face. Then he raised his head and looked at Duguay. He smiled a sort of sad smile and said, "You know, I've been addicted to almost everything you can be addicted to. I've wrestled with everything at one time or another. Fuck. When I think of the shit I've put into my body, the places I've been. You're stronger than me, you always were. I've been trying to find a way to live with myself since I was a kid, you know, to live in my own skin. It's not right, some of the stuff we've seen, the way we grew up. That's why I moved here in the first place, to get away from the ghosts on all the street corners back on the island. Just trying to find a life that works. I've had enough trouble in my life. I don't want trouble any more."

"I know you've seen hard times," Duguay said. "I was there when you were on the needle, remember. Anyway, fuck, I'm not your mother."

Danny took a mouthful of coffee, then wiped his mouth with the back of his hand and said, "Speaking of mothers— you ever hear from the old lady, or are you still an orphan?"

Duguay stirred some sugar into his coffee, and he looked out the window, his face reflected in the grimy glass. He thought his face looked old and worn. The way he felt.

"Still an orphan," he said, "just like you, brother."

Fourteen

McKelvey thought goddamned rain or sleet would be ideal to mark the occasion, but the first day of his official retirement dawned sunny and clear, a fresh morning of early spring. Birds made song in the trees of the neighbourhood backyards. There was a sense of regeneration. He took his time getting ready in the morning, making sure he looked just right. He stood at the mirror and examined himself. He smiled and he said, "This is it."

He got in his truck and drove across town. He took the same route, stopped at the same lights. *It was the last time he had to do this trip.* The last time. Tina Aoki tried to conceal her surprise, but she couldn't make it work. She sat there wearing her best poker face while McKelvey and the over-congenial representative from Human Resources poured over the details of his retirement package. There were issues to be dealt with, items considered: sick days and accrued vacation, months of service stacked against the date of his birth, various solar calculations and determinations that interested McKelvey not at all.

And then it was done, his life as a lawman.

He wore a new suit purchased solely for the occasion, something he'd bought while shopping with Tim Fielding, letting the younger man guide him towards modern cuts, away from the big box stores and their warehouse styles. They went together to these high-end men's shops, places McKelvey had never heard of, and he let out a noise when he turned over the price tag on a simple white cotton dress shirt at a Banana Republic.

"Who'd pay a hundred bucks for a shirt? One shirt," McKelvey said. "I used to buy a whole suit for a hundred bucks. Jesus murphy. Are these people out of their minds?"

Tim stepped over to his friend, turtling with embarrassment. "It's not 1985 any more," he laughed. "Men can't get away with wearing K-Mart dress shirts and blazers from Sears. Women expect more from us. They've got entire magazines and TV channels dedicated to this, Charlie, to men's fashion. You wouldn't believe the number of looks a guy like you would get if you changed your wardrobe. Upgraded a little. You know, send a message to the world that this is one middle-aged dude who takes good care of himself."

"Middle-aged, sure," McKelvey said, smiling and nodding. "If I live to be a hundred and six."

McKelvey walked into Aoki's office like an emperor, dressed in a black Italian suit with a rich cream shirt and a black and gold tie, his face shaved and his hair washed and tousled, looking slimmer and healthier than Aoki could recall.

"Wow, nice tie," she said upon his arrival.

"Oh, this old thing?" he said with a wink, taking a seat. The tie had cost him fifty-five dollars. It was Italian silk. It was mind-boggling.

"What's next for you?" she said.

He saw himself standing in a darkened room, the .25 pistol in his palm, all the days of his life narrowing to one single purpose, one point of light...

"I'll take some time off," he shrugged, "then maybe find something part-time."

She nodded, but she didn't look convinced. "Listen, this is the part of my job that I hate the most," she said. "Everybody wants to organize a retirement dinner, and I'm supposed to find out your view on the whole thing."

McKelvey thought, *but I wouldn't have anybody to bring.* And it was one of those seminal life moments that you imagined a hundred times in your career, your colleagues roasting you, digging up old stories from the graveyard, your superiors boasting about your indispensable talents, your long-suffering wife at your side, the golden years shimmering on the horizon.

"I appreciate the sentiment, but you know it's not really my style," he said.

"We'll get everyone together and go for a beer then, keep it casual," she said.

He stood, wiped his hands on his pants, and leaned in to shake her hand.

"Screw that," she said, "I want a real hug."

*   *   *

That evening Tim came over for dinner to celebrate. The invitation had slipped McKelvey's mind as he brought his papers to his lawyer to ensure Caroline would be permanently listed as the beneficiary of his police pension should anything happen to him. He wanted all of his papers in order. And then he saw him...

It was him. It had to be…

McKelvey was coming out of the lawyer's office when he caught the side profile of his son. Yes. Gavin! It took his breath away, stopped him cold. He squinted against the brightness of the day, and while his intellect looped the impossibility of it all, his heart raced with the potential. What if? What if there

122

had been a cover-up? Stranger things had happened…

He walked briskly, deftly navigating his way through the people on the sidewalk, never taking his eyes from the back of the head. His boy's head. The pace quickened, and he almost knocked a woman sideways as he drew closer. At last, like running after a bus pulling away from a stop, he was close enough to reach out and touch. Which is what he did, he put his hand on the boy's shoulder, and the boy turned sharply and stared back with a snarly look of confusion on a face that was decorated with metal, but altogether not his son's.

"Sorry," McKelvey mumbled, and the kid shook his head and walked away, left him standing on the sidewalk like a lover spurned.

Fuck.

Right now McKelvey pretended not to be surprised when Tim Fielding came to the door at ten to five, a six-pack in hand.

"You forgot, didn't you?" the younger man said.

It came back. *You bring the beer, I'll do the rest.* McKelvey remembered his invitation now. Some friend he was.

"Of course not," he smiled and waved Tim in.

They popped their beers and sat at the kitchen table, an old Gordon Lightfoot song coming through a small radio on the counter. Some guy threatening to deal with anybody caught lurking around his back stairs…

"That stuff reminds me of driving around in the back of my mom and dad's station wagon," Tim said. "They were so proud of their eight-track stereo, they went out and bought every Gordon Lightfoot and Joan Baez album they could find. Don't even get me started on Nana Mouskouri. I think they call it Post Traumatic Stress Syndrome."

McKelvey fiddled with the tuner and brought in a station

playing new pop. Tim kept looking around the place until McKelvey told him that no, he had no plans to buy more furniture or otherwise re-decorate. He had everything he needed.

"Probably list the house in the summer, maybe buy a little condo," he said.

"I was going to say maybe I should move in. Save some money if we split the expenses."

"I've tried that," McKelvey said. "I'm not very good at living with other people."

McKelvey felt a rare sense of ease in the teacher's company. Tim Fielding was a good man, plain and simple. And not a cop, which was good and new. Tim had stopped by the hospital the day after McKelvey's episode, bringing with him a copy of *The Hockey News* and a pair of flannel pyjamas, and that simple act had altered McKelvey's comprehension of the younger man. There were good people still.

"I went on a date," Tim said. "Last Tuesday." He looked down at his beer, turning the can with a thumb and forefinger.

"And?" McKelvey said. "Details, man. A full debriefing."

"She's a teacher at my school. We went out more as friends than anything else. But I got out at least. We went and saw *Cast Away*."

"The one about the guy who gets stranded on an island or something?"

"He washes up on an island and has to learn how to do everything from scratch. Build a shelter. Make tools. Tom Hanks did a pretty good job. It was believable, you know. And I just kept thinking as I was sitting there, how if I were shipwrecked for twenty years, I would want my wife to go on and have a life, to not waste it sitting around waiting for me. And I started thinking about it in terms of my life today. Shipwrecked and alone. And I sort of thought my wife probably would want me to go on…that's right about the time I started to cry, and I had to apologize to my date."

McKelvey looked over at his friend, and the two of them smiled then began to laugh. Tim had a few tears in his eyes, but he wiped them with his thumb and finished his beer. McKelvey opened them each a second can, and he closed his eyes as the cold beer burned down his throat.

"Well," McKelvey said, wiping his mouth, "I have a confession to make."

"I know, you forgot about tonight. It's okay," Tim said.

"How does pizza sound?"

McKelvey ordered delivery, and they sat there talking, finishing up the beers. The pizza arrived, and McKelvey brought out plates and a bottle of red wine. He hadn't had a drink in weeks and hadn't missed it much. But now the wine was going down just fine, wrapping him in a blanket of ease and congeniality.

"Tell me, Charlie, how you became a police officer," Tim said.

McKelvey shrugged and said, "I suppose I should say something about wanting to save lives and make the world a safer place. But the truth is I got off the train and rented a room in an old boarding house on King Street. The woman who ran the place had a son on the force, and one thing led to another. It was easy back then, if you were a decent size and in good shape. I guess I always figured it was a steady paycheque, until I figured out what it was that I wanted to do with my life." He shrugged. "The years went by, and we started a family and I just sort of stayed. They promote you if you stick around long enough."

"Was it fulfilling?"

McKelvey bought himself a moment, wiping his mouth

with the back of his hand. "Fulfilling? I don't know, I never really thought about it that way. Maybe some days. You help somebody in trouble, get them out of a jam. The town where I come from, the men were miners or unemployed miners. Neither of those options appealed to me much. And what about you, how did you get to be a school teacher?"

"It's a family tradition. Both my mother and father were teachers. They viewed it the same way some families view the practice of law or dentistry, a sort of a calling. My grandfather was one of the first trustees back in the Forties who helped name half of the schools in the city. I think it runs in our blood, to be quite honest."

"And is it fulfilling?" McKelvey said with a little smile.

"Definitely," Tim said, "I mean, when they're not throwing stuff at me or putting pencil shavings in my coffee."

"Long as they don't shoot at you."

For the rest of the dinner they managed to steer clear of conversation pertaining to grief or loss, focusing instead on sports, joking about the billions spent preparing for turn-of-the-century mayhem that never arrived. Eventually though, as is inevitable—like co-workers who meet for dinner and try with all their might not to discuss office politics—the conversation found its way back home, back to the shared experience that bound them and had brought them together in the first place. A thread on crime and punishment created the segue.

"You know what really burns my ass?" Tim said. "I mean, our justice system is so light on drunk drivers. This guy Leonard Tilman, a repeat offender, kills my wife. And he gets what? He loses his licence for five years and spends six months in jail, another six under house arrest. If he had walked up to her and shot her, he'd spend the rest of his life behind bars."

"Don't be so certain of that," McKelvey said. "Guys plead

down to manslaughter or make other deals, they do all the right things in prison, maybe start carrying a bible around, and they're back on the street in six, seven years. Early release programs. They've got townhouses where they can live together and watch cable TV. It's just the way it works."

He topped their wine glasses again.

Tim leaned in and said, "I shouldn't tell you this, you being a police officer, but I found out where the guy lives. And drinks. His favourite bar."

McKelvey narrowed his eyes, interested. "First of all, I'm retired. So don't worry about whether I'm a cop or not. And second of all, you shouldn't be doing that sort of thing. You could get yourself in a lot of trouble, Tim. This asshole could have *you* charged with criminal harassment. Some of the repeat offenders know the code better than we do. They revel in the loopholes."

But the truth was, McKelvey liked what he saw, some new depth or angle to Tim's character. Yes, he could see it now, what it would take to get a decent school teacher out tailing the man who killed his wife. Well, wasn't that something. McKelvey was not alone, that was the message. Not alone in his thinking. It was natural, after all. A man, any man, who faced this variety of personal loss would eventually come to this place. Find himself standing on the precipice of the void. Standing there yelling into the blackness just to hear the comforting sound of his own echo...

"I saw him one day when I was out walking. There he was. Just there. I recognized him, but he didn't even see me. I ended up following him for four hours," Tim said. He had a blank expression on his face, as though he were surprised about hearing his actions recounted out loud. "He went into a bar on his way home. I couldn't fucking believe it. A *bar*. This guy's going to drink and drive again, a year after he killed a human being. Like it was *nothing.* I got his plate and was going to call you guys—he's not supposed to be driving or drinking, those were the conditions on his sentence—but something stopped me. I just…I don't know."

"You thought maybe you'd handle it on your own," McKelvey said, finishing the sentence as was his habit from a lifetime of interrogations, leading, always leading. Or as they used to call it, 'keeping things on track.'

Tim's face betrayed him. He was the sort of individual who wouldn't hold up under questioning, McKelvey knew. Even if he was innocent, given an hour, McKelvey could get him to confess to the Hoffa murder. There was a rhythm to these sort of procedures. A small interview room with no air, a pit bull cop like McKelvey calling you a rapist or a sicko, making a grown man cry, or letting on he understood how things got out of control sometimes.

"Listen, I get it. I understand. A little retribution," McKelvey said, emptying the last of the wine into Tim's glass. His own head was weightless, a bobble atop a spindle; he had had enough of the wine. He cleared his throat, and said, "You want to do something to this guy."

"I don't know. I mean it's one thing to sit in your car and talk tough..."

"You saw it with your own eyes, the guy's breaking his conditions."

Tim nodded slowly, the arc of the older man's thinking becoming clearer now.

"You know what bar he goes to?" McKelvey asked.

"Clyde's over on Eglinton East."

"I made some trips there when I was in uniform. That's a rough little joint on Friday nights, or used to be. What does he drive?"

"A blue Ford pickup. I got his plate, too."

"Jesus. You should have been a cop," McKelvey joked.

"It was easy to remember. It's personalized: Tilman58."

"Maybe we'll wait for him one night and give him a little scare."

The utterance of this was like a jolt of electricity through McKelvey's body. It sat him upright, cleared his thinking, and painted an image of how things would work. He saw the layout of the rear parking lot, with its high fence enclosure offering almost ideal seclusion. *Nobody would even see them...*

Tim looked up, disappointment or discomfort on his face, and said, "I appreciate it, but... I don't think I'm cut out for it. I couldn't stand in front of my students and look them in the eye if I did something stupid. I'm supposed to be an *example* to these kids, not some vigilante. You said yourself he could charge me with criminal harassment."

"You don't have to *kill* the guy. Just fuck with him a little."

Tim shook his head slowly, staring into his wine.

"You want revenge, Tim, sure you do. It's only human. I don't blame you. There you are walking down the street minding your own business one day, and who do you see? Curiosity gets the better of you, so you end up following him. You just want to see where this guy lives, what his life is like. You had no idea where he was going, but then you see him pull into a bar. The guy's actually going to *drink* again—after how many convictions for drunk driving?"

"Seven," Tim said.

McKelvey shook his head. "Seven. Jesus. They should throw away the key."

A silence fell between them, and McKelvey saw his lockbox stuffed with clippings, the little pistol wrapped in a tea towel, let his mind wander through the minefield of fantasy. Finally, just when the evening seemed at risk of falling sideways to gloom, Tim offered McKelvey the chance to participate in what he called a "life affirmation".

"I'm getting a tattoo," he said. "Why don't you come with me?"

"A tattoo?"

"The counsellor I've been seeing said it's helpful in the healing process to pick a few things you've always wanted to do. Like take a trip somewhere or dye your hair or…"

"Get a tattoo," McKelvey said.

"Exactly," Tim said, nodding. "I always wanted one. I used to talk to my wife about it, but I just never went and actually did it. Now it's time to follow through."

McKelvey's mind flashed with stark images, black and white, of Gavin's pale arms emblazoned with cryptic designs, incomprehensible pagan symbols. The work he'd magically had done in the time away from home. *His thin arms tucked against his body on the table…*

"What kind of tattoo are you thinking of getting?" McKelvey said.

"Well," Tim said, and reached for his wallet, "I just happen to have a picture with me."

He found a slip of paper in his wallet, a cutout from a colour copy, and handed it to McKelvey. The design featured black and grey lines, intersecting weaves combining in a triangular knot pattern. It was, McKelvey knew well from his ancestral roots, a Celtic trinity.

"The endless knot," McKelvey said. *No beginning, no end,* he thought, *just two lines, two lives intertwined to infinity.* If only it were like that, if only it were the truth about life.

"So," Tim said, "how about it? Are you up for it?"

"A tattoo?" McKelvey said. He thought about it for a minute, then said, "I'll be there for moral support, maybe hold your hand. But I'm not getting a tattoo."

"You're not afraid, are you?"

"God no," he said, "I just don't shed my blood unless it's absolutely necessary."

Tim laughed. "I'll set up the appointment. Who knows, maybe you'll change your mind."

"You can always hope for a miracle," McKelvey said.

⁂

✳   ✳   ✳

With the school teacher stretched out on McKelvey's bed, snoring with a jagged back draft, McKelvey poured himself a cup of tea to clear the boozy fog then crept into the bedroom and pulled down the box he'd moved from the garage to the closet. At the kitchen table, with a single light throwing a soft candle glow, he scribbled the particulars: the make and personalized plate for Leonard Tilman, the name of the bar. Perhaps. Yes, perhaps it was something to be considered.

It was just past two in the morning. McKelvey felt like he was the last person alive in the world. And it struck him that he was in fact an orphan. A man without a family. The clock on the stove ticked. The dogs next door began to bark on cue, and their howls rose in near perfect unison as McKelvey absent-mindedly fingered the new .25 cartridges he'd picked up.

Fifteen

There were memories of touch. Smells. Of breath. Fire and a taste of ashes. A dream, just a dream. Or else she had imagined the memory after hearing the story repeated so many times... Some days she felt there wasn't much difference between a real memory and an imagined one.

*   *   *

The girl with the black hair stepped from the shower and towelled herself, pausing to reflect upon the image of her body in the long mirror against the opposite wall. She had been blessed with good genes. Cursed, more like it. Men back home had been looking at her in that way since she was ten years old. And in her little girl naïveté, she had at first embraced the attention. Her father was dead, and the stories everybody told about him made her feel sorry for him, even though she didn't remember him. How he did what he did and almost ruined them all. A loser, that was the insinuation. She didn't remember him, not really. Just because you never knew someone didn't mean you couldn't miss them.

In another life, in a time that now seemed so distant it was perhaps a lie, the girl had dreamed of becoming a dancer. A *real* dancer. It was true. Putting her aunt's ABBA tapes on the little stereo in the living room and twirling and twirling, her little girl mind filled with the sounds of applause. Happy moments of sunshine memories broken by the sound of the door opening in the middle of the night. The man with the stutter who said words two or three times in a row.

Sometimes she could smell the breath of the man with the strong hands, a memory manifesting itself through the senses, yes, smell the cigarette smoke and the funk of his body, then she felt feathers of his hot breath on her back, and she heard the noises he made, and she closed her eyes and wondered why nobody knew what was happening to her insides...

Now she danced beneath the lights for the hungry eyes of strangers. They called them "exotic entertainers", the whole business regulated through permits and laughable entertainment visas handed out to Russian and Serbian women brought over to fill a skills void. It was a strange business, and the lines were blurred between everything: criminality and drugs and businessmen, and nothing was free and everything came hard.

But it was filling the hole in the floor with the money she would need to leave it all behind.

Duguay was not a nice man. But everything in this world required perspective, and when stacked against the other assholes, he was okay. He never beat the women in his "entertainment agency". That was something, at least. And it was strange, because while she had never seen him so much as raise his hand to a man or a woman, everyone seemed to fear him. He demanded respect and owned a room when he entered it. He looked you in the eye, his cold eyes focused, intense. He was big and tall and thick-chested. He had brought her into this life before the bust on the strip joint and the mandatory drug treatment, in those blurry days after the boy was taken from her, and there were no alternatives for a girl of her position on the street. He said dancing at first, easy money, then he asked for a favour. Just a favour. And then the favours kept coming. He shared the money, though; he was always fair about that. He bought her clothes, and he brought them out for meals at restaurants, Duguay in the centre of the booth with his girls on either side.

"Anybody fucks with you, they fuck with me," he had told her. And she believed it.

But everything had changed so quickly. She'd seen the writing on the wall, how quickly things in this world could change. Like flipping a coin. The man named Leroux had turned rat—and she trusted her instinct, because she had met the man once or twice through the boy and had been left with an uneasy feeling. Leroux's turn to the other side had caused a whirlwind within the club and the men who worked around Duguay. The vibe was electric, dangerous, and she thought someone might end up dead. Then it happened: Duguay was pinched leaving the club early one morning, and that asshole Luc started running things. They said that Luc had come from northern New Brunswick and had killed men to earn a patch with the Outlaws before crossing over to the Blades. These days Duguay was locked up in the apartment, hiding out. Sometimes he'd come down to the club and talk to the doorman, talk to some of the guys—heavies she recognized as regulars.

When they partied after closing time, and Duguay was a little drunk and his edge was softened, he spoke of his father and the life he had led in the small bike gangs of Montreal in the Sixties. The Popeyes, he said, and the name made her laugh. It was a place of mutual understanding, for her own father had met a violent end.

"Those guys were animals back then, and my dad fit right in," he said. "A real tough son of a bitch. They say when he hit someone with his fist, it was like getting hit with a brick. He was raised in Hochelaga-Maisonneuve, the same neighbourhood where Mom Boucher grew up. You know, the head of the Nomads over there. I wonder what he'd think of me now, my old man. All these years in and still spinning my wheels. I should have patched with the Hells when I had the chance."

"My dad was a bank robber," the girl said. "He robbed banks all over the north. Timmins, Kapuskasing. Places like that, right. He got killed in a shootout."

"Was he Indian? You look a little Indian to me," Duguay said.

Her black hair, her olive skin, the shape of her pretty face.

"Métis," she said. "More like half Métis."

"My mother had a little Indian blood in her," he said. "She got crazy when she drank."

"Not all Indians are like that, you know," the girl said. "Not where I come from, anyway. The Indians aren't nearly as bad as the white trash."

"Only Indians I ever really knew," he said, "were in prison. Lots of them in there."

She took a cigarette from him, and he leaned in close when he lit it for her. She drew on the cigarette and sat back, letting her robe slip open a little bit to reveal the tight flesh of her belly. She watched him looking at her body. She was used to it. It's what men did. She wanted to ask him questions about Marcel Leroux. She had so many questions, and yet there was never the right time or the place. And anyway, a man like Duguay didn't answer the questions of a girl like her. One thing she had learned on the street, it was best to stay close to the people you least trusted.

*　　*　　*

It was just like the old days working a stakeout, only this time instead of bad coffee and cigarettes, McKelvey had a bottle of mineral water tucked between his legs as he sat parked across the street, with a perfect view of the rear parking lot of the dive bar. Waiting, watching. He had arrived at the decision a few days after his dinner with the school teacher. It was something he came to with clenched teeth and an existential shrug. When he looked at his friend, when he viewed the facts spread out across the continuum of the young man's life, the scattered debris and the residue, and all the long days of soul-searching yet to come, he was overcome with a desire to *do* something. That was the thing. The frustration of his own life and experience, of watching his wife slip away like a boat drifting from the very bay where once it had sought refuge, it left him with an insatiable desire to act.

The Leonard Tilmans, the Pierre Duguays.
Who the fuck did these people think they were, anyway?

In the end, when perspective and context were put into a sharper focus, it didn't really matter, did it? Not when stacked against what he was planning for Duguay, with the truth that was in his heart. In many ways, he viewed this as an exercise, a training manoeuvre, something to steel his nerves, move it forward. He had finally stopped meandering on the precipice, had crossed the threshold and stepped into the void. It was, he knew, the onset of a free fall. *Let it come…*

There was no point in getting Tim involved, for he was a teacher, and besides, he would not be able to live with himself. That was a fact. McKelvey knew that much about the young man. The kid wouldn't hold up. As for McKelvey, well, he now believed that life was all about figuring out the difference between the things a man could live with and the things he couldn't. Between the two poles there rested a place that promised a version of peace.

So it was that he dressed in jeans and an old flannel work shirt, and pulled his old Blue Jays cap down from the closet. When he saw the broom standing at the back, he got his idea. With an old handsaw from the basement, and working across the kitchen table, he cut a length of the stick. Six inches. Held the stub in his palm, curled his fingers around the shaft.

He stood in front of the bathroom mirror and looked into his own eyes. Searching there for something. A way out of this? No. Confirmation perhaps that he was in the right here. It was a grey area, but not really. Not so grey. He could see that now. He put the length of broom handle in his back pocket and went to the truck.

*　　*　　*

Now he fiddled with the radio, tuning through the static. Pop music, country music, the voice of a young woman talking about the latest thing in cellphones, a card that allowed you to load time on your phone with complete anonymity—perfect for pimps and gangbangers... He paused while a reporter told his unseen listeners how a reputed member of the Quebec Hell's Angels had been implicated in the beating death of a bar owner in Saint-Jerome. "Serge Gallant, a member of the Rockers, has been charged..." *Poor bastard probably refused to let the bikers deal dope in his establishment,* McKelvey thought. A scourge, that's what they were. Uneducated, uncouth, the new bikers resembled very little the professional members of the traditional mob. Back then, things had been so much simpler. The mob only killed the mob. Regular citizens never had to worry about being drawn into the world of organized crime. Now every immigrant faction had its own gang. Vietnamese triads, the Jamaican posses, the Somalian street crews, the

Bloods and the Crips up at Jane and Finch, and always the bikers. It was to the point where the regular citizens couldn't go to a night club without wondering if there would be a shooting, a revenge killing, a stray bullet in the spine while you were two-stepping with your lady. When the smoke cleared, there wouldn't be a single goddamned witness; the affliction of momentary blindness could save your life.

Then he spotted the truck pulling into the lot and confirmed the identity by the personalized plates: Tilman58. Every man had his habits. He watched as the driver got out of his truck and shuffled in his untied work boots over to the back door, which was propped open to let in the air. McKelvey waited a minute or two then got out and followed him in, taking a seat in a far corner. The bar was a workingman's hangout, a plain little American-style gin mill. Dart boards and a pool table, the round wood tables scarred from cigarettes, dented with rings from mugs and shot glasses. McKelvey ordered a draft beer, which tasted stale, and he watched Tilman sit at the bar and bullshit with some other working men. The man drank three pints in less than an hour. He was a professional.

The job hadn't left him, so McKelvey noted every detail for later recall or testimony. Tilman was in his mid-forties, with a narrow, pock-marked face, and a balding head with a long strand of hair saved for a combover. McKelvey felt odd. Lightheaded. His body tensed, slick with sweat beneath the shirt and the jeans. He could feel his heart working hard in his chest. He sat there, playing through how things would happen. He was going to do this. Yes. For Tim. For Tim's *wife*.

He saw himself, and his wife, all those who had been hurt by Gavin's death. He saw each of them in his mind's eye in their various forms of torment. As though they had been poisoned by grief. The silent promises, the pledges, the crying, and he knew this would be easy. Anything would be easy when held up against this thing which they had just come through...

At last the man's seasoned bladder put the plan in motion. McKelvey waited a beat then stood slowly and followed Tilman into the washroom. The room was grungy, dimly lit. Graffiti scrawled on the two cubicles, a battered metal condom machine fastened to a wall. The room reeked of piss and sweat, a deep funk. Tilman was standing at a urinal, head forward and eyes closed as he relieved himself. McKelvey walked up to the other urinal and pretended to unzip. He hauled a deep breath, steadied himself.

"Friggin' beer goes straight through you," McKelvey said. "It's like paying to piss all night."

Tilman made a noise with his throat, some sort of guttural acknowledgment.

"I shouldn't even be drinking. I got a suspension last month," McKelvey added.

Tilman zipped up and took a step to the stain-splattered mirrors, the counter drenched in water and old soppy paper towels. He began to run fingers through his thin hair, adjusting it.

"Just stick to the speed limit, man," Tilman said. "Pigs got no reason to pull you over."

McKelvey pretended to zip his pants as he stepped just behind Tilman now, putting in place the sequence of events like watching a film, how this thing would happen frame by frame, and he stepped outside of himself, his hand sliding into his coat pocket and bringing out the piece of broom handle, bringing it straight out and up with all of his weight behind the thrust, the handle digging into Tilman's kidney like a jolt from God.

The man let out a wild noise, the yelp of a wounded animal, his body twisting sideways in agony. McKelvey grabbed the man's collar and swung him around, bringing the broom handle up again, this time burying it deep in the soft round stomach. A whoosh of sour air exploded from Tilman's mouth as he struggled to comprehend, to keep his footing, red eyeballs stretched wide in surprise. McKelvey took hold of the collar again, tightly, this time driving the head down towards the urinal, pushing the man's face into that porcelain bowl with its glued pubic hair and the old deodorant puck half dissolved from the piss of countless patrons. Tilman's mouth bounced off the porcelain with a sickening smack, and McKelvey saw an explosion of blood, his own jaw clenched to the point of aching because it felt good, and it was all he could do to stop himself, to rein this thing back in.

"...what'd I do to you?" Tilman sputtered, teeth stained red.

McKelvey said, "It'll come to you," and he left the man slumped against the wall. He walked briskly out through the bar, walking with his head held high, with a sense of purpose. He understood this atmosphere, understood that witnesses rarely were able to recall with any vivid description a suspect who did not draw attention to himself in some spectacular way, in fact simply blended into the world around him, his cap pulled low. In the parking lot McKelvey gripped the piece of broom handle and smashed the left side brake lights on the blue Ford pickup with the personalized plate. It took four or five hard shots before the plastic finally gave.

He got in his truck and pulled away from the street just as he spotted Tilman stumble through the back door, a line of blood running down his chin, staining the neck of his shirt. The sort of man, McKelvey knew, who would go looking for some payback. In fact, McKelvey was depending on this vengeful streak within the man's makeup.

McKelvey sped away, taking a left then a right, then ducking down a side street. His breath coming hard now, everything around him soft and muted as in a dream. He used a payphone outside a corner store to report the vehicle and its drunken driver to the police.

"Guy's just pulling out of Clyde's," he said. "Blue pickup, personal plate, Tilman58."

"Can I get your name please sir?" the operator asked.

"He's drunk and he's dangerous," he said, and hung up.

He jogged back to the Mazda. As he pulled away from the curb, he glanced in the rear view and was startled by his own image. He wasn't himself, not then.

Who the fuck are you?

Sixteen

McKelvey pulled into the driveway, ran up the steps, and made it to the bathroom just in time to vomit in the sink. Stooped over, hands gripping the sides of the vanity, his stomach clenching and releasing like a bellows, spewing his poison until he was an empty vessel, nothing left but the dry heaves to wrack his body in rivulets. He began to shake and had to wipe away a line of acidic bile that hung like a newly spun spider's line from his chin, a moist and glittery silver.

He splashed cold water on his face, and it stung, hot then cold. *Christ almighty.* He raised his head level to the mirror, his eyes red, unfamiliar. He wiped the water from his face and waited in the silence for an answer, a clue to the future trajectory of his life. An arc rising, soaring, then falling back to earth. He held his breath, listening to the silence, then the sounds came on: the rush of blood in his inner ear, the slow drip of water from the tap, the drops exploding like thunder against the porcelain.

He towelled his face as he moved to the kitchen in search of a drink to calm his nerves. As he passed by it, the phone on the wall rang, startling him. He snatched the receiver and spoke.

"McKelvey."

"What are you doing?" Hattie said. "You sound like you've been jogging or something."

"Square dancing," he said.

She laughed and said she was on her way over. She had some news she thought might be of interest to him. "A juicy bit," is what she called it.

"Might not be a good time," he said, "I was just getting ready to jump in the shower."

"Oh, I don't mind," she said and hung up.

McKelvey raced back to the bathroom, jumped in the shower, and scrubbed the guilt and the sweat from his body, scrubbed away the residue of his criminal activity. He bowed his head, put his palms to the tile wall, and clenched his eyes shut. *What is happening to me?* he thought. *I'm supposed to be the law... I* was *the law for the better part of my life... Am I lost, or am I found? Was this within me all along, waiting for me all these years?*

He was towelling himself dry as the doorbell rang. He stood there for a moment and took a couple of deep breaths. He tied the towel around his waist and, a little embarrassed, opened the door for Hattie. She was dressed in new jeans and a sweatshirt. She was beautiful standing there with her toes pointed together, a tomboy come to call on McKelvey to go frog hunting, her red hair pulled back into a thick ponytail, unruly strands making their escape. McKelvey thought she might even have been wearing some makeup. There was a faint black line beneath her eyelashes. He thought she looked like a million dollars.

"Come in," he said, "I'm just getting changed. Go ahead and sit down in the kitchen. Well, there's no other place to sit, actually. I'll be out in a minute."

"When are you going to buy some furniture, McKelvey?" she said.

"I was thinking I might take up woodworking, build my own," he said. "You know how retired people are supposed to have all these hobbies."

He heard her laughter as he turned into the bedroom. He tossed the towel to the floor and picked up a pair of boxers from the bed. He was standing there, in the middle of the room, one leg in his underpants, when he froze. He heard the door open quietly, or perhaps felt the presence first, and he turned to see Hattie standing there, a girlish grin on her face, staring at his naked ass. His face rushed with blood, his heart in his mouth.

"My god, you're so *bashful*," she said, taking a step inside, standing with her back to the door now. "That's what I like about you. You're old-fashioned. Even your underwear is old-fashioned."

He put the other leg through and stood there, half-naked before her. He snapped the waist on the shorts and shrugged. He gave her a smile, a boy's grin beneath a head of curls.

"They're just boxers," he said.

"Yeah, like my dad would wear. We'll have to get you some Calvin Kleins or something."

They looked at one another. The tension which had truthfully existed between them from the moment they first worked together was out there now in the three feet that separated them. McKelvey felt himself stir, his cock beginning to flow with life, with possibility. He was standing in the centre of the master bedroom, the bedroom he had shared with his wife, and it felt like cheating. He grabbed a pair of khakis from the bed and slipped them on.

"Come on," she teased, "don't spoil all my fun."

"Hattie," he said.

He moved to the door, but she didn't budge. She closed her eyes and lifted her face to him, waiting, expectant. "Cost you a kiss," she said.

He exhaled and realized he was shaking inside. Like he was fifteen again, slow dancing in the school gymnasium with

Wendy Parker, smelling her lip gloss and wondering when he would get a chance to taste it.

"Fair trade," he said, and kissed her quickly on the mouth.

It was strange at first, because they were friends and colleagues, then they kissed again, and it was good. He put a hand to the base of her back and pulled her to him, to his mouth. Their tongues touched, and she tasted like coffee. Her hands moved across his naked back, and he felt himself fully involved. The room spun in slow circles, and he pulled back.

"Let's have a drink," he said. "Some wine. First, I mean."

They stepped apart, and Hattie fixed her hair as she followed him back to the kitchen. She sat at the empty table while he got half a bottle of red wine from a cupboard. It was all he had, and he told her so. That and a little rum or gin that had been hanging around since some Christmas he couldn't recall.

"I'm a Maritime girl," she said. "I grew up drinking wine made in a bucket and Schooner beer. I can roll a pretty good cigarette with Drum tobacco and Player's papers, too. My dad and his brothers, they were all fishermen. When they worked, they really worked, but when they didn't work, which was often, they were prone to drinking and playing the fiddle. In fact, I bet I could beat you in both arm wrestling and beer guzzling, perhaps even farting and horking."

He poured them each a glass and sat beside her. He felt flushed from the day's activities. He felt like a husband hiding a secret life as they sat there drinking the wine. *I'm a criminal, Hattie,* he heard himself telling her. *I assaulted a guy tonight...*

"I know what you're up to," she said, as though reading his mind.

"Oh yes? And what's that?"

"Don't treat me like that, Charlie. I know what you've been working on, where everything is headed. Why do you think

Aoki asked me to follow you around?"

This caught McKelvey completely off-guard. He raised his head and turned to look at her.

"She got you to fucking spy on me?"

Hattie's face softened, and she smiled benignly. "Don't look at it that way. She's worried about you. What you might get yourself into. I am, too, to be quite honest."

"I can't believe she'd pull something like that," he said. "I can't believe you'd actually do it for her, for Christ's sake. How long has this been going on?"

"I didn't say I accepted the job. I said that she asked me to check up on you. But I don't need to do that to know what you're up to. I know how you think. It's called *harassment.* Duguay was released free and clear. Until the Crown comes up with a new case against him, he's a free man. You can't stalk him, Charlie," she said. "The law aside, I don't think I have to tell you this Duguay guy is bad news. I know you're a tough guy, but these characters don't play by any rules. I checked him out. He's got a solid record. He was mixed up in all that trouble in Quebec."

"What'd you tell Aoki?"

She took a drink and swallowed, shaking her head. "I'm on your side, Charlie. I didn't tell her anything. Listen, you can't go down that road. These guys are *deadly.* The Hell's Angels aren't even worried about the Blades, because they're so bloody violent, so over the top with the TV gangster bullshit, the Hells are just waiting for them to self-destruct like they're doing down south. They know it's going to happen, it's just a matter of when. You don't want to be around when it does."

He was quiet, processing the information.

"Anyway, what if you've got the wrong guy?" she asked.

"What are you talking about?"

"Unless you have some evidence that homicide doesn't have, you couldn't say he's the guy without a reasonable doubt, could you?"

He didn't say anything. He didn't tell her that he had in fact spent a few hours the previous evening sitting in the parking lot of the Dove Gentleman's Club. Sitting there to watch the movement of the clientele, the ebb and flow of the traffic, to get a lay of the land, finally working his way inside to buy an overpriced beer and squint through the darkness at the faces of the bartenders, doormen, managers. He thought he spotted Duguay once, even followed the man towards a hallway leading to the washrooms, but it wasn't him. Arriving home at quarter past three, he was exhausted and simply slipped out of his clothes and into his bed.

"And what would it prove anyway?" she asked. "In the end, what would it prove?"

"What do you mean?" he said.

"If you kill your son's killer—or, to use legal jargon, your son's *alleged* killer—then you become a killer, too. And cops aren't overly popular in jail, in case you hadn't heard."

McKelvey said, "What do you think, I'm going to kill the guy, just like that?"

She looked at him, and she didn't blink. She was a cop, and she could see the truth in a person just as easily as he could. He found a measure of comfort in the fact that they spoke the same language.

She said, "I don't know what to think. You keep everything inside, all your cards close to your chest. I think somewhere along the line this stopped being about justice. This is about being the head of a family, about wronging a right. About being a cop and seeing the investigation get ground down. How am I doing so far?"

"My family was destroyed, Hattie. Do you understand that? It's the first piece of information I wake up to, and the last thing I fall alseep to. This weight on my chest, these thoughts on my mind. It's in every breath, every step. I want to die knowing things were made right. Everything I didn't do to help Gavin when he was alive is what I can do now. It doesn't get any simpler than that," he said.

She didn't say anything. She drank some wine. After a while, she looked at him and said, "Revenge is a funny thing. Makes people do all sorts of crazy stuff. But you have to ask yourself. Is extinguishing this ex-con's life worth turning against everything you worked for as a cop for thirty years?"

"I can't look at it in those terms," he said. "I've moved beyond the moral dilemma."

"Bullshit. You worked on the side of justice every day. You were part of the whole machine, you were part of the *system.* And so you have to believe in the system, Charlie, or it means everything you did in this job didn't mean a fucking thing... It'd make you no better than they are. And you are a better man than that."

"We just sort of lost touch," he said, just talking to hear himself, to maintain the cadence of their voices in the stillness of the house. "We didn't see him much back then, Gavin I mean. I think I might have seen him a couple of times on the street, trying to wash windows or something, down by the highway overpass. Hell, I know I did. But I was stubborn or embarrassed, and I turned away. I know Caroline gave him money a few times. Probably more than a few times. She'd meet him in the food court at the Eaton Centre, slip him a hundred."

Hattie listened, waiting for him to find the words.

"I knew he was screwing around with drugs a year before Caroline even suspected anything. Our line of work, right, you can pick it out. It was just some weed back then. I said to myself, let it go. He's just a teenager smoking a few joints. He'll find his way. Maybe he needs to get into some trouble to learn a lesson. Doesn't mean he'll end up on the street. I remember talking to a few of the guys on the Drug Squad, you know, about getting them to scare the shit out of Gavin and his friends. Bust them in the parking lot of the high school, put on a big show. Just something we talked about, and it made me feel like I was working on something. We just never got around to it. I had my work, and I stayed away more and more."

"What happened?" Hattie said.

McKelvey sighed and shifted his weight. "He started stealing," he said. "His friends got rougher. His moods were all over the place. We'd argue, and he'd put holes in the drywall. He stole some of Caroline's jewellery. It was an ongoing escalation, and it finally came to a head. I guess it always does. He was rude to his mother one night, said something so vulgar that I slapped him across the face. I mean hard. Hard enough to make his nose bleed a little. Then everything went quiet. I told him to get the hell out of the house and not to come back until he was ready to act like a human being. A fucking civilized human being."

McKelvey saw it happening as he spoke it. How many times had he replayed that single night, that single two-minute portion of time? Countless. Over and over and over again, then over again. It was like poking at a hangnail or a diseased tooth; no matter how painful, you couldn't break the habit. It was something he deserved, this self-torture. He felt oddly lighter now, though, much lighter than he had ever felt in all of those closed rooms with grief counsellors and therapists, and all those nights pretending to read those goddamned thick books Caroline brought home from the library.

"I shouldn't have hit him," he said.

"Nobody's a perfect parent, Charlie. It's the same in our job, we have to make decisions in a split second."

"Yeah," he said, "and so did he. So did Gavin."

She got out of her seat and came behind him, locking her arms around his chest, her cheek to his cheek. He didn't want her to hold him like this, but her grip was resolute, and soon he was crying without a sound, and his eyes were closed and everything was gone from his life. Then it was the smell of her and the feel of her skin on his skin, and they were kissing through the tears, kissing in spite of, or perhaps because of, the sadness.

"Shhh," she said, and took him by the hand back to the bedroom, where they fumbled like teenagers new to sex. They were pioneers stumbling though the wilderness here, coming to an open patch of ground that seemed suitable by default. Buttons were undone, pants removed, limbs tangled, confused, as though they were strange dance partners unfamiliar with the subtleties of each another's physiological machinery.

McKelvey stopped, rolling away. He stayed on his back, chest rising and falling.

"What's wrong," Hattie said. "Do I have bad breath or something?"

"It's not you," he said.

Hattie propped herself up on an elbow. She looked at his face, brought her fingers to his cheek. The room was already filling with the closed-in scent of their bodies. "Come on, Charlie," she said, sounding like a child denied, "let's just screw, okay? We're both adults here. I'm not going to get all weird on you after this."

"I'm not myself," he said. "I don't…"

She said, "I've been a cop a long time. I've got my share of baggage, too, you know."

150

"I don't know what I'm doing, Hattie. I've lost my way," he said quietly.

"And you don't want to bring me down with you, is that the story?"

"I don't blame my wife for leaving, let's put it that way. I'm glad she did. She has the capacity to see the bright side, to maybe start again with the time she has left. I think I'm finished. I mean, I can't see anything up ahead that's worth waiting for...working for…"

She moved her hand, playing with the sparse grey hair on his chest.

"Everybody loses somebody," she said. "You know that because you're a cop."

He didn't say anything. His eyes were closed as she continued to touch his body.

"How many doorsteps did you stand on at three o'clock in the morning? A dozen? More? I don't know how many times I told somebody the most important part of their life was *gone.* Maybe fifteen, twenty. I stopped counting after the very first one."

He listened to her voice, and it was the same as when he allowed himself to drift away to somewhere else, to get lost without really leaving, playing through memories and dreams. Hattie said, in the same voice she used for testifying in court, "This mother in Bedford reports her twelve-year-old son missing. She's used to him playing in the woods near their home after school. Kid always comes home for supper at six. It's after nine when I show up at her door to tell her that little Jimmy's been found hanging from a skipping rope tied to a tree. And the worst part was, it was a genuine accident. Kid was trying to swing like fucking Tarzan."

"We become zombies," he said, but his voice was hardly a whisper.

"I remember the faces of the mothers, the fathers. I see over and over again what happened to their faces in that instant I opened my mouth. Like you can see this weight falling on them, this heaviness bringing them down, like they're *dying* right in front of you...they're dying, but they're still standing."

"Sometimes I used to pretend I was in a movie," he said, his eyes still closed. "I had these lines to deliver, and nothing else was real. It worked for a little while, I guess. I just went in and did it and then it was done."

"What was it like when you got the call," Hattie said, "about Gavin?"

"It was my boss."

"Aoki?"

"She insisted on taking it. She called and then sent a ghost car over to pick us up. She was waiting for us at the hospital," McKelvey said, playing through the memory of that goddamned terrible night. The sickest feeling that ran from his crotch to his stomach, then all the way up to his throat, a fear that rang at the very core of his being, utterly helpless. "She's a good woman. She's tough."

They were both silent for a time. Then she turned to him. "Well, I think," she said, and a grin was coming to her pretty face, "I think we should have a screw for every time we had to go and do that, Charlie. It's the worst job in the world. What do you think, sort of like padding the karma for us?"

He smiled at her black sense of humour, the tangled mess of her hair, and the fact that for a night, for no reason at all, he was lying next to her naked body. He was drowning, and the waves were getting higher, and he saw that she was offering a buoy. Something to clasp, to hold onto. He moved to her and felt that her body was chilled. He pulled himself into her, and they made love.

Seventeen

In the morning, Hattie was up early for work. She was pulling on her bra in the semi-darkness of the room. McKelvey lifted himself on his elbows.

"How about dinner tonight?" she said.

He rubbed his sleepy face with his palm and yawned. He shook his head. "I can't make it tonight," he said, still dozy. "I have this thing with a friend. A tattoo."

She looked at him for a minute then continued dressing. "I won't even ask," she said.

He fell back to the bed and closed his eyes. Now that rest had finally come, he couldn't get enough. He drifted for a time, his mind running and running, then he heard the front door close, and he was out cold.

In the dream, someone was knocking on the door, ringing the doorbell. Ringing and knocking. It was just after ten, and McKelvey was still asleep. The knocking and ringing did not cease but seemed to grow in both volume and urgency. He raised his groggy head and listened again. He was not dreaming; it was his front door. He scrambled from the tangle of sheets and, dressed in his boxer shorts and white undershirt, ran to the front door, fumbled with the deadbolt, and swung it open.

"Mr. McKelvey?"

A stocky woman who looked to be in her late thirties was standing on the front step, wide-eyed and breathless. Her face was somehow familiar, but he couldn't place her. It looked as though she had dressed in a hurry, pulling a long coat over Saturday track pants, and her brown hair was pulled back in a hasty ponytail.

"I'm Carl Seeburger's daughter, Anna. I'm sorry to bother you. It's my father, you see, someone poisoned his dogs last night..."

"Poisoned them," he repeated, both tickled by the notion and suitably impressed that one of his seemingly humdrum neighbours owned the capacity to toss some balls of tainted hamburger over the fence. One just never knew.

"...and when he found them in the backyard—two of them anyway—he suffered a heart attack," she said, then paused to draw a much-needed breath.

"Oh my god," McKelvey said, forgetting the long-standing feud, forgetting the midnight prayers wherein he sought specifically this, the deaths of those same bastard dogs.

"He's at Mount Sinai. They have him heavily sedated, and it looks like he could be in for a triple bypass. All of that Limburger has taken its toll," she said and tried to smile but instead stopped just short of breaking into tears. "I have a favour to ask, Mr. McKelvey. On behalf of my father. He was very implicit in his instructions. You're the only neighbour who is still on speaking terms with him."

McKelvey's mind spun. *On speaking terms?* What did the old German need, a few pints of blood for his operation?

"I don't know how I can help," he said. He felt awkward standing there with the door open, dressed in his skivvies. Then suddenly his cop's mind rewound her opening statement, and it struck him in the face with the force of a sledgehammer. '*When he found them in the backyard, two of them anyway...*'

"The Doberman survived the poisoning," she said, "and

154

we have nowhere to put him. I'm allergic to both dogs and cats, and anyway I'm not allowed pets in my condo..."

"Oh no," McKelvey said, shaking his head, "see, I don't really have a thing for dogs."

"I'm begging you, Mr. McKelvey, my father was implicit in his instructions."

"So you said. Still. I mean, I don't..." He shrugged and turned his head, looking around the hallway as though his current situation explained everything.

"The Doberman, Rudolph, is highly trained, Mr. McKelvey, and he's—"

"I'm not home very often, with my job and everything."

Anna squinted and said, "My father said you were retired very recently."

McKelvey was taken aback by the neighbour's seeming awareness of his life.

"Well, yes, but I'm consulting on a project. I have no way of knowing whether I'll be home at night, so the dog could starve to death. Take him to a kennel and board him. That's what those places are for. It's not my responsibility."

Anna's chin began to quiver, and a series of tears formed at the corner of her eyes and began their slow trickle down her rosy cheeks. His jaw clenched. The tears, a dirty trick.

"He never got on well with other people," she said, "but those dogs were like children to my father. He's already in a fragile state, and if he knew his Rudolph was at a kennel, it would kill him. Please, Mr. McKelvey. Let me go and get the dog, and you can see for yourself how well-behaved he is, and I promise as soon as I can make other arrangements, I'll come and get him. He won't be any bother at all."

McKelvey stood there, stunned. If he had been groggy a few minutes earlier, he was wide awake now. His instinct told him the German was setting him up—yes, likely believing McKelvey responsible for the poisoning—and this was a sort of mean-spirited payback. The old bastard. But he hadn't poisoned the dogs, much as the idea had crossed his mind, as many times as he had fantasized about walking over and shooting them in the fucking head with his service pistol. He looked at Seeburger's daughter now and saw within her the desperation and emotion of all the families of victims he had worked with over the years. Her father was ill, perhaps even gravely so. He could always tie the dog up or keep it locked in the bathroom, or whatever it was people did when they didn't want to be around a damned dog. Fuck.

"Christ," he muttered beneath his breath. "All right. A day or two. That's it."

Anna Seeburger was gone from the front step and back within two minutes, with the sleek black Doberman on a leash, a bowl and a small bag of food under her arm. She dropped the dog off like a busy working mother dropping her baby off at daycare.

"Whoa, hold up," McKelvey said as she turned towards her Volvo which was still running at the curb, "give me your phone number or something, just in case I need to reach you."

She came back and handed him a business card. He held it with his free hand while the other held Rudolph's leash. He closed the door and turned to see Rudolph sitting there in a perfect pose, the picture of Zen.

"What the hell am I supposed to do with you?" he said.

The dog stared back with his glossy eyes, blinking. McKelvey moved the bowl and the small bag of food to the kitchen then unfastened the leash and hung it over the back of a kitchen chair. The dog followed him, maintaining an appropriate distance. McKelvey returned to his bed and climbed under the covers, his mind reeling from the strange irony of it all. When he opened his eyes and lifted his head, Rudolph was sitting there in his pose at the threshold to the master bedroom, a protector or a servant. Sitting there like a statue, silent.

"So you're the last man standing, is that it?" McKelvey said.

Rudolph blinked and waited.

McKelvey woke an hour later, and the dog was still there at the door, only now he was curled and sleeping. McKelvey put his feet on the floor quietly, easing his weight from the bed. He took a step, but the dog was feigning sleep and instantly raised his head, eyes open and alert. Rudolph stared with his big moist eyes, and McKelvey took a few steps to the door. He gingerly stepped over the dog then cautiously moved down the hallway towards the bathroom. Rudolph followed at an obedient pace, nails clacking on the hardwood.

"Sit," McKelvey said, turning in the hall. The dog stared at him for a moment. He remembered how the police dogs were trained with German-language signals so they would not listen to false commands. "Christ, don't tell me the old guy speaks German to you."

Rudolph cocked his head to the side. McKelvey slipped inside the bathroom for a long shower. He would be just in time to meet Tim Fielding for his afternoon tattoo.

Eighteen

They had arranged to meet at a coffee shop on the corner of Queen Street West and Spadina. McKelvey came in a few minutes late and spotted Tim sitting at a table with a coffee. He bought a tea from a young man behind the counter who had large black rings expanded through his earlobes. He was reminded of pictures of lost tribes in *National Geographic*. There seemed to be no limit to the ways in which human beings were willing to distort or adorn or impale or otherwise defile their bodies. It was boredom on display in the twenty-first century. He shook his head on his way to the table.

"Somebody looks happy," Tim said.

McKelvey sat down and yawned. "I finally got a good sleep," he said.

He wanted to tell his friend about Leonard Tilman. He'd made a few calls that afternoon and got confirmation of the arrest. Pulled over twenty minutes after an anonymous phone call. Due to his previous convictions and the conditions of his probation, Tilman would be remanded at the detention centre to await a bail hearing. McKelvey shivered with complicity, drawing the cosmic connection between himself and this stranger, Leonard Tilman. And they weren't so different, Leonard Tilman and Charlie McKelvey, were they? That's what he thought now. Just two lost souls, each of them drifting across the painted lines in his own way.

He drank some of the tea and said, "Listen, I thought you'd want to know. I heard a report from a friend of mine on the force. Leonard Tilman was arrested for drunk driving last night."

Tim sighed. McKelvey closed his eyes, pushing away the desire to tell his friend the truth about retribution, how in the end there was no other way for a man to live with himself than to put one foot in front of the other, to swing the hammer or throw the rope, to make things happen when everyone else was standing around with their hands in their pockets.

"Are they going to finally nail this son of a bitch?" Tim asked. That was it, there was nothing left in his voice. He had exhausted himself of violent hatred. He was simply tired of it all.

"I still have some friends at the Crown attorney's office. I'll be sure to put in a real good word for this asshole," McKelvey said.

"How long do you think he'll do?"

"My bet is he'll draw a few years this time for sure."

Tim said, "Thank you, Charlie."

"For what?" McKelvey said.

"You know, for putting in a word on Tilman. I appreciate it."

McKelvey said, "I'm glad I can do it."

"Well," Tim said, glancing at his watch, "I guess there's no point in putting it off."

*   *   *

The tattoo parlour was long and narrow, nestled among the vampire clothing outlets and trendy head shops of Queen Street West. The place was clean enough in McKelvey's estimation, a lingering smell of antiseptic in the air. There was nobody else in the shop on this weekday afternoon. The woman who greeted them at a low counter was dressed in torn black fishnet stockings, a camouflage mini skirt, a black sleeveless top with what appeared to be her bra on the outside, and her lips were painted the deepest purple to match the thick band of eyeliner highlighting an otherwise youthful and attractive round face. Her name was Kendra, and it was a small enough shop that she appeared to be both the receptionist and the tattoo artist. McKelvey found himself counting the number of Kendra's piercings—nine that were visible—while Tim went over the rough sketch he pulled out of his pocket.

"Is your friend getting one too?" Kendra asked as she drew an ink outline from Tim's design, then made a transfer from it. "I'll give you guys a discount if you double up."

"I don't know," Tim said, glancing over his shoulder. "Are you?"

"Not today," McKelvey said. "Maybe for my ninetieth birthday or something."

"Everybody should get at least one tattoo in their life," she said.

"I don't see any on you," McKelvey said, teasing.

"'See' being the operative word," she came back with a little smile. "Check out the portfolios over there on the coffee table while you're waiting. Most of my work is in there, and a bunch of other local artists who work in the shop. There's a picture of my back in there somewhere. Took eighty-five hours just to do the outlining, another sixty hours for the colour work."

McKelvey whistled and made his way to the four waiting chairs and the coffee table piled high with the thick black ledger-sized art portfolios. He looked around at the posters on the walls, the samples of artwork to choose from, a sign going over all the rules and health code information in great detail. Another sign declared: *If you're not 18, don't even bother.* He watched as Kendra brought Tim to a single dentist-style chair just behind the counter and began to prep his flesh for the inking. She put rubber gloves on then shaved the area at his upper left shoulder with a disposable razor, explaining every aspect of the procedure as she worked. McKelvey marvelled at the professionalism, the artistic pride, to be found within this strange subculture of placing permanent designs on the human body.

"Just holler if he starts to pass out," McKelvey said. "He tends to get squeamish at the sight of blood, starts flopping around and the whole thing."

"And yet I'm the one sitting in the chair," Tim said.

McKelvey said, "Touché," then hefted the top portfolio and began to flip his way through the clippings of artwork and accompanying colour Polaroids displaying the finished result. There were entire sections dedicated to themes: dragons and skulls, Celtic and tribal, naval-style and Japanese. Soon the sound of the tattoo machine began to buzz like a sharp electric razor, and McKelvey could hear Kendra and Tim making the time pass with smalltalk. She asked about the design, and Tim told her the story of his wife. She said something about memorials being one of her most common requests, recounting the time she'd inked the portrait of a man's revered father across the expanse of the client's back. It was work that she came to with a sense of artistic and spiritual understanding.

McKelvey was on the third portfolio, skipping some pages here and there, gazing at other spreads absentmindedly, when he flipped a page and stopped. Stopped cold. He couldn't speak, he couldn't move. His stomach clenched. The air in his lungs constricted as he stared at a picture of Gavin smiling, displaying a freshly inked tattoo on his chest above his heart. A girl in the photo beside him, a pretty girl smiling with black hair and olive skin, proudly displaying a matching tattoo.

He lifted his head. The room spun. Noise from the tattoo gun. *Humming*. His fingers fumbled with the protective plastic sheet, then he was beneath it, pulling the Polaroid free. He went to the counter, legs weightless. He stood there, the photo between a thumb and forefinger, and the photo seemed to be shivering.

"Excuse me," he said. "Kendra."

The young woman raised her head, clearly intent on remaining focused on the job at hand. She held the tattoo machine in one hand, in the other a bloody tissue that she was using to dab at the plasma running from the fresh wound.

"This is my son," he said, and held the photo out. "My son, Gavin."

Kendra squinted and nodded. McKelvey felt his chin quivering, nerves. "Well, at least your son wasn't afraid to get a tattoo," she said with a smile.

"When was this taken? Do you keep records of this sort of thing?"

Tim was listening with interest now.

"I did both him and his girlfriend that day. I remember, because they didn't have all the cash, and we worked out a deal where they agreed to clean the shop and make up the difference. We'd have their authorization forms on file, for sure. Randy, the owner, is real anal about all the paperwork."

Girlfriend, McKelvey thought. And it brought back some of the comments the street kids had made. Innuendos, vague utterances. It was never confirmed that Gavin had a steady girlfriend, but then on the street that sort of declaration could be a liability. He had moved beyond the circle of the squeegee kids, graduating to the orbit of the drug peddlers. The kids beneath the expressway and in the drop-in shelters carried only faint memories of the boy by the time McKelvey had got to them, their population transient.

"They got matching tattoos?" McKelvey said.

Kendra dabbed the tissue at Tim's arm, where a line of translucent fluid was forming in a fat teardrop.

"I'm sorry," she said, "I'm a little confused. You didn't know about the tattoo?"

McKelvey stared at the photo. In vibrant colour. His son, smiling, proud of the new artwork on his body. The black-haired girl smiling beside him, their heads touching, the whole rest of their lives spread before them.

"His son was murdered," Tim offered quietly. "About two years ago now."

"Oh my god," Kendra said, and her shock was genuine. "I'm so sorry. I didn't know..."

"Don't be sorry," McKelvey said. "Listen. I need copies of their authorization forms. I need the girl's ID."

"Oh, my god," Kendra repeated, and now it seemed she was trying not to cry, the emotion of the connection coming through. "It's just that..."

"What is it?" McKelvey said.

"You knew they were expecting, right? I mean, the reason they were getting matching tattoos," she said. "Because they were expecting..."

Kendra sniffed, the tears coming now. McKelvey didn't hear anything after that.

Nineteen

Duguay's mind swam with the possibilities, and he took no notice of the white Ford minivan pulling away from the curb as he drove out of the club parking lot. The van kept its distance, then allowed a car to cut between it and Duguay's Mystique. Twice since the meeting at Danny's place, Bouchard had called him on the safe cellular, speaking in code, pushing him towards the dual objectives. He'd gleaned the retired cop's home address, even driving over there and circling the neighborhood, getting a feel for the territory. And for the first time in a long time, Duguay experienced the pressurized discomfort that comes when a man finds himself increasingly wedged between two wrong places.

Duguay saw it clearly laid out: Bouchard would use him to get rid of the dirty cop and the meddling cop—two cops, for Christ's sake—then it would be Duguay who took the bullet in the back of the head. He saw how it would unfold. The call to a meeting. The shot you never heard. His body tied in a sleeping bag, tossed in the lake with a set of weights. Or perhaps they would opt to roll his body into a minivan which would be found burned to its metal frame in a vacant lot in an industrial complex, in true Quebec biker style. No physical evidence, no leads. It would take significant efforts to identify the body. And when it was identified, it would make the front page of *Âllo Police*, then he would be gone from the world as though he had never been born.

With some of the guys it came easy. Guys like the famed Cortez from down south who had a dozen notches on his belt. Duguay had always sensed it was more than just a job for some of them, more than a contract to be fulfilled. It was something, the seeking and the finding, sniffing for the essence of death. With Duguay it was all business. There was no pleasure to be found in taking a man's life. You carried that blood on your hands for all of your days. There had been only one, and he had never talked about it, not with anyone. It was his hope that there would be no more. He wanted money and a string of businesses, a nice home, a truck. He didn't want to look over his shoulder for the rest of his days, wondering when the payback for an old kill might be delivered. It's what they didn't understand, that once it got started, there was no end.

With Balani it made sense. There was no question. The cop had stepped across to the other side, sticking a toe in the waters, accepting envelopes of cash, a hotel room with a high-priced call girl, the exhilarating knowledge that he was in many ways *above* the law. He was the law, and yet he was circulating in a realm of ambiguity, a sense of danger. Happened to the narcos all the time: good cops driven underground for a year or two suddenly found themselves no longer surprised by their own depraved actions. Of course Bouchard was right, it made business sense to get rid of Balani if the drug-addled cop was starting to spread stories.

With the other, this McKelvey, it wasn't so clearly defined. Duguay was puzzled, confused by the man, even more confused by his own feelings. There was no obvious connection, at least not in his memory. He had requested and received personal information on the man, relying on inside sources, police informants. He looked at the stark black and white departmental photo of the man, with his piercing eyes and his square jaw. The facts were plain: the man's son had been murdered. The cop's son peddling dime rocks for none other than Marcel Leroux. That was the connection to the Blades. So what did this have to do with him? McKelvey was retired. What was the point?

Or had he simply lost his nerve? Was he making excuses here?

The man had suffered the loss of his son, a weight to carry for the rest of his life. *So what? People die every day. They die in accidents, stabbings, bombings, from food poisoning for fuck sakes. Why am I supposed to feel bad for this asshole snooping around in my life, making connections, drawing conclusions...*

What the hell is wrong with my head? Duguay joined the traffic merging onto the four-lane highway headed east. His mind finally drifted, and he thought of Chantal LeClair's body and the taste of her, the smell of her, the girl from his street back home, the only woman he'd ever thought of marrying. He wondered, as he did from time to time, where she was or who she was with, what she was doing now, right now. Another missed opportunity, choosing the boys and the lifestyle over a home with babies, Chantal in her summer dress to greet him at the door with his lunch bucket and his little paycheck. They could have made it, he knew. She had wanted to. Get married, get out of the life, get a trade ticket and live like all the rest of the people in their row houses, living for a Saturday night drunk, getting old and your kids coming back home for Sunday night roast beef.

Chantal LeClair. What would she think of him now? It made him smile. To think of the old days and the old places, those nights when they were seventeen and made love in the back seat of a car parked down a dead end street. Probably something he'd stolen. He smiled at the memories of Chantal, the girl he could have had and should have had. Some times when he felt himself starting to go crazy inside the penitentiary, he would go back to those days. Before he'd robbed the bank in Dorval and been caught two days later asleep in a room at the Holiday Inn in Pointe Claire. It was the first time he'd used a handgun, the first time he'd drawn more than a short stint. *Seven years.* Too long for Chantal to wait, even though she would have. She would have waited. But he never gave her the chance.

Duguay pulled into the lot at Danny's place. He glanced around as he walked from the car to the door, quick shoulder checks to scan the field of vision. He sensed the vehicle near him, around him, always just out of sight. He'd made the connection halfway across town. It was Bouchard's man keeping tabs on him, or a Hells associate come to make good on that promise made all those years ago after the Lennoxville Massacre. Sign with us or retire, that was the ultimatum. He knew things, he knew people, he held secrets, and they'd offered him a place with the new chapter, but he had turned his back on them.

Duguay slipped inside the garage with its strong smell of epoxy. He paused at the door to the bay, watching his friend work on the frame of a rare 1981 Trans Am. Danny's hand moved in slow circles across the front quarter panel, shaping the body one invisible layer at a time.

"Sugar plum," Duguay said, "I need a favour."

Danny looked up, smiled. He set the square of sandpaper down and wiped his hands across the front of his coveralls. His eyes were red, and he moved slow, buzzed.

"You're in your zone," Duguay said. "You wouldn't even

notice somebody coming in here to rob you. You should lock the fucking door at least."

Danny came over and stood with a shoulder against the door frame, fishing for his pack of cigarettes. He offered the pack to Duguay. Danny lit their cigarettes and blew a mouthful of smoke toward the tubes of bright fluorescent lighting that made everything, even the flesh on their faces, seem fabricated, plastic.

"Not much to steal around here," Danny said, looking around. His face was dark with ground dust and fibreglass shavings. "Anyway, I got a full set of wrenches that'd knock a row of teeth out pretty quick. Not to mention I still keep an old pistol in the bottom drawer of my desk."

Duguay laughed, said, "Not the same little .38 I gave you, *es ti.*"

"That would be the one."

"Thing probably wouldn't shoot any more, buddy. It'd jam on you. You have to clean them, or they don't work. We'll have to get you set up with something newer. A Taser, maybe. They're getting popular. Bring a guy down without having to waste him, at least not right there and then."

"Come on, Pete, look at me. I don't need to keep a fucking gun around, man. I'm just hiding away in here with my cars, you know? I'm not bothering anybody."

"I brought you into this, Danny. You're *in it.* If Bouchard is looking to get rid of me, then he won't think twice about wasting you. The guy's fucking paranoid."

"What can I do, Pete? Just say it."

"When it happens, it's gonna be big. A real big bang."

Danny pinched his cigarette at the halfway mark, twisted the end and slipped the butt in the front pocket of his coveralls. It was an old habit, and witnessing it brought Duguay back to prison, where cigarettes and decks of smokes were traded with the weight of cash. A man on the inside could have another man beaten for the mere price of a few cartons of cigarettes. Everything had a value: blowjobs from the trannies, a pinch of dope hooped in a con's anus, a copy of the key to the phone in the administration wing. He remembered a green kid coming to the pen for the first time, how badly he'd wanted a deck of smokes, and how Duguay had warned him to wait until the canteen order was placed in a few days, not to borrow a pack. The kid couldn't wait and wouldn't listen to advice, ended up "borrowing" a deck of smokes from a particularly degenerate old con, an infamous and merciless sex hound. The kid's time inside quickly turned to a version of hell when he found out the next day that it wasn't a one-for-one trade; no, the old con wanted a full carton for his single pack. It was inflation in triple digits. The kid didn't have the ways or the means to cover the carton right away, so he began digging himself deeper into the debt of the old con until finally he was owned outright. Duguay saw the kid crying in fear and desperation, coming back to him for help. But the old con's game had been played straight up, it was the code, so Duguay had no choice but to turn his back on the kid.

Whatever happened to that kid? Duguay wondered. *What makes one stronger than the other? Why am I still here, still standing, when so many of us fell back in the day?*

His mind flashed with memories from the penitentiaries, the stabbings in the weight pit with jagged hunks of glass, toothbrushes melted and fitted with a razor blade, an uncoiled bed spring sharpened to a deadly point, the actual smell of fear that settled upon the place like a poisonous gas as a new fish was brought down the line—the ways they tried to maim and kill one another on the inside, it was mediaeval. It didn't happen every day, but when it did, it was brutal, and it was fast. The last stint awaiting trial, it had made him think. He wasn't sure he had it in him to do another long stretch. He couldn't say it, but it was there in the back of his mind, a whisper.

"So what about this favour?" Danny said.

"It can wait a little. Why don't you roll us a joint like the old days."

Danny Madill didn't have to be asked twice.

*   *   *

The marijuana was an analgesic to Duguay's old wounds, broken bones in various places that had failed, for one reason or another, to set properly. It had been a long time since his last toke, because the dope was never worth the price you had to pay on the inside, and now he coughed against the weed's sweet refrain. His body exhaled a sigh, and he twittered a bit, but there was no sense that he was "off", or otherwise dulled. He couldn't afford it. He'd been good about his drinking lately, too. And the cocaine, it was something he had to push away. It wasn't out of reach, though, or beyond possibility, that rush of confidence. There was an itch in the core of his brain, the coiled serpent there hissing for a good dose. He had to keep a lid on it.

"You remember that time when we took off from juvie hall?" Danny said. His feet were up on the desk, and he was splayed in his chair. "We had like ten bucks between us. We made it all the way back downtown, don't ask me how," he continued, laughing now as he relived the memory, his own laughter building with the story's punch line, "and then, instead of putting our money together for a room or some food, we bought a little weed..."

"A couple of amateurs, we thought we were like Butch and Sundance on the lam," Duguay said, smiling so hard his cheeks were beginning to ache.

He looked over at his friend, his oldest friend with the wide face and the brown hair swept back like an eight-year-old boy, and he felt at ease within himself for the first time in weeks.

"We were back in the joint before dark," Danny said.

"We didn't know *anything*," Duguay said, easing through the memory of those times. "We didn't know you've got to have someone waiting in a car, a set of civilian clothes, ID, a safe house where you can lay low for a month, all those *details*. Juvie hall can teach a kid how to fight and how to break into a car or pull of a quick change stunt, but you don't have a clue how things really work until you do penitentiary time."

"I'll take your word for it."

Duguay tilted his head and narrowed his eyes. He said, "You were in, Danny. You did some short time on that vehicle ring years back."

Danny's face changed, and Duguay knew without asking. "Danny?" he said—and it was a question.

"I tried to tell you a long time ago," Danny said. "It just never came up."

"Tell me what?"

Danny shrugged, looked down at his boots.

"I felt like a punk to you, to my brother," he said quietly. "After you pulled that first set of three years when we were what, eighteen? You came back and you were—I don't know, man—you were fucking *hard.* You were a hundred years older than me. I told you they sent me to Collins Bay due to the over-crowding at Archambault. Shit, I only pulled nine months, and I did that in the city hoosegow with a bunch of drunk drivers and quick change artists."

"Why would you lie about something so stupid?"

"I don't know, maybe I figured you wouldn't trust me as much."

"Trust you? After all we've been through? Fuck. You got to be kidding me. I trust you with my *life*. Without hesitation. Shit, Danny, that's nuts. It was me, I'd be happy as hell to say I'd never spent a single fucking night in a penitentiary..."

In the silence that fell between them, Duguay understood something intrinsic about their relationship, something he'd missed along the way, or more likely something he'd seen yet wished not to believe.

"You never had to do anything to impress me," Duguay said. "Talk doesn't impress me, you know that. Those fucks are a dime a dozen on the inside. Tough guys talking about big jobs they pulled or guys they wasted, and it's ninety per cent bullshit. When the dice hits the mat they always show their true colours, and it's usually yellow. I'd want you covering my back any day."

They sat there together. The room was stale, warm, and there was a scent of rust and hand cleaner. Danny pulled the ashtray to his lap and began absent-mindedly fishing through the jumble of butts with his already-blackened fingers.

Duguay said, "Danny? If something happens to me. You know. Or if I ever call you and give the word, would you do me a favour?"

"Name it," Danny said.

"I got some money stashed away. If I don't get it in time. I mean, if they get to me. I want you to find Chantal and give her the money. Okay?"

Danny shook his head slowly and smiled. "Chantal LeClair. Haven't heard that name in a while," he said.

"I been thinking too much lately," Duguay said.

"That's never a good thing."

"You ever miss the old days, the old neighborhood?"

Danny said, "Sometimes, sure. I miss the smoked meat. I miss the quarts of beer in the *dépanneurs*. But everything looks better from a distance, man. I moved here to get away from that place. The people who tie you to your family name, to the things your father did or your older brother. I would have died if I had stayed, Pete. I know that's the truth. I'd be dead right now. Or pulling a life sentence like my brother."

"I just can't get used to it here," Duguay said. "Everything's different. The women are stuck up, and all the cons are working on ten-year plans. I've been thinking a lot lately, you know. Maybe I should make a move. I can't sit here like a lame duck, you know?"

"Where would you go?"

"I don't know," Duguay said. "Home, I guess."

"You could expect a nice homecoming from the Hells," Danny said. "From what I hear, things are only getting worse again between them and the Rock Machine. Heat was coming down on everyone for whacking those prison guards. It's a goddamned butcher shop back home these days."

"It's the only place for me."

"They'd kill you, Pete," Danny said. "You have to know that. You can't just walk back into the old neighbourhood and start up again like nothing happened. Like you didn't turn away from them and side with the enemy."

"I have nothing to hide," Duguay said. "Nobody ever owned me. I never ratted anybody out in my life."

"You're old-fashioned, that's your problem. You believe in the old-school days, honour among thieves and all that bullshit. But these guys today, they're fucking animals. Blowing kids up, taking hits out on those prison guards like that—and a chick, to boot. They all turn over to the cops as soon as they get picked up. Anyway, honour ain't much use if you're dead."

"If it's coming, I'd rather face it in my own way, with my own people. Not here, not in this city. It's all strangers. My English is good, Dan, but I miss speaking my native tongue. I miss driving around the city, you know, the old streets."

"I don't know, maybe you could go back. If you talked to some of them," Danny said. He fiddled with his lighter and said, "If anybody could beat the odds, it'd be you."

Duguay held his hand out and said, "Light another, will you, Danny? I've got something to ask you. A little backup plan for these motherfuckers. I need some place to draw them in if everything goes to hell. A last stand."

*   *   *

It was a dark sky night of no stars when Duguay pulled out of the parking lot. He bought a coffee at a corner store to shake off the last of the head buzz and sipped it while scanning the magazine rack, pornos and bike mags. He bought a magazine featuring a new limited edition Harley Davidson on the cover. All sleek chrome and badass muscle, all shine and gleam, and Duguay stood there feeling like a kid staring at his first nude centrefold. It was something he'd wanted back in his life; he'd been almost a year without a hog of his own. There were many things he wanted back in his life. And some things gone from it. Is this what happened to a man as he edged up to his fortieth year?

When he pulled out onto the boulevard, he noticed the white van turn in behind him from a side road. He fixed the rear view, checked the side mirrors, ran through the options.

He could make out two of them, a driver and a passenger. He wasn't carrying, not this soon after being released. He had a baseball bat in the trunk, but it would mean pulling over, popping the trunk, and making it to the back before they opened up on him. A baseball bat against a gun; the odds weren't worth the calculations.

He took a few quick turns, circling a block, and the van stayed on him. His heart was beating fast now, his mind playing through the possibilities. He pulled over on a dark stretch of road. The van eased up a few yards behind him and kept the headlights on, then flicked the high beams. The blast flooded Duguay's car so that his every move was visible. He squinted, trying to remember the license plate from the quick glances he'd managed in the rear view, but it was gone. Back in Quebec during the war, he'd become adept at memorizing plates and car makes of the rival dealers and associates, cataloguing them away for later recall, slips of paper kept in the glove compartment.

Duguay hit the gas and the engine whined. The van pulled out and was almost touching bumpers when the passenger rolled the window down and fired once, twice, with a handgun equipped with a silencer. One of the bullets hit the driver's side of the car, exploding the side mirror in a spray of plastic and glass, and Duguay tried to drive with his head below the console level. He managed to break away from the van by taking a sudden turn down a narrow side street, scraping the side of a parked car in the process, sparks shooting into the dark night like fireworks. He got himself out of the maze and back onto a main street, joining the flow of normal citizens.

"Come on!" he screamed, hitting the steering wheel with his palm, the adrenaline running through his body like an electric current. "Here I am! Come and get me!"

He pulled into a laneway, backed the vehicle up behind a parked trailer and sat there for almost an hour, smoking cigarettes with a shaking hand. It was then that he understood the decision had been made for him. He had no choice but to make the drive out to the small town bank, make his final withdrawal, and leave the failed experiment of this city behind him. He wondered, as he sat there in his car with the broken side mirror, if Chantal LeClair would run away with him if he showed up on her step in the middle of the night. He thought she'd probably say something like, "It's been ten years, Pierre..."

Twenty

True to his reputation, the loyal dog stayed up with him through that long night, the first night of his newfound faith. Hattie came by just past midnight with the file folder on the girl. There was a vibration of hope and desperation all at once, and always, this faint hope that all of the searching and the dogged harassment would come to fruition with this, the startling news of the existence of a *child*. McKelvey was unable to eat or sleep, and Hattie said he looked like a college kid strung out on speed during exam week.

The girl, she told him, was named Jessie Rainbird.

"She's in CPIC. She was picked up in that sweep on the strip clubs last fall. She was charged and got rehab in lieu of jail time. I got a friend to pull the court reports. She's a runaway from Manitoulin Island. Grew up in Sudbury. Same old story, small town girl blinded by the big lights of the city. No education, no job, no fucking chance. She has a history with the Children's Aid. Looks like an aunt is her legal guardian. There was no mention of dependents, Charlie."

"Maybe she lied. Maybe she gave it up," he said. "Could be any reason."

"For all we know, she could have made the whole thing up for Gavin's sake. To keep him. A knocked up girl out on the street, that's got to be absolutely terrifying."

"Why are you saying all this?" he said. "I haven't had a

goddamned ray of hope in two years, Hattie. And now I find out I might have a piece of my son out there somewhere, and you want to bring me down?"

"Charlie, nobody wants to see you happier than I do. I just don't want to see you get hurt in this. Maybe take some time to think things through, that's all. These people, they're from the street. They tell lies they way you and I say good morning."

"I wondered why I called Tim Fielding that first night, you know. I could never figure out what made me do it. It's not like me to reach out like that. But something made me pull over and make the call that night, Hattie. And now I know it was Gavin. There are no coincidences in life. If I hadn't called Tim that night, I would never have been at the tattoo shop today..."

She watched him, and she nodded, but he could tell that she didn't believe him. Or she didn't believe that he believed what he was saying. They both knew how far the families of victims can carry things when they hang onto hope just a little too long.

"Let me see the file," he said and held out his hand.

Hattie sighed and handed it over, and said, "It's official. We're both breaking the rules now. Only you don't have a job to lose."

"I hear the work's overrated anyway," he said and gave her a little smile.

McKelvey flipped through the printed reports. "She was picked up at the Dove," he said.

"Blades' unofficial clubhouse," she said. "Must be working for one of their agencies."

He glanced at his watch. It was twenty past twelve. The strip joint would be stumbling headlong into its final hours. There was no tomorrow, no day after that. It was right now, right here. This was everything.

"I'm going to ask you to go home," he said.

"What are you talking about?" she said.

"Go home and stay by your phone. I'll call you to check in."

"Charlie, no," she said. "Let me stay here at least. I'll be worried sick."

"I have to do this on my own," he said. "You can understand that. Please."

"I can't just let you leave here to go after Duguay. Printing a few files is one thing, Charlie, but I'm not going to be an accessory…"

"Shhh," he said, and leaned over to take her face in his hands. "I don't give a shit about Pierre Duguay, Hattie. I want the girl, that's all. I want to find my grandchild."

"She might not even work there any more," she said. "Christ, she could be anywhere."

"She's there," he said. "I can feel it. She's still there."

⋆　⋆　⋆

Duguay parked the car in the lot of a motel a block down from the Dove. The passenger side was trashed, streaked with black scratches and peppered with paint flecks from the car he had side-swiped, something in burgundy, and the driver's side mirror hung there like a popped eyeball. He walked back to the club, came in the front door and slipped past the doorman. He spotted a few of the hangarounds standing at the bar, guys who did the gang's dirty work while awaiting their promotion to "prospect" status. He would have them get rid of the car before it drew any more heat to him. Duguay slipped the keys in the jacket pocket of a hangaround named BB.

"Car got shot up. Get Davey to follow you and drive it out of the city," Duguay said. "Take it up to Orillia or some place. Strip the plates and light it up."

"What's Davey supposed to do?" BB asked. His mouth was open, and he had big teeth.

"Drive you back, asshole," Duguay said and brushed past them on his way through the club to the apartment, using his shoulders to clear a path through the patrons. These were the soldiers Bouchard had sent to open a franchise, to raise a flag. Morons and crackheads. The thing was doomed from the start. And now his ass was on the line.

The sweat was drenching his T-shirt as he began to throw his clothes into a duffel, cursing his own stupidity for throwing in with this crew. He'd felt like he was in a no-win situation after the bad business in Lennoxville. He should have taken the hand extended by the Sorel Hell's Angels, moved past the fact they had killed a few of his good friends. Yet here he was. Pride or hatred, or perhaps both had prevented him from shaking hands with those people. He'd been sitting in a bar near the Montreal airport waiting for a flight attendant from Air Canada who imported cocaine for him on her body. That's when the friend of a friend had seen him there and made the introduction to Jean Bouchard. The old man had liked him right from the start. And that's when everything had changed for Duguay.

He went around the rooms of the apartment, and it was always this way in the end, it always came down to this: trying to decide what to carry with him, what to leave behind. He was in the living room zipping the bag shut when Luc, the acting boss, came through the door. He stood there regarding Duguay for a moment, and Duguay did not like the trace of a smile on the man's mouth.

"What's the joke?" he said, and straightened up.

"BB told me you came in, said your car got shot up," Luc said. "What happened?"

"Why don't you tell me?" Duguay said.

"What are you talking about? Why would I want to hurt you?"

"Don't fuck around with me," Duguay said. "I'm not playing games here."

Luc took a few steps, careful not to move too fast, and sat down on a love seat. He was a tall man, but lanky, and his stringy black hair had always bothered Duguay, always hanging in the man's eyes. And he wore too much jewellery—like most of the bikers did—which Duguay saw as unnecessary and boastful. All show and sizzle.

"I swear on my life, I would never put a hit out on you, Pierre. It's the Para-Dice Riders, I bet. We're starting to get heat from them, too. The Hells on one side, the Riders on the other, both of them starting to squeeze our nuts. Loners are the only ones who will even sit and talk to us about an alliance. Have a drink with me, Pierre. Relax. Sit down and have a drink," Luc said.

"It's all a mess," Duguay said. "Nothing's organized. They sent us here to fail. The Hells own this place. It's a death wish trying to carve out a territory in this city with a bunch of fuckheads."

"Listen," Luc said, glancing at his watch, "I've got to run across the city to see a few of my guys. I'd like to have a beer when I get back so we can talk. But tell me what you need, Pierre, tell me what I can do right now to help."

Duguay said, "I need a piece. Something big. A .45."

He would make it through the night. Make it until morning, when he could hit the bank and grab his rainy day money. With a gun in his jeans, he could make it all the way back to the streets of Montreal.

Twenty-One

It begins with the bass line to a new song, and the curtains part to reveal the first glimpse of the dancer. And so the ceremony begins beneath the dim lights, the stage cool to her bare feet, the funky scent of liquor and perspiration in the air.

Feeling unknown
And you're all alone...

Bathed in steel moonlight, yes, the dancer moves liquid to the beat. Men watch, many of them believing they could find religion where her thighs meet, the delta of some deeper well. The prize they have sought for all time. Men pause with pool cues in hand, their eyes dialed in to the stage. This is what they have come for.

The girl with the coal black hair arches her back, rolls to her side and lifts her head. McKelvey stares into her eyes, and he sees only a girl, the girl his son perhaps loved, and this leaves him feeling lightheaded. The room begins to rotate on an axis, and he doubts himself, doubts his ability to follow through with all this. But the doubt is fleeting. The training comes back. The years of walking the beat, driving the streets of the division. He slows his breathing, focuses on the task at hand.

Lift up the receiver
I'll make you a believer

Someone howls, then there is clapping as the dancer rises from the floor, a goddess come alive, and she slips back through black curtains. It is as though she simply dissolves. It takes a long time for McKelvey's eyes to adjust to the dim lighting, or more like the absence of lighting. He is no stranger to these establishments, but it has been a while.

She is just a girl, just a kid. Somebody's daughter, he thinks. He moves through the tables, past the girls on the stools touching their toes for private dances, through groups of young men with dozens of beer bottles on their tables, and he moves to the hallway at the rear that will lead him to the dressing room.

＊　＊　＊

Experience had taught McKelvey that to be in command, a man must believe he is in command. "Fake it if you have to," is how the old veteran cop had put it to him his first day on the job all those centuries ago. Now he had the .25 pistol shoved in the back of his waistband with his untucked dress shirt covering it, and he reached back and felt it, a slight comfort, as he slipped down the hallway and on past the set of doors for the washrooms, crossing the final threshold of his life. At the end of the hallway, there was a set of stairs. He took the only other route, a short hallway to the left. At the end of it he turned the knob on the door and pushed it open, coming into another long and blue-lit hallway. Now the music began to thump in his chest as the next dancer came on stage and the men clapped in half-hearted appreciation. He opened the door at the end of that hallway, and he was inside the dressing room.

It was very dimly lit. Three women were in various stages

of dress and undress, they were all smoking, and only one of them, a tall and skinny blonde girl, seemed to take notice of him. The blonde eyed him while she brushed her phoney hair. McKelvey pulled out a cigarette from a package he'd bought just that afternoon after the nuclear devastation of the tattoo shop, his first transgression in months. That initial draw sending a dose of dope to his head, good old dependable nicotine. It made him feel guilty to give in, to surrender once again, but Christ, it didn't really matter any more, did it?

He had just finished lighting the cigarette when the girl with the black hair came into the room from the stage hallway. Dressed in a short kimono now, carrying the blanket she used on stage.

"Jessie," McKelvey said.

She squinted and gave him a look. She got closer to him, but not too close.

"Who are you?" she said.

"I'm Gavin's dad," he said then reached into the back pocket of his pants and pulled out the Polaroid from the tattoo parlour. She stared. She seemed transfixed, on the verge of breaking down, then suddenly her body language changed, and she was defiant, tough.

"I don't know what you're talking about," she said. But she was visibly shaken. He knew the truth without asking. Years of questioning drivers, crooks, garden variety assholes, had honed that sixth sense to a sharp edge. He saw her life and her connection to his boy in her eyes.

"It's right here in the picture. You got matching tattoos. Because you were pregnant. The girl at the shop told me the whole story. Come on, Jessie, cut me some slack here. I just want to talk to you for an hour. Just an hour of your time."

The other girls were listening now, pretending to curl their hair or apply thick mascara. Jessie tossed the comforter over in a corner and took a cigarette from the ashtray, took a haul.

"He was my son," he said. "I only had the one. I just want to talk to you, Jessie. It's been a rough couple of years. Would you do that for me?"

She looked at him, and as he spoke, she visibly softened. She liked him, just something about him. Then she knew. She knew the parts of her boy that she saw in this man standing there in front of her. The curly hair, the intense blue eyes, that handsomeness that was neither conventional nor easy to explain.

"Well, I'm sorry you came all this way," she said, "but somebody lied to you. There's no baby."

"Come on, Jessie," he said. "Don't fuck with me, not tonight."

McKelvey saw the expression change on the blonde girl's face, and he turned to see a stocky man coming through the door. McKelvey did the calculations quickly. The man was about his height, but a good bit heavier, more solid. A bouncer or paid muscle.

"This guy bothering you, Jess?" the man said and wagged a thumb at McKelvey.

"He was just leaving, Gerry," she said.

"Now just wait a minute," McKelvey said, but Gerry took steps towards him, and it was McKelvey's experience that once the distance was closed, there was no going back. So he reached behind his shirt, pulled the pistol free and brought his weight down through his arm and his hand and cut the man across the head, a short and deep gash across the forehead that instantly opened up and flowed. Gerry blinked and staggered, but only for a second.

"Get Duguay!" one of the girls yelled.

Gerry put his hand to his face to wipe away the blood but kept coming on, all rolling shoulders and thick arms, and

McKelvey absorbed a hard shot to the left cheek before employing a manoeuvre he'd been taught thirty years earlier, one he'd used on more than one occasion in the outdoor parks and graffiti-splashed hallways of city housing complexes, and he side-stepped a quick shuffle, got hold of the man's neck and had him off balance and on the floor with a sharp knee to the back of the leg. He felt quickly for the cuffs at his belt, an old habit, then stepped off with his back to the wall, the pistol trained.

"Gerry!" Jessie cried, and went to his side, using her blanket to clean the blood that was rushing from the gash. She looked back up to McKelvey, hatred in her eyes, and she said, "He was just doing his job, you know. He was trying to protect me. We get a lot of creeps around this place. You don't have to be such an asshole."

"I need you to come with me," McKelvey said, and he realized how drained he was from the brief scuffle, too old for all this. His heart was hammering, and he was winded. His cheek was beginning to throb now, and he could feel the flesh rising, tightening. In the excitement of the moment, he had failed to recognize the power of the punch.

"I'm not going anywhere with you," Jessie said. "I told you, there was no baby!"

McKelvey was about to reach across and grab her arm when the side door opened and Duguay came in, the blonde girl behind him, her eyes hungry for a fight. The two men stared for a long moment. Duguay recognized McKelvey from the black and white photo he'd gleaned from a source, a shot of McKelvey in uniform, young and fresh-faced and unsmiling in his serious policeman's pose. And McKelvey recognized Duguay from the file of photos, from the very images, both real and imagined, that were scorched across his memory. All of the fantasies, all of the dreams of being alone in a room with this man, it was suddenly here and now, and McKelvey wanted nothing more than to take the girl and find his kin.

Duguay said simply, "I didn't kill your son."

"I didn't come here to settle with you," McKelvey said. "She's coming with me."

Duguay shook his head. "No," he said, "she belongs to me."

McKelvey pointed the pistol at Duguay's face.

"She doesn't belong to you any more," McKelvey said.

"Are you going to protect her like you protected your son?" Duguay said.

McKelvey's eyes flickered, his jaw clenched, but he came back with a shot of his own, one that would hurt Duguay in the worst place: his street credibility. "You don't know anything about me and my boy. You know what makes me sick about you assholes? You kill people, you steal from them, and you put little girls to work on the street, then when you get caught, you're not even man enough to do your time. Your friends here know you turned over and made a deal with the Crown your last go-around?"

The dancers didn't say anything, but they all looked over to Duguay. McKelvey knew the gossip would make the rounds, and the number who disbelieved it would matter not at all.

"I'm not making any deals, fucker. You're already a dead man, so you might as well pull the trigger. Nobody shoves a gun in my face, not in my house. Come on. Do it."

McKelvey pulled the gun back a little and said, "I'm taking her with me. I'm taking the girl. And if you try to stop me, I'll kill you. If I see you again, I'll kill you, I swear to God."

"I will see you again, make no mistake," Duguay said.

McKelvey motioned with his hand, but Jessie stayed where she was, holding the blanket to Gerry's face. Duguay nodded toward the door. This girl he had lifted up, offered work to.

"Go," he said. "You're done here."

Jessie rose slowly, confused, her arms wrapped around her chest. She glanced between the two men, the girls she worked with, her fate once again and always completely beyond her grasp.

"Go!" Duguay hollered. "And take the fucking pig with you."

McKelvey took the girl's arm and walked backwards out the door.

Twenty-Two

In the little truck, the girl changed again, everything about her. Her body language gave McKelvey the idea of somebody who didn't seem heartbroken at the prospect of being pulled away from the club. Duguay had said he was done with her. Perhaps she understood the finality of things in this life much more profoundly than other girls her age. When she did protest, he felt that she was going through the motions.

"This is fucking crazy," she said. "He'll come after you, you know."

"Probably," he said, and he drove.

"So what's your plan now, Sherlock?"

"I just want to talk with you a little, that's all."

"What are you going to do if I jump out of the car the next time you stop?" she said.

"Handcuff you to the door."

She looked at him. He stared at the road. He was staying away from the main streets. It was dark, everything turned a brown-yellow from the dim street lamps. He felt her eyes on him, his face illuminated each time they passed beneath a light.

"You wouldn't," she said. "That's confinement or something. It's a crime, right?"

"Yes, it's a crime," he said. "And yes, I would."

He let the threat of handcuffs hang there while his mind tallied the half-dozen charges he was already facing. He shivered through one of those very rare moments when it becomes glaringly clear that your life has taken an entirely new direction. He saw himself from a whole new angle; saw something that had perhaps been there all along, maybe just beneath the surface. Who knew. It was a question of environment. Working as a cop in the city had changed him. In ways that he couldn't even fully articulate for himself, let alone for Caroline. It didn't matter; unless you had been shot at in the middle of a lonesome night by a seventeen-year-old with a stolen handgun, unless you had hurt men and been hurt by them in the course of wearing a badge, unless you had been *The Law* in a city like this with its immigrants and its extremes of poverty and riches, unless you had *done it,* there was just no way you could understand how the job changed a man from beginning to end.

He pulled up the driveway and shut the engine off. They sat there, the engine ticking. He looked over at her. Just a girl. A child. The last person to love his son.

"I'm going to get out of the truck and head inside. I'd like you to come and talk to me. But I'm too old, and it's too late at night for me to run after you. That's the truth of it. So it's up to you," he said. "I do have some clothes you could wear. And I make a pretty good grilled cheese."

"You're an asshole," she said, "hurting Gerry like that."

"I wish I hadn't done it," he said.

She glared at him for a long minute.

"I only like grilled cheese with the yellow kind," she said. She was so serious. Tough.

"Cheddar, sure," he said. "It's the only way I make them."

*　　*　　*

The girl named Jessie Rainbird was a walking contradiction.

She was small, yet she seemed a large presence. She was scared, yet she was aiming for threatening. In her hazel eyes there was a fierceness that McKelvey thought he recognized. The defiance, the smouldering anger in his boy's eyes. It was there. From where did this originate, he wanted to know. Was it something inborn, or was it developed? Was it generational angst that was beyond comprehension or explanation? Was it his fault, his poor parenting, or was it an inevitable character trait? His boy had always been stubborn, strong-willed. His favourite phrase was "no, me do" by the time he was three. But still, there had been a child there, a happy child…

"Gavin told me a little about you, you know," she said. "How you're a cop."

McKelvey was standing at the stove, flipping a grilled cheese. She was seated at the table dressed in a pair of his jeans, the legs rolled up and the waist cinched with a belt. She wore one of his T-shirts and a fleece over top, her black hair pulled back in a ponytail. Rudolph was sitting there watching.

"I bet he had lots to say about that," McKelvey said.

"I think he wanted to be one some day. He said it would have made you proud."

"I wouldn't have liked it very much," he said. "It's not a job I'd recommend."

"He never really said anything bad about you, in case that's what you want to know. Just how you guys argued all the time, and it got to the point where he couldn't stand being in the house."

He gave the frying pan a flip with his wrist and shot the sandwich onto a plate. He used the spatula to slice it in half on the diagonal and presented it to Jessie.

"Can I get you a drink?" he said, then doubted he had any fresh milk in the fridge.

"You have any rum?" she said and levelled him with stone eyes. Unblinking.

He looked at her for a moment and thought he was looking into the eyes of a fifty-year-old. He had to remember that she took her clothes off for rooms full of strange men, and who knew what else. Those charges which had sent her to rehab were for prostitution. This was no innocent angel. A rum in the grand scheme of things?

"Why not," he said. He went to the cabinet in the living room and came back with two glasses and a bottle of Captain Morgan's dark rum that was a little less than half full. It was what he and the school teacher had gotten into that night. After the wine. Now he measured out two shots. He pushed her a glass then took his own and brought it to his lips, smelled the rich woody scent, hoped the stuff would steer him clear of the usual sadness tonight.

"Sorry, no Coke," he said.

She shrugged and said, "Just waters it down anyway."

"I wasn't the world's best dad, but…" McKelvey began. He cleared his throat, started again. "We didn't see eye to eye on some important issues, and…well, you know how it goes."

"It was dope at first," she said. "The dope and the skate-boarding and the whole lifestyle. Gavin changed when he was out there, though. He wanted to get off the drugs. And he did. And then…"

He waited. Had been waiting a thousand days to hear this. But it was too much, and she changed subjects like throwing a switch.

"I never knew my dad," she said, then took a bite of the sandwich. She chewed. "He was a hockey player. He was good at it, too. A goalie. I wish I could at least remember something about him. It'd be nice to have something to try to forget."

"Did he play in the minors or the NHL?"

"I don't want to talk about all that," she said.

He drank, and the booze burned his throat. The sting of the hard liquor reminded him of winter nights spent in cold patrol cars, that good belt of rye or rum waiting at the bar at the end of a shift. He looked down into the glass and thought of the nights he had gone to the bar straight after work, killing a few hours before heading home. Hell, more than a few hours. Just like his father. The nights he kept looking over at the clock, his buddies roaring about something, always finding a reason to stay another five minutes. What was he avoiding? What had he missed all those years?

"They're overrated," he said.

"What is?" she said.

"Fathers."

Jessie finished half the sandwich then took a long drink of the rum. She barely winced, and McKelvey knew without a doubt the girl could drink him under the table. He was already softening at the edges from the meagre mouthful of rum. So this is what had become of the young man hanging on until closing time, grasping at a shot at immortality.

"That's not very nice to say," she said. "I bet you got to know your dad, that's why. Or else you wouldn't be saying that."

"My dad was a good man, it's true," he said. "He was just never comfortable as a family man. But then neither was I. You see things a little clearer as you get older. I don't hold anything against him. He was just a jackass like me trying to make it through the best he could, putting one foot in front of the other. He got up every day, though, and got back in the game."

With that he raised his glass in a toast and downed it. Jessie shook her head. "Fuck, you're a box of giggles, aren't you? Gavin said you could be pretty intense."

"I'm sorry," he said. "I never should have said that about fathers. You're right, I don't know what it's like not to have a father."

"Apology accepted," she said.

"So what about your mom?" he said and did not want to reveal the fact he had information on her background, the social workers, the involvement of an aunt.

"She's a loser," she said. "Useless. End of story." She took a drink and said, "Were your parents proud of you being a cop?"

"I don't know about that. My dad was a miner, and he wanted me to be a miner. Where I grew up, the boys were miners, and the girls were miner's wives. I took off for the city and joined the force. My dad and I never really talked too much after I moved away. We had less and less in common."

"What did your mother think?"

"I broke her heart, moving away like that," he said. "But I think she was proud. She'd tell everybody back home about where I was working, show them clippings from the *Sun* that I'd send her."

McKelvey finished his drink and thought about another. He knew without a doubt that Duguay or some of his guys would make a run for him. He had known that the moment he brought the gun out, the moment everything turned sideways, that they would make a play for him. The thing was to get a step ahead. He and the girl would leave at first light, and if they made good and steady time, they would be on Manitoulin Island by late afternoon. A call to Hattie with the details. She could put a cruiser on his house. And the dog. Jesus. He'd forgotten about the dog. He'd call Seeburger's daughter again, for the fifth or sixth time, and leave another message. He was beginning to see the truth, that Seeburger wasn't coming home again, and the daughter was long gone.

Seeburger's last laugh from his deathbed. *Well played, old man.*

"Help yourself to another if you want," he said, and indicated the bottle. "I think I forgot to feed the dog. The owner gave me a little food, but it ran out. Do you know anything about dogs?"

Jessie poured herself a drink and took another long swallow.

"We had some dogs at my aunt's place," she said. "Retrievers and labs mostly. What have you been feeding him?"

"I gave him some toast this morning, that's about it."

"Toast?"

She looked at him with a curled lip, the look of disdain that only a teenage girl can muster. McKelvey shrugged. He got up, moved to the fridge and held the door open. He read out the contents. "Some eggs, cheese, an onion, half a loaf of bread, olives, yogurt..."

"Do you have any canned tuna?" she said.

He went to the cupboard, rummaged a moment and pulled out a can of the budget tuna they sold for a dollar at the grocery store. He got the can opener out.

"Dogs like tuna?"

"They'll pretty much eat their own shit, but yeah, they like tuna. It's good for their coat."

"This dog's a purebred or something. I can't believe how quiet he is. Starving like that. It must have been the other dogs that howled all night. This guy is as quiet as a mouse. I almost like him."

McKelvey dug the chunks of dark grey tuna from the can and mixed it into a bowl. He set the bowl on the floor, and Rudolph walked over, tail wagging. He sniffed the food then sat there. He looked at the bowl, then he looked at McKelvey.

"He's well-trained," Jessie said. "He's waiting for you to give him the okay."

"Eat up," McKelvey said, and snapped his fingers. He motioned to the bowl, and the dog finally moved to it, leaned in and began to eat, tentative. The bowl was clean in less than a minute. Rudolph licked his chops, turned and sat beside the table.

The girl went to fill her glass a third time, but McKelvey sat down and took the bottle from her hand before she could pour more than two fingers' worth in her glass. He emptied the bottle into his glass and took a mouthful. It burned, and it was good, crawling in a slow warmth from his stomach to his limbs, spreading the false sense of ease which had steered humanity through shit storms for two thousand years. He needed it, something to help bring him back down. His mind was moving too fast, his body still tensed from the fight at the club.

"Let me see that," Jessie said, as though reading his mind. She leaned across the table and touched his cheek where the bouncer had struck him with a hard right. He winced when she touched it, pulled away. It hurt more now that he was sitting, the adrenaline ebbing.

"It's all right," he said. It felt as though he'd taken a sledge-hammer to the cheek.

"Gerry was a boxer," she said. "You're lucky he didn't get hold of you. I saw him beat a guy pretty bad one night out behind the club. Some rich asshole who thought he could get a blowjob for the price of a table dance."

"I believe it. He has a good jab," he said. And he thought, *one more like that, and I would have had to shoot him.*

She looked at him with her strong eyes. The eyes, he thought, of an old soul. She was such a pretty girl, so pretty in such a natural way, that he could see what she would like when she finished growing up, the woman she would become at thirty or forty. If she let herself get that far.

"Have you ever shot anyone?" she asked.

"I've shot *at* someone. And had someone shoot at me. Missed on all counts."

"I've seen things," she said. And that was it.

He had a drink, and he watched her. She was gone somewhere, looking into her glass, suddenly morose. Then she began to cry, and her shoulders were heaving. He moved a hand across the table to touch her hand, but it wasn't enough. He got up, went around to her, crouched beside her chair and put an arm around her. She allowed it for a moment, then just as quickly pulled herself up, wiping the wet makeup away with the sides of her thumbs, drawing back into herself. Then she sprang from the chair like a cat. She was halfway to the door when McKelvey caught up to her and got a hand on the loose bulk of his sweater. He stopped her and held her shoulders. He looked into her eyes and held her there.

"I told you," he said, drawing some air, "I'm too old to run after you. Now what's the problem? Was the grilled cheese really that bad?"

Jessie almost laughed, but she held it back. Then she was crying again. "What am I supposed to do now?" she said. "Where am I supposed to go?"

"You're hanging around a very dangerous man. Pierre Duguay is not a nice guy. He was involved in Gavin's death. You must know that much."

"Duguay?"

"Sure he was, sure. Listen..."

"He helped me when I needed it, that's all I know. Now I have nowhere to go, and no one to protect me. I have some money saved up, you know. Now I'll never get it back. And anyway, there was no baby. Okay? Get it through your head. It's what you want to believe. But that doesn't make it the truth."

197

"I'll help you, Jessie," McKelvey said, and he was suddenly overcome with emotion, new ones and strange ones, and everything was right there in front of him, the mother of his grandchild, just a single degree of separation from the blood of his blood. "Let me help you. You can start over again. Wherever you want. God, you're just a kid. You have the rest of your life to look forward to. Don't waste it on some asshole like Pierre Duguay. You saw how quick he was to cast you aside."

"I loved Gavin, you know. I loved him," she said, then she broke into tears that became silent, shaking sobs, and he pulled her close, and he put a strong hand across her back and felt the beating of her heart.

"Well, we have that in common," he said.

Twenty-Three

A mouthful of cotton, a taste of iron in the back of his throat. Danny Madill sat there at his cluttered desk holding an old rag to his head to staunch the bleeding. They had knocked first, and when he slid the deadbolt, the metal door had swung open with the force of a sledge. He found himself sprawled, dizzy. They were on top of him before he could get his bearings. He was lifted and dragged to the back office, any trace of his perpetual buzz lost to the surge of adrenaline. So much for locking the door…

"Call him," the bodyguard said. The same monstrous goon who had accompanied Jean Bouchard on his visit to the shop to see Duguay after his release. This time there was no Bouchard, just the former wrestler and a dark-skinned accomplice, a man who looked to be of Indian descent. This second man stood with his back to the door, arms folded across his chest, watching.

"Fuck you," Danny said.

The bodyguard swung his huge arm like a pendulum, belting Danny across the head with a backhand. Danny toppled off the chair and took a moment to shake it off, on all fours down there on the cold concrete, timing a move for the middle drawer and the old .38 Duguay had given him all those years ago. He cleared his throat and spat a mouthful of blood on the floor, pulling up. He took his seat again. He saw clearly where things were headed.

"Get Duguay out here, and you can go home," the dark-skinned man said. He was tall and broad-shouldered, the beginnings of a pot belly hanging over his pants, and he was sweating, puffy-faced.

"You must have the wrong guy," Danny said. Then he laughed, his tingling lips already swelling, a line of dark blood drying on the side of his face. No, he was the right guy. He was exactly the right person for this.

"What's so fucking funny?" the bodyguard asked.

"You remind me of a guy I knew once," Danny said. "A guy named Meat."

"Oh, yeah? Well fuck you, asshole. I'm giving you one last chance to make the call."

The bodyguard reached into his jacket and produced a buck knife. He spread the blade wide open with his thumb, a flash of death, the tempered steel thick enough to split ribs. There was an understanding of great lengths exceeded, limits pushed and barriers broken. The room closed in, and everything—the tool charts and girlie posters on the wall, the ashtray stuffed with roaches, the old coffee mug with the greasy fingerprints—took on a new importance. Danny was all there.

"Let's just settle down here a minute," the dark man said, stepping forward now, a mediator. "There's no reason we can't do this like men. I need to see Duguay. I need to talk to him. It's important. I need you to call him and ask him to come out here, okay?"

"Who the fuck are you?" Danny said.

"This is who I am," the man said and reached inside his jacket. He pulled out a police badge on a neck chain and flashed it like a crucifix. His eyes were red, disconnected orbs. The pallid, candle-wax flesh. Danny well recognized the effects of a cocaine binge.

Danny saw the plot line, made the connections. The grooves and the slots all fit together. The dirty cop Duguay had brought into the fold. Balani was the name. Everything all mixed together, Leroux and the dirty cop cutting their side deals, the cop's murdered son, all of the heat which had fallen on Duguay as a matter of sheer circumstance. Duguay was innocent of all this, and yet he was guilty through association, for he had introduced the elements. And in the end, nobody would care. It was his word against the word of a cop.

"You want to talk," Danny said, nodding. "Just tying up some lose ends?"

"Something like that," Balani said. "Now are you going to call him, or are you really that stupid? Your friend Duguay is going down one way or the other. Why go down with him? His own friends think he's making a deal with the Crown, and he's drawing heat for the murder of a cop's kid. I know you Irish can be rock-headed, but do the math, fuckhead."

Danny saw the .38 in the drawer, buried beneath old invoice pads. It would require a few seconds—open the drawer, get his hand on the gun, bring it out ready to fire. Would he even make it to drawer? Would it even fire after all these years? He hadn't fired a gun in fifteen years, not since his older brother Mick had leant him a stolen .22 to shoot bottles down by the river. It left him with the last remaining option, the backup plan Duguay had put into motion, the favour he'd asked. *I'll need a place to draw them in if they come for me...get them in one room together.*

"Okay, enough. Jesus. Let me try his number," he said and moved a hand slowly to the pocket of his coveralls. He was sweating now, something that came on like nausea, and everything was as clear as it needed to be, the flash of himself and his brother down by the water, his older brother smiling before all the years of prison and violence that were to come, back when they were just kids, and they whispered back and forth across the room long after their mother had turned the lights out…

The bodyguard stepped back and kept his eyes locked on Danny's hand. Balani stepped to the side, a hand moving on instinct to his sidearm. Danny drew a deep breath, all sounds shut out, and there was only this—the hum from inside.

"Easy," Balani said.

Danny took the rigged cellphone in his palm, recalling the three digit code Duguay had given him. Always covering the angles, that was Duguay. Always a back door. A charge wired in the filing cabinet against the far wall. A cellphone linked to the detonator. Tricks learned and passed along during the war in Quebec. Cars and warehouses and beds and toasters—anything could be used as a gateway to the great beyond.

A droplet of sweat fell from the cop's puffy face.

Danny sighed. He was glad it was him.

He pressed the third and final number. He didn't feel anything at all.

Then they were gone, all of them.

Twenty-Four

She told him her life story, or a version of it, and McKelvey guessed he could tell the true parts from the lies, the embellishments. The cop sitting there at the kitchen table playing a role, switching his stance when required in order to draw the information out of her. It was, for the most part, a story he'd heard a hundred times before. And Hattie was right, at least about the runaway girl part, and the part about getting lost in the city. For a time Jessie had wandered and fallen to trouble, lessons learned the hardest way. Then there was Gavin.

"He was putting posters up on the poles along Queen Street," she said, "getting paid twenty bucks cash to staple five hundred flyers advertising a rave. I was bumming change on the strip there. I thought he was cute, and we started talking. Just like that. The way it happens in the movies."

"You guys kept it a secret?"

"We didn't have to, really. Gavin was getting me out of a life," she said. "I got in with the wrong people, and I made a few mistakes. But he was getting me out of all that. We were making a life. He was going to stop selling dope and get a straight job. But it was hard, because he was making a lot of cash for these guys."

"What guys?"

"Bikers. The Blades."

"Does the name Marcel Leroux mean anything to you?"

She shrugged. "Sure. He got the street kids to owe him something. You owe him, and you have to pay it back. Everybody's got something they can sell. The boys, it was fronting dope, the girls it was...well, you know."

"Did Gavin work directly for Leroux?"

"Leroux always had different guys around. You know, wannabes and hammerheads. After Gavin got enough money together to rent us a little apartment, Leroux wouldn't leave him alone. He wanted Gavin to deal from the apartment, and Gavin was trying to go straight. He had that prescription, and he was talking all the time about saving enough money to open a skateboard shop on Queen Street."

"What was the prescription for?"

"He went to a walk-in clinic through the shelter on Yonge, and they sent him to another doctor. A specialist. He didn't talk about it much. He'd just say how the pills were going to help control his mood swings so he could get clean and get a job, a real job."

"Leroux was coming around and muscling him?"

"Him, yeah. And the other guy too, probably."

"What other guy?"

"I told all that to the cops, but they didn't do anything about it. This guy came around in a car one time with Leroux, and Gavin was down in the lobby finishing a smoke, and he saw this guy sitting in Leroux's car, and he recognized him or something. I'm not sure. When he saw Leroux, he called out to this other guy he had seen in the car. The guy in the car followed them up to the apartment, and they were all yelling. I hid in the bathroom closet because I was...I was too high to go out. I heard them talking to Gavin, like they were trying to convince him of something. Then Leroux and the other guy took off, and Gavin was, I don't know...I'd never seen him

204

like that before. He wasn't even high, he was just freaking out. He was paranoid. I couldn't make any sense out of him. He told me to take a bag and go to one of our friend's places for a while until things cooled down."

Then she broke and began to cry again. He reached out and touched her hands, but she pulled them away to wipe her eyes.

"The next day I heard on the radio. On the *fucking radio,*" she said. "He was found in that field by the overpass. He was right, you know. To be paranoid. It wasn't just the drugs or whatever. *He was right.*"

McKelvey exhaled a long breath. He had seen everything, the crime scene photos and the body itself on that cold table, but hearing her speak of the *impact,* the human impact of that single action made everything fresh again. Like a wound coming open, splitting stitches, the blood beginning to flow once again across the scar tissue. He breathed, and refocused.

"Listen, I told the detective all of this stuff, and nothing ever came of it. I asked the investigator before I went into rehab if Leroux was going to go down for this. He said he was still working the angles. Bullshit. Cops don't know their assholes from their brains."

He took a deep breath to quell the butterflies in his stomach. "Were you brought down to the station and interviewed?"

"Nope. I called the number they listed in the paper and talked to that one cop. We met in a coffee shop up there at Jane and Finch. He didn't even take any notes or anything. He wanted to know if I was home when Gavin went out that night, and I told him he had sent me away. And that was about it. He said the best thing I could do was leave town, start over somewhere else. Fucking asshole was even going to give me some money, can you believe that?"

McKelvey blinked and tried to retrain his focus. An image

was emerging here. "Would you recognize the cop if I showed you a picture?" he said.

She shrugged and said, "Sure. I think."

He went to the bedroom and took down the box with his scrapbook and the spare .25 shells. He opened the box of shells and spilled a dozen into his palm, slipping them into his front pocket as he returned to the kitchen with the book. He stood there and flipped through the pages until he found the one he sought. A black and white photograph taken of the boys at the old division. He turned the photo so that she could see it and put a finger beneath one of the two dozen faces. "Is that him?"

"Yup," she said. "That's the asshole. He's uglier now, fatter, but that's him."

He gritted his teeth and held himself upright as he stared at the face of Detective Raj Balani.

"Are you guys friends or something?" she said.

But he didn't answer. Instead he closed the book, pushed it across the table and finished the last of his drink.

"Listen," he said, "it's late. You can sleep in the master bedroom."

"Where are you going to sleep?"

"Don't worry about me. I'll take the chair in the living room."

She looked tired the way children do, with her eyelids dropping.

"What are we doing in the morning?" she said. "I have to get all my stuff."

"Let's just worry about tonight," he said.

* * *

Duguay moved across the city in the middle of the night, the window in the borrowed car rolled down to let in the air. He thought of calling Danny to ask him to meet up at the shop first thing in the morning but chose to let his friend sleep. When he was finished with this, he would wait outside the auto body shop until the sun came up, then he could say his goodbyes to Danny and head up to Midland to collect his cash. From there it was wide open. Another new start. It was getting harder to imagine. Thoughts of roots and a home, some place to leave and come back to. Streets you walked down half asleep, corners you turned without even thinking.

He reached out and turned off the radio just as the news was coming on of an explosion in the east end. An industrial complex. Firefighters were on the scene. There were reports of casualties, but details were few.

He drove and thought of how he had been willing to let the cop McKelvey off the hook, how he had tried to convince Bouchard to let it slide. And he was rewarded for this softness with what? A fucking gun in his face? On his territory? In front of his girls? There were no further negotiations to be held. The man had left him no choice. It was beyond pride and street reputation; McKelvey had made it personal. And he moved backwards in his thoughts as well, from McKelvey back to Leroux and from Leroux to Balani. Allowing the crackhead Leroux to saddle up with the dirty cop was his only major error in judgement in an otherwise solid career. Just like you, Duguay; if you're gonna fuck up, go big.

His dog rode in the back with his snout to the window, watching and breathing and waiting to please his owner.

Twenty-Five

M cKelvey woke in the earliest hours of the morning with the clear knowledge that someone was coming into his house. He lifted up, immediately awake, and reached beneath the chair cushion for the pistol. Rudolph rose with him, a sleek and silent shadow, and followed without hesitation. The training kicked in, and McKelvey slowed his breathing as he made his way down the darkened hallway, all of the moments of his life converging to this one point. He stopped at the bedroom, where the girl was sleeping. He crept up to her and put a hand over her mouth. She startled and let out a muffled noise, her legs kicking in protest.

"Shhh," he said, "stay in here with the door locked. Don't come out, no matter what you hear. Use the phone on the desk to call my friend Hattie. Her number's written on the pad there."

She nodded and stared at him with wild eyes, but she did as he said. She was curling the blankets around herself as he backed out of the room and closed the door.

When he heard the locks slide then the chain rattle free, he took Rudolph by the collar and stepped just around the corner into the living room. Suddenly the door was open, and the pit bull was charging into the house, nails digging for purchase across the slippery hardwood, the big man just a step behind. Rudolph tore from McKelvey's grip, all musculature and momentum, and the two animals were at each other's throats in the hallway, their toothy snarls and growls too sharp and too loud in the small space, the sounds of a fight to the death.

McKelvey gripped the small pistol, and for the first time doubted his choice of weapon. The lazy choice, because it had been there all along, but now it felt too small in the palm of his hand. His service Glock was what he wanted, the weight of it. Everything was slowed down, surreal. He stepped into the hallway as the dark figure passed by, and he called out, a word or a command, and the intruder turned, coming around, his hand moving behind his back, reaching for a weapon. They were swathed in shadows, but McKelvey could make out the man's face, the whites of his eyes. *Duguay.* He set his legs, drew his bead, and fired. The gunshot was a sharp crack, and the noise rang, a stink of cordite in the air.

Duguay fumbled, still reaching, pulling a big black pistol out of his waistband, but McKelvey got off another shot, and Duguay slipped or lost his balance, and he went down, squeezing off two shots as he fell. The higher calibre shots thundered like artillery in the small room, deafening. McKelvey was winded, stunned, and by the time he got his bearings, he was not standing but slumped against the wall, with no recollection of how he got from there to here. His back against the door frame, he reached down with a hand and felt the inside of his right leg, close to his crotch. It was sticky with blood. *Warm.* The wound was numb, then it began to sting, and it buzzed with full-on pain. He needed to tie his leg. A tourniquet. Elevate the leg, slow the bleeding...

The dogs were in the kitchen now, and the noise was from hell itself, the awful sounds of two beasts fighting for their lives. Then just as quickly, there was only the sound of low whimpering, murmurs. Duguay made a sound, trying to pull up or move, his heel against the hardwood. McKelvey grunted and gritted his teeth and, keeping his back against the door frame, used his good leg to pull himself to a standing position. He was woozy, and he felt like he might get sick. He had the pistol in his right hand. He brought the weapon up, checked the safety, and moved to the wounded man in his hallway. Duguay's gun, a thick Browning automatic, was held loosely in his palm, too heavy to raise, and McKelvey kicked the hand then kicked the pistol free. It slid down the hallway. He looked down upon Duguay, aiming the .25 at the man's head. Duguay had taken a shot to the neck. He was attempting to speak, but there was only the buzzing of blood forming bubbles at his lips.

The rage and the adrenaline spun, and McKelvey was down on a knee, his hand working across Duguay's face, the butt of the pistol hitting bone and flesh like a hammer, but Duguay was out, and McKelvey was drained, and the blows petered out like a car running out of gas. McKelvey's heart was hammering, and with each beat it sent a spasm of pain through his leg. He needed a tourniquet, he needed to get the girl and get out. Somebody would come looking for Duguay, of that he was certain. Had to call Hattie. He rose and gave Duguay a final hard kick as he limped up the hallway and stooped to release the clip from Duguay's handgun. He slid the clip in his pants pocket and continued on, his ears still ringing.

The girl was crying in the closet when McKelvey came through the door. He went to the dresser, found one of his old neck ties, and tied it tightly around the top of his thigh. He sounded as though he had run a marathon, his chest heaving, his hands bloodied.

"It's okay," he said, "it's okay. Come on, we have to get out of here."

"Where are we going?" she asked, and her voice sounded like a little girl's now, all of the street smarts and attitude vanished in an instant. She wanted a teddy bear, she wanted her blanket.

"Home," he said. "I'm taking you home."

He grabbed a knapsack from his closet and threw in a pair of jeans, then added a pack of bandages and gauze from the medicine cabinet in the bathroom. He paused long enough to wash the blood from his shaking hands. Jessie followed him without a word. He put the pistol in his waistband, covered it with his shirt and limped out past the carnage in the hallway, and it was strange and it was horrific, and the scene suddenly reminded him of a call to an armed robbery he'd taken years back. How he'd come through the door of the Korean's convenience store, a place where he bought coffee now and then on the midnight shift, how he'd found the old man sprawled by the tumbled display of potato chips, a pool of blood at his side. It was amazing how much blood the human body could hold, and spill.

Jessie was crying and confused, and McKelvey had only a moment to look in on the dogs. He saw the bodies beneath the kitchen table, all of the chairs upturned, the matted fur, the streaks of blood, and understood it had been an epic battle, and now both the combatants lay mortally wounded. He looked at Rudolph, the dog's face turned to the side, tongue hanging slack between blood-stained teeth, his eyes open and glassy, seeing everything and nothing all at once, and McKelvey was filled with a sense of gratitude. *You were a good dog.*

McKelvey told the girl not to look as they passed down the hallway, but she stole a glance, and he heard her draw a sharp breath as he guided her past the body.

"You killed him," she said quietly, a statement of the facts.

He tightened his grip on her arm and said, "Don't stop. Don't look back."

*   *   *

Footsteps, voices, then a door slamming shut. Duguay opened his eyes. Blinked. He stared at the blurry ceiling, at the walls, then he moved a hand to his face, and he saw the blood, his blood on his fingers like grease. His face swollen, his throat closed. It was there now, like the fragments of a dream recalled in the confusion of morning. He touched his face, and his jaw was numb. His tongue. Thick. He could not open his mouth properly.

Not like this, he thought. *Not like this. On my back. I want to be standing up...*

*   *   *

The prison psychologist had wanted Duguay to talk, always to talk, asking him about his childhood and his crimes and his victims and how the scores on his IQ tests suggested he was too smart for the life he had chosen.

"Maybe I should be a doctor or a lawyer," he said. "Or a shrink like you."

"With your intelligence, I imagine you could be anything you want," the doctor said. "But as with everything in life, it takes hard work. You have to apply yourself."

Duguay laughed. He looked at the psychologist, a man of forty dressed in a cable knit sweater and khakis, his hands as soft as butter, his face as smooth as a baby's ass cheek.

"Have you ever been in a fight? I mean, a fist fight?" Duguay said.

The psychologist's face screwed itself into a knot, un-accustomed and uncomfortable with the roles being switched here. The interviewer becomes the subject.

"I got in my first fight when I was about seven. I mean, my first real fist fight with bloody noses and black eyes. It was an older kid named Lameroux. They were a tough family. Real tough kids. I was scared, you know. This Lameroux kid was going to kill me. But it wasn't the pain that scared me. It was the idea of getting beaten in front of my friends. That's all it was ever about for me. Maybe it was pride, I don't know. I just had to win, no matter what. And I did. I beat the crap out of this Lameroux kid. I mean, I messed him up pretty good. It was awful for him going home with a broken nose and a missing tooth. Some seven-year-old down the street kicked his ass. I heard his old man busted his collar bone, he was so pissed at him for losing the fight... I was too busy trying to make it out of the street, man. I didn't have time to look through those fucking glossy catalogues they got for the colleges. But I think I did pretty good. I did pretty good for myself."

"You're in prison, Pierre. I don't see that as success."

"I'm alive, right? I made some good money."

"But you're not a free man."

"Neither are you. Not really."

This frustrated the doctor, and he scrawled a long note in his pad. Duguay didn't tell the doctor the truth about his life, about the time his mother slit her wrists and he found her in the washroom, drunk and dying and still crazy and crying. He didn't tell the doctor about the man he had killed behind a bar in St. Luc, the way the man's eyes went when he turned and saw the gun, the sound of his death. There was so much to tell, but there was no point. There were no textbooks, no videos, no courses that could properly educate on the life he knew, the birth lottery.

"Nobody's going to look after you," Duguay said. "We all stand alone..."

He was staring up at the barrel of a big gun, a red-headed woman behind it.

"Don't even think about it," the woman said. Only a cop would say something like that.

Think about what, he wanted to say. The cop saw the Browning further up the hallway and stepped over the bloody footprints, the wads of dog hair, and examined the weapon. The clip was missing. McKelvey.

Duguay went to speak. To ask about his injuries. *How long?* he wanted to know.

He thought about his father, how the man had died in a stairwell at the prison. What was it like to be stabbed that many times? Did it feel the same as this? Pain and the absence of pain all at once...did his father think of him then, lying there with the life leaving his body? Did he think of his boy?

He thought of his mother and what she was doing, and what would she say when she got the news—would she be sober enough to care? Thought of how all the anger and the love withheld seemed so worthless in the end, how he wanted to see her one more time...his mother. Tell her that she'd done what she could, and it was better than what she'd had.

He wondered about his dog.

He heard the woman calling in on her cellphone, calling for "a bus".

"An ambulance is on the way," she told him.

She was pretty. A girl cop. Soft in the face like an angel. Sent just for him.

His luck. It sort of made him smile.

If Danny could see him now, he'd say something about Duguay always ending up with the girl. Danny and his crooked smile, the juvenile detention centre, the days of the old Camaros and those first little bikes, the Hondas and the Kawasakis.

Duguay. That's me. I'm supposed to live forever.
It's okay...

Twenty-Six

McKelvey and the girl headed up Highway 400, passing a growing stream of commuters moving like drones toward the steel grey metropolis at the first burning of the dawn. It was a choreographed show, wave after wave of rolling yellow headlights rising and falling across the lay of the land. Jessie drifted off for a while, and McKelvey called Hattie on his cellphone. She answered on the first ring.

"Where the hell are you?" she said. "Your house is on City TV."

"Balani," he said. "He was mixed up with Leroux."

"What are you talking about, Charlie?"

"He's dirty," he said. "The girl identified him. He's in with Leroux. Or he was. Maybe Gavin recognized him that night. He would've seen the son of a bitch at police picnics, for Christ's sake."

He heard her speaking to someone else in the room, and there were muffled voices, then she came back on.

"This doesn't make any sense," she said.

"I don't have time to explain everything. Is Duguay gone?" McKelvey said.

"No, he's not dead."

"He looked dead."

"You clipped his neck, and he lost some blood, but other than that... He must have been knocked unconscious when he fell back. He had a large gash on the back of his head. You messed his face up pretty good. He's up at the hospital now under guard. Tell me where you are, and I can send some help."

"I can't do that, not yet."

"You're going with the girl," she said. "To find the baby."

He didn't say anything. He looked over at Jessie. She was asleep with her head against the window. Her face was puffy from lack of sleep.

"This is crazy, Charlie. You're scaring me. You need to stop while you're ahead here."

He didn't say anything. He drove, the leg wound pulsing.

"What if there is no baby?" Hattie said, softer now. "What then? Everything to this point can be explained or at least dealt with. Duguay came into your home, we can work with that. But stop and think this through, Charlie. How it looks, you taking off like this."

McKelvey said, "It can't be any worse than it is already. I'll take my chances."

"You're wanted for questioning. A girl at the club reported the girl missing. Or kidnapped. They said a gun was involved. A man was assaulted…"

Jessie sighed and adjusted herself, folding her arms across her chest. She looked to McKelvey like someone who was not entirely unused to sleeping in strange places, strange positions.

"You're on the way to Manitoulin," Hattie said. "Thinking the aunt has the baby. That's what I'd be thinking, too."

"Give me a couple of hours. I'm not asking you to lie, Hattie. I'm just asking you not to volunteer that information just yet."

Hattie was quiet, background noises filling the dead air.

McKelvey said, "I'll call you. I promise."

He hung up, rolled the window down and tossed the cellphone out like an apple core. A little bit of calculus and voodoo, and they would have his last known position traced to the mile. It was something the bikers and gangs were starting to get smart with. Hitmen were removing the batteries on their pagers and cellphones while criss-crossing the country on their dubious business. His thigh was throbbing, the pain in tune with the beat of his heart. His pants were stained with dried blood. He would need to pull over to check the wound before long.

Jessie rubbed her eyes and stretched. She turned to him, and he felt her watching him. He had so many questions to ask her, about his son, about their time together, about her life and her family, but he focused on the road ahead, the task at hand. It was this sort of behaviour that had driven Caroline crazy; she was always asking for a metre reading on his feelings, his thoughts. In his line of work, keeping the silence was not only a legal right, it was a means of self- preservation. He would take things slow with this one. He knew it wouldn't take much to make her bolt. He could see it in her eyes, waiting him out.

"We should call your aunt before we show up, shouldn't we?" he said.

"This was your idea, remember. I'm just along for the ride."

"You know her better than I do, Jessie."

"I'm kind of glad, to be honest. I mean to see her again, to go home for a while. I haven't been back up in about three months. She sends me money to take the bus back every month, but shit happens, right."

She was quiet for a little while, then she cleared her throat. He thought she might be crying softly, but he didn't want to turn. He felt the balls of his jaw clench and release, waves of pain rushing over his body. He gripped the wheel and held on as the road rushed past them, all around them.

"Are you going to tell my aunt...you know, everything?"

He gave her a quick sideways glance, caught the expectant look on her face. No matter what she had done, where she had been, the rooms and the men and the street and the drugs, she was a child at heart, whether she knew it or not. Hell, none of them knew it. That was the point. The big fucking irony of the whole crazy experiment called life—you didn't know jack shit until you were too old to do anything about it.

"I mean, you don't have to tell her what I've been doing and all that, do you?"

McKelvey said, "Listen, I'm not interested in fucking up your life."

She was visibly relieved, and she said, "It's just that Peg has been so good to me. She thinks I started going to school to become a hairdresser."

"Have you ever thought of that?"

"Hairdressing school?"

"School, period. College, university. It's how most people get good jobs these days."

She shrugged and said, "I never really gave myself a chance."

"You're a smart kid," he said. "I bet you could be anything."

She turned and looked at him hard. "You don't even know me," she said.

"Well, you survived the biggest city we've got," he said. "That's good enough for me."

The scenery of southern Ontario changed shape, the box houses of Barrie dissolving into the rugged woods and jagged grey rock cuts of Muskoka cottage country. Highway 400 became Highway 69, then they were a world removed from the unforgiving city. Here even the most widely used roads seemed forever unexplored, the air was colder and fresher, and busted up pickup trucks took the place of expensive SUVs parked in the laneways of modular homes and trailers.

It had been years since he'd moved beyond the ever-expanding perimeter of the metropolis, and as the countryside engulfed them, he was reminded of his boyhood home. The northern country where woods could swallow a man who did not treat them with the respect they deserved and demanded. McKelvey remembered how every few years, a crew of businessmen would go missing in the sprawling woods of Gogama, city slickers up for a long weekend of drunken amateur moose hunting, and it was men like his father who were called in by the fire department to assist in the search. The hunters were invariably found, wet and cold and embarrassed, huddled in their expensive designer khakis beneath a tree. But sometimes they were not so lucky. As with the sea, the woods of the north swallowed up their share of souls. His father had told him as a boy never to set foot in the woods without a compass, a pack of matches, and a jackknife, even if he was only going on a short hike. "A man can get turned around real easy," his father used to say.

"What are you thinking about?" she said.

"I haven't been up this way in a long time," he said.

"You used to live up here?"

"Are you hungry?" he said, suddenly aware of the time of day.

"I'm fucking starving," she said. "I need some cigarettes, too. And I need to pee."

The gauge was hovering at the orange safety marker, and McKelvey had no choice but to cease the momentum. He pulled into a ramshackle gas station and convenience store on the other side of Parry Sound, for the summer town was far too busy with Greyhound traffic and a detachment of the provincial police. The odds were high that his plate number was already making the rounds. The notion that he might be considered an outlaw was strangely exhilarating.

"I'll gas up then see if I can look at this," he said, indicating his leg. He stepped out of the truck, reached for the knapsack and slung it over his shoulder. "You can wait in the store for me, see if you can find something for us to eat."

"Dressed like some fucking backwoods hick?" she said, lip curled in disgust.

He shrugged and looked at her sitting there in his old clothes. It made him smile.

"Fuck you," she said, and slid low on the seat, arms folded across her chest.

A boy of eighteen or nineteen came across the gravel lot dressed in work boots and old jeans, a John Deere cap pulled down over a thick head of hair. McKelvey handed the kid a few bills. He saw the kid looking at the bloody stain across the crotch and thigh of his pants. McKelvey gave him his cop's stare in return—the "it's none of your business, keep moving on" look—and the boy busied himself with the fuel.

"Washroom open?" McKelvey said.

"Just follow your nose," the kid said, wagging a thumb over his shoulder.

McKelvey limped across the lot and found the washroom door ajar. He pushed it open with the toe of his shoe, his face wrinkling at the stench of shit and closed, fetid air. Beneath the single forty watt bulb, he steadied himself with a hand to the brick wall and managed to get his ruined pants off. He felt for Duguay's ammunition clip and slipped it into the backpack, then balled the jeans up and tossed them in the garbage can. The wound was scabbed with dried blood, and he had to dab at it with some of the wet gauze before he could get a glimpse of its severity. The bullet had sliced through several layers of flesh, and when he parted the wedge with his fingers, fresh blood came to the surface, along with an ooze of yellowish fat. He winced and let out a groan. It was deep, but not as bad as he had imagined. Lucky, considering its proximity to the femoral artery—not to mention his balls. However lightly used of late, the latter were something he aimed to keep in their original condition. He clenched his teeth and pressed the two flaps of his flesh together long enough to apply a rectangle of gauze and tape. With his wound dressed and his new pants on, he washed his face in the brackish water then stepped back outside, hauling the fresh air into his lungs.

The gas attendant was back inside the store now, sitting on a stool behind the counter. McKelvey went in and looked around. No sign of the girl. He looked out the dirty window to the truck. It was empty. Of course.

"You see where she went?" he said.

The clerk pointed up the highway.

"Women," McKelvey said, and the clerk gave him an understanding nod. McKelvey took a hobbled step then remembered the list: food, smokes. Something to drink. He shuffled to a wall of coolers and grabbed a litre bottle of water, a dozen packaged cake donuts from a stand in front of the cash, and ordered two packages of cigarettes. With his sack of supplies stowed in his knapsack, he cut a line to the truck as quickly as he could, wincing with each step. He tossed the knapsack inside and tore out of the station in a cloud of dry dust.

He scanned the shoulder of the road on both sides, squinting to decipher human forms from the rows of rural mail boxes. There were ways of bringing this to a conclusion, with or without her. He had taken her—kidnapped her, perhaps—so she was entirely his responsibility. His mind flashed with images of her on the side of the road, sprawled in a ditch, or picked up by some maniac. *Fuck,* he thought. *Give me a goddamned break today, please. Just one day, that's all I'm asking.*

He knew she couldn't have made it far in the time it took for him to dress the wound, so when he spotted a bungalow-style truck stop diner up the road, he pulled in. The lot was filled with a half dozen family sedans and four tractor trailers. Sure enough, he saw her standing in a phone booth at the far end of the lot. He hit the gas and pulled up in a choking billow of dust, the front of the truck a foot or two from the doors of the phone booth. Jessie was not on the phone. She was standing there with her arms crossed, her eyes shooting arrows of hatred into his chest. He honked the horn and motioned for her to come. She shook her head and turned away. He revved the engine and honked the horn again, then resorted to lazy parent tricks by pulling the cigarettes from the knapsack. He rolled the window down and lit a smoke. He had almost forgotten how much he missed that simple ceremony, that rush of nicotine to the brain. He set his arm on the window and took a long, leisurely drag on the cigarette. She watched him, and her eyes were full of a base, uncomplicated hatred. It was a stalemate. He watched a big rig roll by, and in that moment envied the life of the driver. Long hauls. A radio and some good coffee. Just the road.

"Want one?" he said, waving the cigarette like a smoking baton.

She gave him the finger and mouthed something he couldn't make out.

"Get in the truck, Jessie," he said in his cop's voice. "You could've run away last night, and you didn't. So unless you want to be left here in the middle of fucking nowhere, I suggest you get your mopey little ass in here. Right now."

She didn't like it, and she took her sweet time making the

move, but she finally flung the folding door open, got in the truck and without even looking at him grabbed the door and slammed it shut.

"Give me one of those," she said and held out two fingers.

McKelvey obliged and lit her cigarette, then they were off again, rolling northward. The sky was changing its mood from grey to a dull yellow, then it was full sunshine and the cab of the truck was warm. They smoked their cigarettes and ate their packaged donuts in silence.

They sailed through Sudbury, with its giant nickel statue paying homage to the mineral which made life possible for the city. It was an odd sight, a goliath coin set against the backdrop of golden black slag heaps and rock cuts.

"Ever been to the Big Nickel? I went there when I was a kid," Jessie said. "You can take a tour of the mine. They grow food and stuff down there, you know. It's pretty cool. My aunt Peg took me and my friend Katie there one summer."

"To be honest, I've never been one for small spaces like that," he said.

"You're claustrophobic?"

"I wouldn't say that exactly," he said. "I just don't like being underground. Figure I'll do enough of that when I'm dead."

She laughed, and McKelvey gladly accepted the point as a small victory. He stuck his foot in the door of opportunity and held it open a while longer.

"Were you raised by your aunt?" he asked.

"After my dad went away, my mom had trouble looking after me and my brothers. Her sister Peggy had a decent job working for the town of Little Current, so she tried to help out the best she could. When my oldest brother Tom was eighteen, he joined the army and moved out west. My other brother George got sent away to a foster home because he was breaking into houses all the time. He had a learning disability, but nobody took that into account."

He didn't trip her up with her changing story about her father, the way he would have tripped up a suspect. Had the man died or left them? It was a mystery.

"And what about you, Jessie?"

She shrugged and flicked ashes out the window. "My mom is so needy. Pathetic, really. She always needed a man in her life. It was good for her, I guess. It wasn't so good for everybody else. Some of them would get into fights with George after Tommy was already gone. They picked on George because he was a little slow. And some of them, well, some of them wanted more than what my mom was giving them, I guess."

"You were abused," he said.

"Call it what you want."

McKelvey saw his son, Gavin, and the change that had taken place between fourteen and sixteen, two years of utterly confounding transformation. The cowlicked boy spreading hockey cards across his bed suddenly emerged one day as a moody, sullen impostor. It was a question he had asked himself a thousand times, playing through any and all possibilities for the opportunity of abuse, and he always came up empty. Gavin had played pee wee hockey, but the kids were never alone with the coaches, not like that. Beavers and Cubs, it was the same thing. So what then? What had been the catalyst for the startling transformation? Could it have been manic depression all along, or some other condition to which they were oblivious? What if a simple prescription could have spared them all of this pain? Why hadn't he bothered to dig beneath the surface of things, search for medical records? Instead he'd become fixated on a single man, a single crime. But it wasn't so clearly defined; Hattie was right, he had become blinded. It was the investigator's most unforgiveable sin.

"When did you start drinking and drugging?" he said.

"I don't know. Eleven, I guess. A friend stole a bottle of cooking sherry."

"Jesus," McKelvey said, making a face. "I'm surprised it didn't turn you off for good."

She shrugged. "Tasted like shit, yeah, but the buzz was good. I felt like...I felt like was *out of myself,* away from myself. You know?"

"I think I do, sure."

McKelvey could piece the rest of the story together for himself. "When did you run away?" he said.

"I was living with my aunt Peggy because George was gone and Tommy was gone, and my mom couldn't take care of me any more. That's what she said, that I was too much to handle. Can you fucking believe that? Her boyfriend's coming into my room at night to get his rocks off, and I'm the problem?"

Jessie reached for the pack of cigarettes and lit one with a shaking hand. The talk had upset her, dredging up memories from the past. And right now, right here, she was defenceless. No booze, no drugs, no place to run.

"Peggy's the only one ever gave a shit about me, if you want to know the truth," she said, curling up, drawing on the cigarette. "I took off the year I turned fifteen. I mean, you can only take so much bullshit, right? Peg wasn't so bad, it wasn't her. She tried everything to get me back. She got the cops involved, and when that didn't work, she even hired a private detective to come down and find me and bring me home."

"Sounds like she really loves you," he said.

Jessie didn't say anything. She smoked her cigarette, her head turned to the window, the trees blurring to a single wall of green. The sun was strong through the windshield, and the cab of the truck was beginning to smell of smoke and dust and body odour. McKelvey rolled the window down a little to let in a rush of cool highway air.

"She's a good person, she just doesn't understand what it's like. To go from there to here. To live on the street and do...things. She doesn't understand that you can't just flick a switch and go back to being a little girl playing with Barbie dolls. You know?" she said, and turned to him. Her eyes were glossy, and McKelvey saw that she was close to crying, in search of assurances.

He said, "There's always a way out. It's never too late to turn things around. Look at you. You're young. You may not feel like it, but when you're my age, you'll look back and realize just how young you were now. The past is the past, Jessie. You can't change it, but you can learn from it. It's all any of us can do."

"Where did you read that bullshit?" she said with a snigger.

McKelvey laughed and said, "I don't know. Some pamphlet probably."

"All the counsellors at the detox say the same fucking slogans over and over again, like you can just walk out the door and become a completely different person. But people can't really change that much. You still have to live with who you are and what you've done. What's been done to you."

"You said you saved up some money," he said. "What's that for?"

"After Gavin died, everything went crazy. I had nowhere to go, no money. And Duguay was there, and he offered me work in the club. I didn't want to do that, you know," she said, and turned to him, and he knew she was looking for something.

"You don't have to apologize," he said. "We all have to survive."

"I was pregnant and alone and broke. I lived in the women's shelter until they got me into this program for teenage mothers. They were trying to get me to give my baby up," she said, and her voice began to break, "but there was just no way. You know? I mean, she's all I had left."

It was the first genuine admission about a child, and McKelvey took a deep breath.

"I went back home for the last two months. After she was born, I left her with my aunt until I could save up enough to make a new life. It was supposed to be a couple of months, but they make it hard to save enough money. You always owe them for something. Duguay said I owed him for the time off I took with the baby, for the last few months when I couldn't work for him any more. Anyway, I started tucking a little away, and I have almost a grand under the floorboards of the apartment they keep for us, for the girls who come through on the circuit. I was going to head out to Vancouver maybe and start all over again where nobody knows me. Gavin and I used to talk about Vancouver all the time, because it doesn't get too cold. I figured when I had enough money to support me and..."

"What's her name?" McKelvey said.

Jessie was quiet, and she stared at the road ahead. Just when he was beginning to think she would never give it up, she turned to him with red eyes and said quietly, "Emily."

*   *   *

Uniformed officers wove a spider's web of yellow police tape around the perimeter of the blackened rubble, the scorched and twisted remains of the auto body shop. They closed the street at both ends. A police cube van was brought in to act as the situation headquarters. As the sun rose, the city's media assembled at the periphery, television stations jockeying satellite trucks to provide live feed from the scene. The beamed images recalled days of Gaza, Belfast. The victims would be identified through dental records and DNA.

One of the vehicles parked outside the shop was traced to a new member of the city's organized crime task force, Detective-Sergeant Raj Balani. There would be many questions raised, leads followed to their end points. Links would be drawn between the deal made for one of Balani's top civilian informants, a Marcel Leroux, and Balani's involvement in the milieu. What was he doing at the auto body shop, and what went wrong?

A gas explosion was ruled out, and the journalists filled the air with their assumptions of organized crime, drawing conclusions by what was left unsaid, relaying the scant information provided by the public affairs officers. A photograph on the front page of the *Sun* the next day would show cops dressed in white space suits carting three black body bags from the still-smouldering ruins.

Twenty-Seven

They crossed at the old swing bridge at Little Current. Something about the island immediately reminded McKelvey of the east coast, a trip he and Caroline had taken through rural Maine the year before Gavin was born. They'd stayed in a Cape Cod-style bed and breakfast, slept in late and made love in the mornings, laughing because they tried so hard to be quiet. It brought back good memories, the sense of this place. Cut off from the mainland, life here was slower, better. People lingered at the Post Office to talk about the weather and who had cancer. Boats on trailers in long gravel laneways and wild flowers growing among the weeds in the ditch, mailboxes with red flaps sticking up, and even the air smelled fresher, like it was a place where people could live a good life and be happy.

He pulled over to the dirt shoulder to check the backpack for the printouts Hattie had provided, but there was nothing. The clip for an automatic pistol, heavy calibre, the box of gauze, a half-dozen cake donuts. He had forgotten the papers in the confusion of the night. Jesus Christ. Scenes from those dark minutes rushed forth, the sounds and the smells, the deep fear that surged through his crotch as they met in the dark—he was fighting for his life in that hallway. He squeezed his eyes shut then opened them again. He knew the address was on Government Road. Christ, the island wasn't that big.

Ask a gas station attendant. He chewed at the skin of his thumb a little and looked out the windshield at some black birds fluttering among a stand of trees across the road. It was the wound that was making him lightheaded. His life energy ebbing, he could feel it.

"Are you going to ask me for directions," she said, "or are we just gonna sit here?"

He looked at her. The face of her, the girl and the woman. His son's lover, a girl for whom he would have given his life. It made him proud to think of his boy in this way. Reverence for the mother of his child. It made him feel close to this girl in a way that he could not explain; he did not know her from a stranger, truthfully, and yet he knew he would give her anything she needed in this life.

"Kidnappers generally don't ask for directions," he said.

"Is that what this is, a kidnapping? Officially?"

"That all depends on you," he said. "Perspective is everything, kid."

A coy grin and the wheels turning, the street-savvy con performing the calculations.

"I guess I do have some juice here after all, eh?"

"Whatever you want to call it. Sure."

"Relax, Charlie, I'm not going to lay charges or anything," she said, and it was the first time she had called him by his name. "The way things were going back there, it was just a matter of time. You think Duguay's a bad dude, that asshole Luc was a real son of a bitch. I heard rumours he was setting Duguay up, spreading stories to the big boss. Just keep going up here. Stay on 6. I'll tell you when to turn off. It's a white house with an old barn off to the side."

McKelvey pulled the little truck back onto the road and shook off an overwhelming rush of fatigue. His eyes were raw, and his leg was pulsing with pain, and there was a nightmare awaiting him back in the city. But all he needed to do right now was keep the truck aimed between the lines of this road which had been waiting for him all along.

*   *   *

Just outside Providence Bay, they pulled into the long dirt lane of the home Jessie had described. It was late afternoon. McKelvey sensed the shift within the girl, her body tensing, anxious. She was silent, sitting forward, twirling her hair with a finger as they eased up the laneway. McKelvey parked behind the only other vehicle, a Dodge minivan. He cut the engine, and they sat there. A dog barked. The late day sun was stepping back, giving way to a golden sacred evening of early summer. McKelvey smelled the absence of the big city, the fetid air blown through sidewalk vents, and it was good. It reminded him of the smell of summer back home, the wild flowers and the hay browning in the sun, the smell of lakes and creeks and rivers drying out.

"Looks like she's home," he said.

She nodded. He heard her draw a long breath. She was out of the truck and halfway to the side porch when the screen door opened, and a woman with a strong family resemblance was standing there. Her face was heavier with age, and the black hair was beginning to grey, but there was no mistaking the woman was Jessie's aunt. Her hair was tied back in a ponytail, and her hands, he noticed, were stained with mud or earth. He pegged her at forty-five. She stood there squinting, trying to comprehend. Her niece standing there, the context and the confusion. McKelvey slipped out of the truck but stood behind the door, an interloper.

"Jess?" the aunt said.

The stripper and the street urchin dissolved in that single moment, right there and then, transforming back into the girl she had been and could be again. Jessie cried as she took the four steps in two jumps and was wrapped in the arms of her aunt. McKelvey looked away, over to a golden retriever tied to a long rope, lying in the last of the sun. He thought of the old German's dog, Rudolph, and how he figured he liked dogs after all.

"My god," the aunt said, "I didn't expect you home. What's happened? Jess?"

But Jessie just cried, and she clutched.

"Who's your friend?" her Aunt said.

Jessie turned toward McKelvey as though she had completely forgotten her guest. She wiped her nose and she said, "This is Gavin's dad. Charlie McKelvey."

The aunt's face told McKelvey that she knew the story of the boy, of *his* boy, and his place in all of this. He stood there behind the door of the truck, and he gave a little nod.

"I don't understand," the woman said. She looked Jessie up and down and laughed and said, "My god, child, what are you wearing?"

Jessie sniffed, and she glanced at McKelvey, her swollen eyes pleading.

"There was an incident," he said, the first thing to come to mind. He indicated the shiner raised beneath his eye as explanation. "With her employer. She's okay, don't worry."

The aunt narrowed her eyes and was about to speak when McKelvey saw her face change shape, and it was a look he instantly recognized. He saw his wife standing in the kitchen years earlier as they discussed, or argued about, the son who was drifting from them. The look that fell across Caroline's face was the look on the aunt's face right now, and it was a look McKelvey understood was born of defeat, or worse, the acceptance of that defeat. This woman knew that where the girl was concerned, the stories were necessarily embellished. This is what happened over time to the lover or the friend or the parent of an addict, too. It was always something, always some new emergency to deal with.

"You folks must be starving," she said.

McKelvey closed the truck door and limped towards the porch. The aunt followed him with her eyes, but she didn't say anything. He grunted as he hefted himself up the stairs, and his forehead broke out into a sweat. The aunt held out her hand and said, "Peggy Rainbird."

"Charlie," he said. "And I'm pleased to meet you, m'am."

Inside the house, it smelled of freshly baked bread and something else, fresh soil, and it reminded McKelvey of his grandmother's house. It was a century home, an old shotgun farm house with a kitchen three times as big as any other room in the house. They stood in the kitchen while Peggy put a kettle on the stove. He saw down the hallway to an open door and spotted the reason for her muddy hands. There was a chair and a pottery wheel set up, a square of canvas set out for a drop sheet.

"Go on and get changed," she said to Jessie. "Your room's still in the same place."

Jessie went through the kitchen and up the stairs. Sounds of drawers opening and closing, then water running for a shower. Peggy turned to McKelvey and said, "You're Gavin's father. Pardon my surprise. I understood from Jessie that his parents were killed in a car accident some years ago."

He made a face and put his palms up.

"My sweet girl always has a good story," she said.

She reached above the sink to a shelf, pulled down a tea

pot and dropped three bags in. McKelvey liked her. The way she moved, the way she looked him right in the eye. A no-nonsense sort of woman. Something in her reminded him of Hattie, and he thought of her back in the city, dealing with the mess he'd left behind. How he wanted to be with her.

"Jessie has not had an easy go," she said, turning to face him, folding her arms across her chest. The stance gave McKelvey the feeling he was in for a declaration of the state of affairs. This small woman with the youthful face was not a hayseed or a pushover. "I don't know what story she gave you, or what version. She grew up in Sudbury, a rough section called the Donovan. Her father passed out on the couch one night when she was four years old, burned the house to the ground."

"Jesus," he said. "I didn't know about that."

"Her father was killed in the blaze. My sister was hardly capable of raising children on her own. She could barely look after herself. And Jessie, well, she fell through the cracks."

"She mentioned there was abuse," he said.

Peggy nodded slowly. She said, "My sister wasn't overly selective when it came to companions in those days. Jessie was molested at the age of seven by a man who was living with her mother. By ten she had developed a personality disorder. And then, of course, like adding gasoline to a fire, she discovered the great escape of drugs and alcohol. From there it was like watching a line of dominoes fall."

"She said she never really knew her father," he said.

"Jessie doesn't know what she remembers or what parts she made up."

"She's lucky she had you," he said.

"I never had any children of my own, Mr. McKelvey."

"Call me Charlie."

"You probably see a middle-aged woman living out here in

the country, and you make one of two assumptions. She's gay, or she's one of those crazy cat ladies. I'm neither, and yet here I am. I like life out here, Charlie. We're just away, that's all. Away from the noise and the constant movement."

"I'm starting to dislike the city myself lately," he said.

"I realize that it's hard for her to come back and live here again. I give her the distance she needs to get things sorted out. She's not ready to be a mother yet. I know about the drugs and charges for prostitution. I've been through the whole thing, so I can only imagine what brought her home this time."

"She was hanging with some pretty rough characters, it's true," he said. "But I think she's trying. She's not on drugs, I know that much. None of the hard stuff, anyway. You can tell by her eyes."

He decided against further extrapolation at this point. It wasn't his place, and the aunt seemed to have the situation well covered.

"When she's ready to get the counselling she needs, when she's ready to stop hiding in drugs and alcohol, then I'll be here. With Emily."

She poured herself a glass of water from a jug in the fridge, filled a glass and handed it to him. He drank the cold water, and it was the best he had ever tasted, clean and tasting of river rocks and the earth.

"I'm sorry about your son," she said. "I never met him, of course, but I know what he was trying to do for Jessie. Has there been any progress in the investigation? Jessie said one of the detectives told her that there were no suspects. She mentioned that man's name, the one on the news a few months ago. The biker who hung himself in his cell..."

"Marcel Leroux," he said.

"That's the one."

It was too complicated a thing to open up right here, right now. The pieces were falling into place. Marcel Leroux working out a plea bargain to net Duguay and also avoid charges in Gavin's murder. Duguay serving as the big prize for the Crown, and also Balani and Leroux's convenient fall guy. Balani the one pulling all the strings, playing both sides. It wasn't the first time a good cop had lost his way, but still, it was the ultimate betrayal.

"Things have gotten a little complicated," he said. "Anyway, it's not important right now. I want you to know that I'll be around if she ever needs anything. If she needs someone she can trust down in the city. I'd like to help get her into a college or something. I could help with that."

"I always had a soft spot for Jessie. You should have known her when she was a little girl. Always carrying a little pail around trying to catch frogs or minnows down in the creek when she'd come to visit. She was happy. I'm just sorry that I didn't step in sooner. I'll always wonder what would be different if I had taken her in with me sooner. Before everything went to hell. Maybe I could have changed her life."

"You can't blame yourself," he said and immediately felt foolish for saying it.

"No? Who should I blame then? My sister? Her father? It's just life, Charlie. We all draw sticks, some short and some long. I stopped wondering why all of this had to happen to one girl a long time ago. There's no answer. It just is."

McKelvey said, "I think I know where you're coming from."

"You should eat something," she said, "you look tired. You're pale."

He eased himself into a kitchen chair and sighed because it felt so good to take the weight off his leg. He thought of all the questions we ask ourselves across the days of our lives, all the wasted hours spent trying to answer them in silence. *Why? Why me? Why now?* The whistle blew on the kettle, and Peggy filled the teapot with steaming water. Then Jessie was coming down the stairs again. She came into the kitchen dressed in old jeans and a sweater, her hair wet and combed back.

"Hey, Charlie, come here," she said. "I'll introduce you to Emily."

The bedroom upstairs was warm and smelled of blankets and baby powder. McKelvey held the child, and the tears came so easily, so naturally, and they came without a sound. It was a wonder, a miracle, all soft skin and good smells, and McKelvey thought only of his wife and the news he would deliver to her, this gift from their son. In that moment, standing in the small hot room with the taste of tears in the corner of his mouth, he saw what he had done, how far he had come to once again hold the flesh of his flesh, the blood of his blood. He was overcome with gratitude, and nothing else mattered, least of all the cost. The child's small hand explored his face, squeezing his nose. He laughed and kissed her forehead, and he closed his eyes. He looked ahead for the first time in years, saw himself with silver hair, photos hanging on his wall capturing the progress of a little girl.

*   *   *

It was getting late in the day, and he knew there would be a call out for his license plate. Peggy insisted he stay for a bowl of soup, and he did so gratefully. His mood was lifted to its highest point in years, regardless of the consequences, the wounded. He could feel the energy leaving his body, a new brand of exhaustion threatening to fall. He wondered about his ability to get back on the highway, make it home. He wondered for a minute about his own death and knew he wasn't ready. He shook the doubt and filled himself with the beef barley soup and three thick slices of warm homemade bread. Outside, dusk was falling, turning the sky the lightest shade of purple.

"I need to get back to the city," he said and glanced at his watch.

McKelvey knew he had to get moving, or he would stay the night, perhaps longer. Yes, fall into the simple and good rhythms of life in the country. All of the aspects of life back home he had run from. The rural mail boxes and the cars on blocks, the same conversations at the barbershop and the grocery store, and the good people who arrived at your door with pies and stews at the first sign of familial need.

After she cleared the dirty dishes, Peggy got an address book down from a cupboard and got McKelvey to create a listing for himself. She handed him a folded piece of paper with her own information printed neatly in pen. He put the square of paper in his shirt pocket and suddenly recalled the moment he had accepted the note from Paul at the hospital group. That night in the hallway, the soft-spoken moderator catching up with him. And he thought of Tim Fielding. The school teacher had left three or four messages on his machine following the confusion at the tattoo parlour. Despite the promise of peace in the country, he was pulled back to the city with its awful deeds and white noise and subway smells and the school teacher and Hattie and all the people who were his family now, waiting for him to come home and do the right thing, to close the loop on the endless knot.

"I apologize for the surprise today," he said, "but I appreciate your hospitality. You have a real nice place out here, Peggy. A real nice place."

Emily was down for a nap, and Jessie was out on the porch having a smoke. He took out his wallet and put a hundred dollars in cash on the kitchen table. Peggy shook her head.

"With all due respect, Charlie, I don't need your money…"

"Please," he said, "for diapers and all of that. It's not much, but it's all I have on me."

She shrugged and left the money sitting there.

"Thank you, for all that you've done. For Emily," he said. "And for Jessie. I'd like to stay in touch. I'd like to visit again, too, if that'd be all right with you."

"You're welcome to visit any time, Charlie."

He put his hand out to shake, and she looked him the eye as they shook hands. He limped to the porch, the blood rushing to his head, dizzy, and he stepped out into the early evening. He found Jessie in a wicker chair, smoking a cigarette with her little feet tucked up against her bottom. It was the sort of slow and warm country evening perfect for sitting in a chair and counting cars on the highway.

"I'm going to get that money you saved up, and I'll wire it."

"You won't get it back," she said. "Not from those people."

He said, "I'll get it back. And with interest. Should be enough for your tuition."

She nodded, and her eyes welled up.

"You have my number. You ever need anything, or if you come back to the city and need a place to stay…"

It was harder to leave than he'd imagined, or it was the exhaustion and the wound, or perhaps it was simply his getting older that made a lump form in his throat as he moved to her. He put an arm around her and smelled the cigarette smoke clinging to her young body like all the bad memories.

Twenty-Eight

A t a gas station phone booth on the side of the rock-cut highway, he slipped his credit card into the machine and called his wife on the west coast with the news. Tractor trailers roared past or downshifted as they slowed to pull in for fuel or food. Caroline was slow to comprehend, to absorb the information, and she cried, then they cried together, and he told her how sorry he was for all of the things that had happened to them. It was like a dream, a story someone told you on a train.

"She's real, Caroline," he said. "I held her with my own hands."

He looked up to the darkening sky, cloudless and still, and he felt tired but strong. He was stronger than he knew. He could keep going if he had to, go on forever for his wife and his son and the idea of this family he had made. He thought of his father, and he wished the old man were alive to see how he had come through.

He hung up and dialed Hattie. She answered before the first ring was completed.

"Jesus murphy, Charlie. Where are you? Are you all right?"

"I'm okay," he said.

"They're ready to put a bulletin out on you," she said, "but I promised Aoki that you were coming in with your lawyer. She's been handling this whole thing like a bulldog. "

"I just held my granddaughter. My granddaughter," he repeated. "She's beautiful. Her name is Emily…"

"God," she said. "Charlie."

He could hear Hattie's soft crying, the emotion coming uncoiled, and he reached into his shirt pocket to take out his cigarettes. The lighter flicked, and he took a long drag, his chest whistling. He was so tired, the weight of the years slipping from his shoulders. It was as though he had walked a thousand miles, and only now, at the end of the long journey, could his body finally admit its true exhaustion. *What a strange trip, this life. It's a dream we live,* he thought.

"Charlie," Hattie said. "You have to come home now."

"I guess I'm in some trouble," he said.

He sounded like a little boy, the simplicity of it all, and it made her laugh through her tears.

"You're in a little trouble, yeah. But we can deal with it. It's self-defense. Just come home safe. Aoki's already been talking with the Crown, Charlie. Professional Services is all over Balani's house, his files. There's talk of a full internal investigation," she said. "We can work through this. I'll be there with you."

"I have a picture of her," he said. "I think maybe she's got my nose or something."

"The poor girl," Hattie said. They listened to one another breathing across the static line. He took the small picture from his pocket and looked at it until his eyes watered and his throat felt tight. Finally, Hattie said softly, "Come home, Charlie."

He filled up the little truck and bought a day-old coffee at the gas station. He bought a package of Tylenol and sprinkled four tablets into his palm then swallowed them down with a snap of the head. The road was wide open, and it was where he wanted to be, where he belonged with his head full of thoughts. His thigh was burning again, and he was lightheaded.

Tired, so tired. He lit a cigarette and rolled the window down. The air smelled of early summer evenings in the country, freshly mown grass, wild flowers. And the wind felt good on his face. It would help keep him awake on the long drive home.

Twenty-Nine

Upon his release from the prison in Kingston, Pierre Duguay moved through the underside of life, carving out a place for himself in rented rooms in other cities, in other towns. He made some good money for a few years cutting his own deals. But the work and the life became harder, then it was impossible. He was old at fifty-two. He worked the door of a tavern in north-western Ontario, manhandling drunken tradesmen, miners and peddling dope by the gram. He took a job working construction for a time, then got on with a painting crew, mostly ex-convicts looking to stay out of the system. He moved across the yellow and brown landscape of the prairies like a pioneer seeking new frontiers, finally coming to the oil camps of northern Alberta, where a man could re-invent himself without raising questions. He let his hair grow out and kept a beard most of the time, lines of steel grey laced within the black. He drifted from the life he had known, and those he worked with or drank with learned to respect the deep silence within him. He went by a different name, and in time it no longer stuck in his throat or sounded foreign when called out across a room. The polished crease across the flesh of his neck sometimes brought inquiries from the bold and the curious, and he invariably dreamed a different story until the truth was distorted even to himself.

He was often with a woman, but it never meant anything

beyond a warm body and a break in his loneliness. None of them held a light to Chantal LeClair, who had ruined him for love, for she had known him, known his potential. He understood he was in a holding pattern of sorts, biding his time. He could lose hours sitting on the edge of his bed in his rented room, hovering there, lips working in silence as he sorted through the details, what he would do if he could relive those years again, where he had gone wrong. In this way Duguay became an old man who never stopped looking over his shoulder as he manoeuvred through the days of a life lived beneath the surface.

Now and then, Duguay would think of his mother, wondering where she was or if she was even alive, calculating her age against his own. And it was during these moments that Duguay truly understood that he had fooled himself into believing he had escaped the fates of the men in his old neighbourhood. He had watched them stumble through lives filled with prison records and bad teeth, poverty and despair, living for Saturday night quarts of beer. Eventually the muscles slackened, and the stomach began to hang, no matter how tough you were. He thought he was smarter than all of them, faster and stronger. But he was exactly the same, because he was their son.

*   *   *

In the middle of a winter's night. Dark and quiet. He finds himself standing barefoot on cold tiles in the bathroom taking a long piss, head back, fingers tickling his belly. He yawns, closes the toilet lid and moves to the sink, splashes warm water on his face, slicks the water through his hair with his fingers. He pats his face dry with a hand towel. Then he notices it, an extra toothbrush in the holder on the counter. He picks it up, turns it in his hand. Pink, a perfectly traditional match for his blue toothbrush, and he sees the bristle ends are frayed where Hattie has brushed too hard, like a little kid. He sets the brush back in its place. It looks good there, he thinks.

Earlier the room had been filled with the scent of their love, but now the dark bedroom smells only of linen and closed air, the way any bedroom smells in winter. He lifts the heavy comforter and crawls inside. Slides against Hattie's body, warm and soft. She is still half asleep, and she adjusts her body so that a strand of her long hair falls across his face. He reaches up to move the hair, and he smells the fruit shampoo she uses. He notices everything. The freckles on her shoulder blades, the curve of her hips, the feel of his big hand across her soft belly.

"Charlie?" she says in a sleep-thick voice.

"I'm right here," he says.

"I had a dream about you," she says, her voice drifting.

"Was it a good one?" he says.

But she is already gone again, lightly snoring. He closes his eyes and listens to the sound of her breathing, and after a while he can make out even the faintest ticking of his wrist watch on the night table. He holds on to her body beneath the winter blankets and believes that he can measure out the time that remains to him in easy moments such as this. He sees that it can be done, that a man can believe himself destroyed, and yet still find something, anything—a single blade of grass—to clutch. He understands something profound has been forever altered within his being, within his very heart of hearts, and there will never be another family like the one he made from the ground up. But he sees that it can be done, that a man can in fact be annihilated, yet rise from the ashes, rise up from the depths of hell itself and learn to breathe again, and yes, even smile, and never again take for granted the simple luxury of a woman's touch.

Earlier, fingering the patch of flayed grey flesh at his thigh, Hattie had said, "Does it hurt?"

He'd said, "Not too much. Only when I pick at it."

"Then don't pick at it," she said with a laugh.

"I can't help it," he'd said. And it was true.

Now Charlie McKelvey closes his eyes and lets out a long breath. His arm is falling asleep, turning to pins and needles. He adjusts himself so that he will not wake her, slips his arm from beneath her side. He rests a forearm across his forehead, the way he remembers his father doing when they took midday naps to escape the apex of the summer sun up at the camp in the woods of the north, his silent father's strength there with him now, and he feels an unsolicited tear roll from the corner of his eye as an image forms, a flashing arc. His one and only boy. Gavin is turning slowly, smiling up at him. They are skipping stones across the green-blue water of a lake. He feels the presence of their bodies as strong as the sun on a hot day, hears each of their hearts beating, just slightly out of time.

C.B. Forrest began his career in Journalism and currently works in Communications and Marketing. His fiction includes the award-winning short story "The Lost Father" as well as the novella titled *Coming To,* which was adapted to the stage in 2001. His poetry has appeared in *Contemporary Verse 2, Bloodlotus Journal, Bywords Quarterly Journal* and *Ascent Aspirations,* and has earned praise from writers as varied as George Elliot Clarke and Stephen Reid. He lives in Ottawa with his wife and daughter. He is currently at work on a second McKelvey novel.

He can be visited online at
www.cbforrest.com

With gratitude
to Sylvia McConnell and Allister Thompson

Acknowledgements

The author wishes to gratefully acknowledge Gary Marsh, Chris Nuyens, and Gord Rowland for providing invaluable reader comments on early drafts; Pauline Braithwaite for reading those stones and never losing faith; Greg Poulin for the adaptation; spiritual encouragement from Patty Brundritt; mom and dad for the first typewriter; and B.W. Powe for the condensed MA in Creative Writing.

Several sources of information were helpful during the writing of this book, including offline conversations with a few ex-convicts, most notably P.M. and R.D.; knowledgeable former C.O.'s at the Kingston Penitentiary Museum; an interview with inmate 'S.D.L.' at Collins Bay Penitentiary; observances at Courtroom #5; and solid crime reporting in the *Montreal Gazette,* the *Toronto Star*, the *Toronto Sun,* and *Âllo Police.*